DEADLY WATERS

Christopher H. Meehan

William B. Eerdmans Publishing Company

Grand Rapids, Michigan

Christopher H Meehan

Dedicated to my wife Mary

The cover digital illustration created by Aaron Phipps
was composited from nine separate photos using
Adobe Photoshop 3.0 on a Macintosh
7100/66 computer.

Copyright © 1995

William B. Eerdmans Publishing Company
255 Jefferson Ave. SE
Grand Rapids, MI 49503
All rights reserved

Printed in the United States of America

Library of Congress Cataloging-in-Publication Data
Meehan, Christopher H., 1949–
 Deadly Waters / Christopher H. Meehan.
  p. cm.
 ISBN 0–8028–4068–X (paper : alk. paper)
 I. Title.
PS3563.E292D43 1995   95-33064
813' .54--dc20   CIP

S quaring himself, shoulder dipped, eyes riveted to the front of the racquetball court, Bradley DeHorn had the look of a bulldog about to bend metal with his teeth. A broad-beamed and burly Christian warrior, he swung back with one hand, flipped the ball up with the other, and moved his arm with ferocious energy. The blue ball banked against the right wall, smacked the left corner and shot back to DeHorn. With pugnacious speed and surprising deftness for a man his size, he stretched and flicked the ball wall-ward again. He didn't know yet, or at least wasn't letting on, that I was there. Stepping closer to the thick pane of Plexiglas that separated us, the scene made absolute sense: His only opponent was himself. He embodied the powerful need for self-conquest that I sometimes found so rife in our church. His demeanor, his crab-like stance, reminded me of the stolid, single-minded stubbornness that kept our Dutch denomination a still largely ethnic enclave on the mainstream margins of modern Christianity. In DeHorn, I saw my father as well as myself. We were often a people torn, trying to maintain our-selves in a corrupt world not of our making — but a world that, nonetheless, demanded our participation.

After he dished up a serve that slammed the wall directly in front of him, the president of Redeemer Seminary cut quickly to the right, dipped, and swatted the ball. It careened up, popped against the ceiling, and continued toward the front.

DeHorn, speeding toward the wall, swung and missed. As the ball dribbled back toward me, he crashed chest-first into hard wood; he turned abruptly, his face flowing sweat, and cursed, "Damn!" At this point he saw me, glowered, and dragged a forearm across the broad plane of his brow. His chest heaved inside the sweat-splattered gray Redeemer College T-shirt. His white gym shorts, flared at the sides, hung low on his belly. Dropping the racquet to one side, his arm dangling, he nodded and motioned me on. I looked down at my dirty running shoes. He shook his head; it didn't matter.

"Who's winning?" I asked, stepping inside.

"Me."

A blanket of light fell from the transom windows behind me. The sweat on DeHorn's face looked like motor oil.

"You ready for some snooping around, Turkstra?" he asked from behind the shirt. Sopped as it was, I couldn't see how it would help.

"Sir?" I asked.

"You know, poking around."

"That's why you asked me here?"

Snooping is a form of theology for me. A way of getting at the truth. The greatest mystery of all, of course, is God. I had suspected just that — a mystery of some sort — is what had brought me on a Monday afternoon in August to the place where I had learned a good deal of what I knew about God, at least the formal Calvinist version. I was now at Redeemer, in the familiar gymnasium. DeHorn had called me the night before and asked if I would meet him after his daily workout. Actually, he hadn't really asked. Didn't really demand. Just made it clear he wanted to see me.

"You play?" he asked. A curious smile appeared on his block-shaped face laden with pockmarks.

"Haven't for awhile," I answered. "Not since I hurt my shoulder last summer playing softball."

"Too bad," he said. "It's a good game."

"Especially if you can't lose."

The smile evaporated. The brow bent inward. He turned and hit the ball against the wall. "Rough part," he said, "is keeping score. Sometimes I cheat."

I laughed. "On which end?"

The flat-topped head appeared over his left shoulder. "Both."

I shook my head. Leaned against the glass wall. Noticed the polished surface of the floor catch the swift shadow of DeHorn's body as he took a couple more swipes at the ball.

"So," he said, finally stopping, "let's talk. But let me shower first."

✌ ✌

As water drummed the stall in which DeHorn stood, I sat on a bench across from a bank of sinks. From my vantage point, I could see the top portion of my body in a mirror. A long, slanting face, blondish-brown hair combed back, pinpoint of a nose, pencil-line lips. How many times, I wondered, had I been in this same locker room, after gym classes in college and following basketball practice in my freshman, sophomore, and junior years. I'd been a forward on the college team. I had done well, but had not played in my senior year. That is when I'd come to the conclusion that playing drums in a rock band in Grand Rapids, and the accompanying lifestyle, was far more important than running up and down a court in pursuit of a ball and opposing players. The memory of myself, all arms, pounding the drums in that sorry, silly band called "Do-Wa-Did-Dee" made me wince, an expression the mirror shot back at me as if in accusation.

"Indigestion?"

DeHorn stood nearby, a towel wrapped around his expansive waist, water pouring from him onto the black-and-white speckled tile floor.

I rubbed my stomach. "Something like that."

Turning in my basketball uniform for the long hair and raggedy clothes of a late '60s-era hippie had been difficult for my father, Henry, who had sat in the stands and had watched

3　　　　　DEADLY WATERS

my every game from high school on. As for my mother, Rita, my decision had been a necessary act on the road, she had said, to maturity. That I was still on that road, and a long way from growing up, was no real surprise to my mother, who now lived in a nursing home in nearby Grand Haven. As for my dad, he died of a heart attack in 1974, when I was serving in the U.S. Navy on a submarine in the South China Sea, off the coast of Vietnam.

"Well," said DeHorn, peering into the mirror and digging something out of a small acne crater above his mouth. "Let me fill you in." He wiped the crud on his towel. "You see," he said, digging through a shaving kit he'd set on the ledge below the mirror before his shower, "I thought we'd had it all arranged until late last week. Then that damned article yesterday topped it off."

Immediately the reason for the summons came clear. The article in The Grand Rapids Press. It had been a hot topic of conversation during yesterday's church picnic in Dorr.

"You read it?" he asked, slapping foamy lather on his blocky face. A pelt of gray hair covered his back.

"The one about Sid Hammersma, you mean?" DeHorn nodded at his reflection. "Hard to miss it." It had taken up a chunk of the front page. A photograph of the missing history professor's wife had accompanied the story. She had looked teary-eyed in her wheelchair.

"And?" DeHorn dug a razor out of his bag and twisted it under the tap, which dribbled water.

"Seemed a rehash of the facts, except maybe the part about life insurance."

A path of skin showed on his neck as he set the razor to work. "Exactly."

The story had sketched the situation. Hammersma had gone out in his sailboat one Friday night in mid-June and had not returned. He'd left the marina in Holland about dusk; police discovered the boat, empty, the following morning drifting near South Haven. The presumption was he had drowned. But so far the body had not appeared. Stories had showed up periodically in the paper and on TV, rehashing the little that was known. The life insurance twist was new.

"First, Turkstra, before I get to what I want," the president went on, jerking the razor up and down one cheek so hard it looked as if it dug off flesh, "tell me what you think of the professor's death." Above the slab of flesh that served as his nose, Bradley DeHorn's dark eyes gleamed.

"What's to think?" I said carefully. "It sounds like an accident."

DeHorn flicked foam and whiskers from his upper lip. "Simple as that?" he asked.

"Do you know something the public doesn't?"

He rubbed a wadded towel across his face. "Just asking, Turkstra."

I watched as he twisted a piece of towel in each ear, rooted around as if trying to yank out wax, or maybe even pieces of brain. "Don't you think it was that?" I wondered.

He shrugged, opened a bottle and slapped sweet-smelling aftershave on his cheeks. "I'm not sure what to think, which is partly why I called you here." I noticed scrapes under his chin, a raw spot on the right side of his nose.

I waited. He stenciled the bloody spots with what looked like a piece of chalk, combed fingers through his bristly hair. He had a large, bearish body, full of hard-looking, ruddy flab.

"Let me bring you up to date. Tell you where you fit in."

Two years before, Sid Hammersma, the seminary's premier historian and a writer of some popularity, informed DeHorn he had received an offer to assume an endowed chair in Reformation-era historical theology at Harvard School of Divinity. Hammersma said he found it a deal hard to pass up. But he was torn. His ties — and especially those of his wife — were to West Michigan. Suffering from multiple sclerosis, Virginia, his wife, didn't want to move. And yet it was a wonderful opportunity. The school in Boston offered a six-figure salary, plenty of fringe benefits, had even thrown a stately old town house into the deal. The offer had come on the heels of the publication of "Torn But Still Whole," a searing, highly readable look at how the Protestant church had suffered from the wanton exploits of some of its TV and radio evangelists. The book, filled with juicy anecdotes about Jim and Tammy Bakker and a host of other electronic pulpiteers, had actually been bolstered by the way Hammersma compared modern evangelistic mistakes with strikingly similar ones made by Martin Luther and his gang. Hammersma, as he often did, had neatly and entertainingly explained our present predicament by bringing in the past.

In any case, said DeHorn, it turned out that the trustees at Redeemer Seminary, on learning their star historian was about to skip town, came up with a package that matched, and in some ways went beyond, the one offered by Harvard. Bottom line, said DeHorn, Hammersma ended up with an endowed chair in history, plus a variety of financial incentives, among which was the life insurance policy mentioned in The Press. "So," said DeHorn, rubbing his scalp with a brush, "we went tit for tat with Harvard, and kept him here."

I stood up, stretched. I vaguely recalled some of the negotiations to keep Hammersma, one of my own professors in seminary, on campus. It had occurred about the time I moved back to West Michigan from Chicago, following Monica Smit, a preacher I had hoped to marry. We didn't make it to the altar, but I had remained in my home community, pastoring a country church not too far from where I'd grown up in Overisel. As for Monica, she remained, too, as a youth minister at a swank non-denominational church in Holland.

"Where do I fit in?" I asked.

DeHorn sprayed deodorant under his arms. "I'm almost there."

Virginia Hammersma had been waiting patiently, or as calmly as she could, to see if her husband's body appeared. Still, as the vigil wore on, she found herself in dwindling financial circumstances. The complications were many. Suffice it to say, she had petitioned the college to cough up some money, be it a chunk of the life insurance, part of her husband's pension, or even extended salary benefits. She needed the money and answers from her church.

"I don't begrudge her this," said DeHorn, plopping his towel-draped butt on the edge of the sink and facing me, arms folded over his chest. "I think we do owe her. Question is how much, given the circumstances."

"Because the body's missing, you guys are holding back?"

He frowned. "There is a swamp full of legal technicalities here." I sat on the bench again, waited for him to go on. "I need to make a report on this business to the seminary board a week from today."

I heard voices deeper in the locker room. Metal clanged. "And …" I prodded.

"And I want you to make a few inquiries for us. Gather some information."

"Such as?"

"Put to rest a few rumors, if nothing else."

"Which rumors?" I asked.

"That our illustrious professor rigged the accident and left."

"Isn't that a job for the police?"

DeHorn's hairy chest rose as he sucked in a deep gulp of air. "So far they've been next to useless."

"You really think Sid Hammersma would just up and leave like that?"

"I've run across stranger things in this church."

Founded in The Netherlands, our historic church held to a strict Calvinism that believed any of us, at any time, was capable of next to anything. Our actual denomination, begun in the late 1800s by Dutch immigrants to this part of Michigan, believed the same — pretty much the theology that we were all shit. Only God's grace could take away the rank odor.

"Any other rumors?" I wondered.

"C'mon, Turkstra, you had to have heard them, too."

I had. That Sid was murdered by angry right-wing church members because of his liberal views. That he'd been sick and killed himself. That he had a student lover, male or female — take your pick. That, and this came from the Baptists in town, he'd simply been raptured away that night on the lake. "You want me to serve as your rumor control?"

DeHorn leaned away from the sink, lifted and examined a foot, picked dead skin from a toe. "More than that. Basically make the rounds of a few people I'll put on a list for you, and ask them a few questions."

The task was similar to a couple others I'd done for him. The other times involved background checks on one professor and a student, who were supposedly engaging in shady activities. In the professor's case, someone thought he'd been pilfering information from the school's computer system and switching seminary investment funds into an account of his own. It had proven he was guilty. He was quietly fired. The student had been from a mission station in El Salvador. A few folks thought he was smuggling drugs into the area, that his seminary stay was just a cover. He was innocent. So the proposal regarding Sid Hammersma intrigued me.

"So," said DeHorn, "will you do it?" He padded off toward his locker. I followed.

"You want the information for your report to the board?"

"I want to give them a thorough rundown so they can make a reasonable decision for Mrs. Hammersma."

"I hope reasonable doesn't mean to leave her in the lurch."

DeHorn cracked open his locker and scowled at me. He let his towel drop. I looked away. The seminary president's full frontal nudity was less than appealing. "Whatever happens, we'll be fair," he said.

"What I'll give you for your trouble is one of our top theology students for the next week or so for pulpit help. You tell him what you need done. Do this for me, and I'll let you have my cabin for a week up on Whitefish Bay. It'll be yours any time you want, except over Labor Day."

I pretended to think it over. "The only thing I want," said DeHorn, pulling up boxer shorts decorated with the flags of the world, "is that you keep your inquiry discreet."

"Inquiry?"

"Whatever it is. Just talk to the people and report back."

"And you say the police haven't been of much help?"

"Zilch."

"Wonder why?"

"Incompetence springs to my mind." He stuck his arms through the sleeves of a stiff white shirt.

"I don't suspect they'll be pleased to learn I'm nosing around."

"Who knows, maybe it will get them off their duffs." His nostrils flared, mouth opened, closed. His hands worked buttons through holes. I could trace a lunar landscape of small pores along the ridge of his nose. His brownish gray hair, cut so short, made me think of corn rows in the fall.

"Do you have any theories about what happened to the professor?" I asked.

"None."

"No?"

He shook his head. "With Sid, you never know."

I wasn't sure what he meant. But I didn't ask. DeHorn finished dressing without another word.

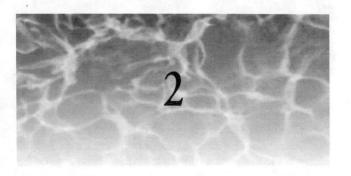

2

Surrounded by trees, the late afternoon sun dripping through branches, I sat and waited as Marlan Oosterbaan read through the list of people DeHorn had handed me. Scratching his reddish-brown hair with one hand and holding the crisp piece of paper with the other, he nodded, chewed his lower lip, worked his nostrils side to side.

"I suppose this group ought to do you," he said, handing it back. Oosterbaan's pale blue eyes caught shards of light filtering down. In them I saw arrogance and hints of friendliness. He was watching me with that cop's cynical surliness — a practiced gaze that made me feel less than human.

I had called Oosterbaan, Holland's police chief and a childhood friend, shortly after leaving DeHorn's office. The chief's name appeared on the list. I figured he'd be the best person to talk with first. Over the phone he'd suggested meeting on Lakeside Boulevard, just east of the expressway, at a miniature golf course he and his wife had built and opened earlier in the summer. A second job, a hobby for him, a full-time job for her and one of their three children. Soon after arriving. we'd strolled along a wood-chip path on the edge of the course, and Oosterbaan had explained the way police had handled Hammersma's disappearance. Because the college professor's boat left from a marina in Holland, Oosterbaan's department took the initial report. Since the actual disappearance apparently occurred on the lake, the Ottawa County Sheriff's

Department Marine Division had become involved. To that end, another blast from my past — Bruce Slade, this man no friend — had done the investigation. Slade, a detective, had performed a bulk of the follow-up interviewing. I knew now why his name also appeared on the list.

"From yesterday's story in The Press ..." I started.

Dressed in casual slacks and an open-neck white shirt, Marlan held up a hand, karate-style. Checked me with those eyes. Freckles dotted his ruddy skin. Thick lines creased his neck. As kids we'd been friends for a few years — until he grew older and involved himself in a harder, harsher crowd, which included Slade.

"That story was half-cocked," he interjected.

"Something wrong about it?" I asked.

Down a small slope a toy windmill turned, the blades intermittently blocking access to the hole beyond. A handful of people played on the bright, carpeted greens. I could hear the faint click of balls, snatches of laughter, the burble of water rushing down a small waterfall on the far edge of the putt-putt course near the highway.

"Nothing wrong. It's just that whatever you say to them always comes out half-assed," said Oosterbaan although he didn't look particularly perturbed. His round, rough face remained placid. He leaned his hands between his knees and directed his gaze to the golfers below. Colorful flowers, freshly painted fences, scattered benches, a hole featuring a rendition of a Hollander in wooden shoes and baggy blue pants, and a bank of pop machines spread before us. A well-tended field of play. As for the story, I figured cops never liked what came out in the paper.

"But was the story true?" I asked.

"Which part?"

"Where you said you're not sure what happened yet and prefer to leave the case open?"

The story said Oosterbaan's department had the final say on the case. Oosterbaan's name had to be signed somewhere

11   DEADLY WATERS

to finally close the book on the inquiry. In the Press story, he'd been clear — he wasn't ready to do that.

"More or less," he said.

He watched the activity on the course for a few seconds. He wore shiny brown loafers and beige socks decorated with diamonds. He pressed his outstretched fingers together, closed his knees under his wrists. He turned to me. "Whatever I say, you put in your report to DeHorn?"

"Not if you ask me not to."

"I can trust you, Turkstra?"

I nodded, made an attempt to show him an innocent face. He smiled, glanced back toward the small building in which I'd met his wife and his teen-age daughter.

"Anyhow," he said, turning and scratching his neck. "I think your board ought to keep this on the shelf awhile longer."

"Something's about to break?"

He frowned, tugged on the bridge of his nose. Always large, Oosterbaan had filled out. His belly and chest strained against the buttons of his shirt. "If it is, you know I can't tell you that."

"But …"

He went on, "Turkstra, we don't have a body. Until we do, it's anyone's guess whatever the hell happened."

A young boy whooped with delight on the holes below. He held his putter high.

"Couldn't that be forever?" I asked.

"Most times bodies that go down in the big lake show up some place or another," he said.

"But not always."

Insects buzzed around us. Mulchy wood scent rose from the ground. Shreds of sun poked through leaves. Families moved from hole to hole, tapping balls. One man missed a three-footer and slapped his forehead.

"Nice place," I said.

Oosterbaan nodded a few times. A lump of muscle showed under his shirt, below the shoulders. Even as a kid, I'd felt comfort, yet fear, in his presence. An odd mixture —

the nature of which was borne out in childhood experiences. He'd been something of an older brother who one day turned away and rarely looked back.

"We've been talking about building it for years."

"Must've cost a bundle."

He flinched, as if I'd criticized him in some way. "My wife came into money when her father died last year."

He stood abruptly. So did I. We started walking the path.

"Slade?" I said. He glanced at me, offering me an opening to go on. "He think the case should be kept open, too?"

"Doesn't matter what he thinks. We're not closing it without a body."

"So," I tried, "he's of a different mind?"

"Ask him."

We circled the far edge of the course by the road. Cars rushed by, disturbing the calm of the landscaped putt-putt place.

"You think it was a suicide?" I asked.

Hands stuffed in his pockets, Oosterbaan shrugged. Pale hair covered his forearms. Freckles, the size of pencil pricks, dotted the backs of his hands. "That is one of the theories," he said.

"You buy it?"

He rolled his tongue inside his mouth. "No real evidence of it."

"He wasn't despondent?"

"Far as I know, no."

"Did you interview folks who knew him?"

He stopped, pulled an ear. "That was mostly Slade."

"But you still figure he wasn't depressed?"

"I've read all the reports. Doesn't really sound like it."

Atop a small hill, we could see from one end of the golf course to the other. It was a tidy arrangement, a self-contained little world.

"What's your opinion?" I asked.

He hooked his thumbs through the waistband of his pants. He seemed to look out a little paternalistically at his miniature golf kingdom. He smiled, narrowed his eyes. "I

13

told you. Let it be. For now." His face shifted in my direction. A hint of something, a warning, formed in his eyes.

"Simply because no body has been found?"

"That's the easy answer."

We stood in the midst of towering oaks. Shadows stained the ground. I could hear the sucking rush of traffic on the nearby expressway. A mother looped her arms around her son and helped him putt into a swooping tube below us. A creek meandered to our right, carrying reflected sunlight, twigs and who knew what else, through a huge metal tunnel that led under the highway. On its way to Lake Michigan, I thought.

"You have a deeper reason?" I wondered.

"Ask Slade."

"Ask him what?"

"Exactly why your professor hasn't washed up on the beach yet."

3

Heading up the driveway that led to Sid Hammersma's Allendale home, I recalled coming here once, probably six years before, for a party. A stuffy academic affair. I was struck then by the well-tended but not overly manicured look of his lawn, flower beds, trees and even his home. A solid red brick structure with tall windows looking out like probing eyes, the home had enclosed the world of a church historian known for his richly conservative, although compellingly contemporary ways. Rounding a bend in the drive, I was surprised how different it looked now. The grass was bulky and clotted; mounded clumps lay here and there. Pale, almost wan flowers were arranged on the sides of the walk that led up to the arched front doorway. I parked in a spot to the right of the garage and just stared out for a moment.

Looking out the window of my Ford Ranger pickup at the Dutch Colonial home, I felt a twinge of sadness. The two-story structure looked worn, seemed to sag — not the vital, colorful place I had come to years before.

As I got out of my truck, it struck me that sadness wasn't all I felt. A flicker of fear, or more accurately apprehension, was there as well. I wasn't sure why.

Following Virginia's instructions, I knocked on the back screen door. Inside, I smelled chilled air, something sweet, and heard the echo of my knocking. Further in, I detected the humming of a television set, or possibly a washing machine.

Standing on the redwood deck, I knocked again. Still waiting, I turned and surveyed the back yard. To the left was a large enclosed garden. Again, there was derangement, stiff stems, piles of leaves, overgrown weeds. Nothing new had been planted this year — or, if it had, it hadn't been tended.

"Yes?" I heard, and turned to see a woman standing behind the screen. I couldn't make out her face.

"I'm Reverend Turkstra," I said. "I called earlier and talked to Mrs. Hammersma. She asked me to come by after dinner."

"I think she was expecting you."

By my watch it was almost 7:30. She evaluated me a few moments. I met her gaze with mine, tried to look pastoral and charming. "I'll go see," she said.

⌣ ⌢

Windmill cookies sat between us on the deck table on a plate. I had taken a lawn chair facing the yard. Eunice, the visiting nurse who had answered the door, had eased Virginia Hammersma and her wheelchair into a spot across the table from me. As we sat, orangish sun floated down and touched her snowy head and sweater-draped shoulders. She looked kinder, softer, and yet much weaker than she had appeared in the previous day's Press picture. In the time before dusk, with the summer night sneaking in from the woods on either side of the yard, I recalled how this same woman had once been a bundle of energy as she moved from seminary student to seminary student at the party. She had served drinks and food, flinging back her head in laughter, her face illuminated with a vigor I suspect some of us envied and more than a few of us would-be preachers feared. Her vitality had been matched only by the aloof grandeur of her historian husband.

We sat in silence. "Pleasant night," I finally said.

"It is." Her words came out slightly slurred. Her chin slung to one side as she spoke.

"You say you were here years ago for one of the parties?" she asked.

"I was."

Her eyes moved over my face. "I'm not sure I remember you."

That didn't surprise me. I was tall, gangly, fairly nondescript in the department of good looks. And at gatherings such as the one she and her husband had hosted, I always hovered on the periphery, listening, watching, rarely offering any words. "I was one of many," I told her.

She smiled, then offered me a cookie, reaching out and pushing the plate in my direction with a shaky hand. I took one, then another. I hadn't eaten dinner.

"Have some more," she said, watching me munch. I took another, then held back.

"What church do you pastor?" she asked.

"Overisel."

"Do you like it?"

"Very much," I said.

Her right hand idly moved on the table. She seemed to be talking to it when she said, "Sidney's first church was like that. In North Dakota, near Fargo — such a long time ago. It was right after we married." I was silent as she seemed to savor, or possibly rid herself of, the memory.

Then, as if rousing herself, she said, "Your questions? You said you wanted to ask." Under the sweater she wore a yellow silky dress with a scarf at the neck.

Crickets had started to chatter around us. "I was hoping you could just tell me what you know or recall," I said.

"Recall?"

"About your husband's disappearance."

She smiled, not sourly, but not pleasantly either. "Sorry, Reverend, if this gets you off track, but as I've told the many others, in my opinion nothing led up to it."

"Ma'am?"

"Nothing. There was nothing, not a thing, out of the ordinary in the days, the weeks, before that night. Lord knows I've tried to think back and uncover something."

I knew this was probably familiar territory for her. I knew

I was being redundant. I replied dumbly, "Nothing?"

She shook her head, giving me a sidelong glance, as if gauging my reaction. "Nothing unusual, nothing strange. No odd bumps in the night. No unexplained phone calls, knocks on the door or strangers lurking in the driveway. Sidney was not involved in anything unusual. Believe me."

From the overgrown garden came a croaking symphony of frog burps. From the lawn itself I heard a faint buzz, as if wires crackled underground. The sky overhead grew deep orange and a chill filled the air.

"What do you think happened?"

Her eyes looked past me at the house. Above and to my right, Eunice was working at the kitchen sink. "I wish I knew," Virginia Hammersma said in a firm, low voice. Her eyes flipped back to me, almost imploring.

"You have no idea?" I asked.

The years seemed to weigh heavily on the history professor's wife. I leaned slightly forward, twirled the plate holding a few remaining cookies. She gazed hard at my face; hands wrapped around a glass of iced tea. "I think this is where Malcolm wants me to be circumspect."

"Your brother-in-law?" She nodded. He was an attorney in Grand Haven, and represented her interests before the seminary board.

A silence stretched between us. The sun, heading west over the lake, shone through slashes of cirrus scattered in the sky above the back yard. "Can I ask you this?" As she looked at me, sorrow sketched shadows under her eyes.

"Is it possible …?" I said, pausing. I asked myself if I really wanted to open this door, but I continued. "Do you think your husband could have …?" Again I stumbled. "There are rumors that say he might …"

She finished it for me: "Have committed suicide?" I nodded. A hand lifted and touched hair on the side of her head. "This rumor isn't new."

"Does it have any credence?" I asked.

"About as much as the people spouting it," she said, with passion, eyes flashing fiercely.

I recalled another rumor. "Then was your husband sick?"

"With what?" Wariness had slipped into her voice, a caution that surprised me.

Here I was in the middle of the river, I thought, so why not push for the other side. "Cancer?" A couple people had ventured as much at our church picnic the day before.

She sat up straight, one hand placed atop the other on the table. "If he had cancer, he certainly would have told me."

"Certainly," I said. Her expression told me she didn't believe my response. I didn't believe it either. I wasn't sure why.

"No husband or wife, if there was any love between them, would deny the other person such knowledge," she then said.

"Even," I said, "as a form of protection?"

"Even then," she said flatly. She gazed at me intently, as if trying to convince me. Her hands rested flat on the table top.

The night was closing in, a blanket of soggy warmth. "It's getting cold out here," she said.

"I don't have much more," I said.

I thought of her mounting bills; the state of her home and its ground attested to them.

"I was just hoping you could tell me. What do you think happened to him then?" I asked.

She looked away, at some spot on my right. She seemed to think this over for a few moments. "I'm sure," she finally said, "it was an accident." The planes of her face had fallen. I tried hard to determine if she was telling the truth.

"I understand he went out on the lake by himself often?" I prodded.

She turned back. "If you define twice a month in summer often. "

"That night, or even day — what can you tell me about it?"

"The police have all this in their report," she said.

"Would you mind," I probed, "just sketching it for me?"

Her husband had awakened early, before 5 a.m., as was his

custom, and had gone into his den to write. About 8 or so, he helped her out of bed, and they ate breakfast about 9. He took the dog for a walk, and when he returned he wondered if she wanted to go in to Holland for lunch. She didn't. When Eunice, the nurse, came about noon, Sid left to run errands and to stop by his office. About 4 or so he called and asked if it would be all right if he took the boat out for the evening. He had called Virginia's sister, Lucy, who was free and could stay with her at their home. Virginia had said fine. She had asked how late he would be and he said he wasn't sure. He would call later and tell her. The day was so nice, he'd said, and evening promised to be the same. At this point, she fell silent.

"Did he call later?" I asked.

"No."

"Was that out of the ordinary?"

"With Sid, not really. When he got out on the boat he lost track of all time." She'd shrunk into herself, shoulders pinched, head bent slightly.

In the air was the scent of new-mown grass and manure from a nearby corn field. Faint stars winked above. I watched them glow, thinking of bobbing on the water in a boat.

"You know," she said, pulling the sweater close to her shoulders, "before I got sick, I used to go with him. We spent many nights out there together."

I don't know why I asked my next question, but I did.

"You have no children, do you?"

Her face shot up, almost frightened looking, possibly apologetic. It was almost a sin, a rebuke against God, for a good Christian Reformed couple not to have offspring.

"What made you ask that?"

"I shouldn't be so personal."

She chuckled. "How can anything you came here for tonight be anything but?"

I took the comment as an entry into what I figured was my last line of questioning. "Your husband sailed by himself at night a lot?"

"I think what I've said is that was his occasional habit." I now detected bitterness in her tone.

"Had he ever gotten himself into trouble before?"

"What kind of trouble?"

"On the water," I explained.

"Are you a sailor?" she asked.

"Not unless you count canoes."

She smiled. "Then you wouldn't know, but, yes, plenty of times." I said nothing. She went on: "The lake can be capricious. The wind comes up suddenly from all directions. Once, years back, sailing at night near Leland, the wind just roared out of nowhere. We nearly tipped. It had been so calm, but then this … wind. It was very frightening."

"So, anything could have happened to him out there?"

"Yes."

"Such as …?"

Her eyes shone across the table at me, a hand clutched her throat. She stared. I stared back, letting her make up her mind about something. Finally she did. "I've only told the police. And, of course, my brother-in-law. But Sidney liked to …" Her white hair was washed with the deep red of the sunset. "My husband liked to go skinny-dipping."

"Out on the lake?"

"The further out the better."

I tried to imagine it — the history professor diving in. Naked. He couldn't restrain himself. In an almost sexual gesture, alone, he swam. "You think he drowned that way?"

"Maybe."

Had she been trying to convince me? The peace of mind that had seemed to come over her as she said this, though, was a little surprising.

"But," I said, "if he'd done this often … if he was a good swimmer …?"

"That's the thing," she said flatly. "He wasn't."

"He liked to swim at night alone, but wasn't a good swimmer?" I asked.

"Basically that's true."

She had verbally taken me by the hand and was leading me somewhere. "Why didn't he drown before?"

"He always took a life jacket."

I let it play out in my mind. It didn't compute. Swirling far in the distant sky was a jet, trailing strands of puffy white, scrawling nonsense. "He liked swimming alone in the lake in a life jacket in the nude?"

"Let me clarify something," she said. "I'm telling you this because I believe your cause has merit. But what Sidney did wasn't swimming exactly. He'd slip into the water in his life jacket. He loved it. Looking up at the sky. He would drift away from the boat and then pull himself back in."

"Pull himself in?"

"With a rope. He usually made sure he was secured to the boat and that the boat was anchored before he went in."

"This time the rope broke?" I asked. Her eyes locked into mine.

"Yes," she replied.

"Is the water in early June warm enough for what he did?"

"Apparently so."

"Then you figure his rope broke, wind came up and he slipped out of his life jacket? That he just went under?" I asked.

She blinked, three times, as if ridding her eyes of a bug, and then said, "What else, what in the world else, could have happened to my husband?"

I certainly wasn't sure. Had the police found a rope dangling from the boat? A missing life jacket? "Mrs. Hammersma, did your husband take others out on his boat?" I asked.

"What are you asking?"

I thought that had been fairly obvious. "Did he like to socialize with others when he was out there?"

"You mean another woman?" I nodded carefully. She snorted her reply. "No, if he were socializing, it wouldn't have been with another woman."

I gazed hard at her face. "I'm not sure what you're saying, ma'am."

She rubbed her temple. "Neither do I."

"Could you explain it?"

"There's nothing more to explain."

We faced off over the table. She gazed at me with keen, probing eyes, chin up, mouth pursed. "One more thing?" I asked. She didn't reply. The fingers drummed on the table. "There's been mention of another will." I'd heard that rumor from DeHorn and from a couple others. There had even been a hint of it in the Sunday newspaper story.

She stared, leaned slightly forward, face shaking as if with slight palsy. "Absolute, utter, irrevocable trash."

"Another rumor?"

"A vicious lie." Her voice trembled with anger.

DeHorn told me Virginia Hammersma last week had filed her husband's will in probate court — a will naming her as his sole beneficiary. A will citing a life insurance policy's restriction demanding payment within 90 days of the death. I had called the court after speaking to Marlan and learned, through some wheedling, that no other will had been filed contesting the first. Apparently the need to file, plus the many debts, had pushed her to come to the board.

"There is no way," I said, "that your husband might have done something like that? Had another will?"

Face thrust toward me, she asked, "Did Bradley DeHorn tell you to ask me that?"

"No, ma'am."

"Then who?"

"It's what I've heard."

"Is this what Bradley DeHorn is having you do, track dirt in my house?" A wild glint flashed across her face, making her looked slightly unhinged. Her hands rose a few inches and hung there like a pair of trapped birds.

I did feel a little dirty, but I pressed on. "Why would such a rumor surface?"

"To take what is rightfully mine," she shot back, head wagging, eyes watery.

"So you've heard it."

"Yes."

"But who …?"

The hands dropped with a soft thud to the table. "No one," she replied. "You go back and tell Bradley DeHorn no one. And that he damned well better be ready to deal with me. I've tried to be kind, but this has gone on too long. If he and the board don't work with me, we sue."

I sat back, struck by the fierce edge to her anger. She shook — an ailing woman in a wheelchair. Her eyes shone. "Tell him that, will you, Reverend Turkstra?"

"Yes, ma'am. I will."

"You'd better." Pain mixed with fear nailed hard edges onto her words.

Or else? I thought. Or else what? I also answered. Frail as she seemed, I could clearly see the power of her emotions. For some reason, I asked, "Your husband, Mrs. Hammersma — were you two having problems?"

I felt a presence behind me in the doorway. Eunice.

A croaking sound stuck in Mrs. Hammersma's throat. The hands flapped to life as if shooing me away. "Eunice," she said, "please take me back in." I scraped back the chair, stood, and watched her — waiting for an answer.

The visiting nurse appeared behind her, grasped the wheelchair handles. "Please," Virginia Hammersma said, "Reverend Turkstra, don't come here again. I have nothing more to say to you."

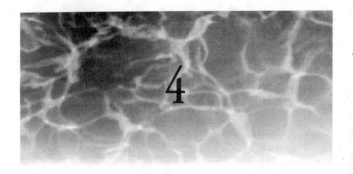

4

Water lapped the sides of the sleek, expensive boats, making them bob, filling the night with slurping, soupy sounds. Otherwise, the South Ottawa Marina was mostly still. I'd been here a couple of times, but never liked it much. Too crowded, too intensely festive. I am no bumpkin, but I've never been very sociable. As I stood on the end of the dock, I watched two lights slowly beam through the shimmering waters of Lake Macatawa. Black Lake, the Indians once called this body of water because of its great, haunted depths.

This was the first place, this inland lake, that settlers from the Netherlands landed before pushing east into the mucky farmlands that became their home and formed the area in which I served as pastor. On the run from persecutors, bad debts, failed lives and a dwindling European land mass, these, my forebears, established tiny, highly conservative Dutch colonies. Almost unique in this New World, these settlements thrived in West Michigan and, with their own brand of the Calvinist work ethic, set a tone for the area. In many ways I was one of them, and yet in others — largely because of my Roman Catholic mother — I was apart. Perhaps it was this ongoing duality of spirit, a kind of inborn objectivity, that allowed me to serve as a detective among my own kind. I didn't dally, though, over my special makeup. I let my attention move out into the night. Beyond the lights of an incoming boat, unseen in the dark, I looked out toward the channel

25

leading to the big lake. I stretched my arms and I took in a deep breath, thinking of Sid Hammersma's wife and the story she had told. She knew the professor better than anyone. I tried to imagine him stripping to the buff and floating free in the lake at night, pondering his theological thoughts under a dripping welter of stars. Standing there, I pictured him drifting in the heave of the water, allowing the chill of the night to clear his mind. It just didn't ring true.

"Help you, bub?" I heard behind me.

I turned to face a small, silver-haired, bowlegged man.

"Sorry?" I said to him.

Even in the dim light of the marina, I could see the square-jawed set of his face. He reminded me of Popeye. And something else resonated in memory — a familiarity.

"You lost?"

In my T-shirt and jeans and baseball cap, I probably didn't look like a respectable seagoer. "No," I answered.

"Then what's your business?" the man asked in a grouchy voice I tried to place.

"Trying to get the lay of the land."

His fists turned to balls. He squinted up at me. Around us lolled a sea of moving masts, tall match sticks in movement. "A smart aleck?" he growled.

Then I remembered — Jack something. He once worked at the Grandville landfill where I miserably labored the summer before college. He drove a bulldozer, shoving garbage into piles, which others and I spread out and buried. The stench still came back to me sometimes at night. Every summer before that, I'd worked on my dad's farm. But my wayward ways, my long hair, hippie friends, and surly attitude, caused a rift between my dad and me that drove me — gladly — from the farm.

"I think I know you," I then said, switching tracks in the conversation. He squinted even harder, as if trying to read hieroglyphics on my face. "Years back," I said. "At Fewera's in Grandville. Jack Boland — right?" I stuck out my hand.

He looked as if he wanted to bite my fingers. "Bolling," he said. "I don't remember you."

I shrugged, my hand still out. "I was a lot younger than you." He took my hand and quickly let it go. "You drove the bulldozer," I said. "I shoveled the junk."

He stared at me hard, a finger digging something at the back of his neck. "Tell me your name." I told him. "You were the minister's boy?" he asked.

"That was my cousin, Barry. My dad was a farmer. Out toward Zutphen. Henry Turkstra."

"That was a long time ago," he said.

"More than 20 years."

He nodded and then spat into the oily-looking water below us. "What brings you here?" More friendly now.

I remembered him bouncing around on the dozer, the exhaust pipe belching smoke, the huge, ribbed wheels crunching refuse. I recall he used to swear at us as we sorted and stacked and stuffed garbage in holes.

"I was taking in the night," I said.

"Try again," he sarcastically replied.

"Maybe I'm meeting a friend," I tried, thinking the friendliness was slipping away.

"Who?" he asked.

From my long-ago experience with this man, I knew the answer to the question I was about to ask. I asked it anyway. "Are you always so testy?"

"I am when I see someone sneaking around my docks."

To the left, up the bluff along the shore, shone lights from huge gabled homes. From behind, I heard the steady drone of the boat that a few minutes before had been a pair of approaching dots. "Can we start over?" I asked, having stuck my hands in the front pockets of my jeans.

"I'm just wondering why you're snooping around."

"I'm not snooping," I said — which wasn't true.

He didn't react to this one way or the other. I changed the subject. "Do you own this place?"

"Does it matter?" he asked.

I thought it was time to act haughty. "It might if I have to report you to somebody."

" Is this grade school?"

"No, but I'm here for a reason. "

We watched as the boat behind us began to maneuver around and into a slip two docks down. It was a large-hulled, two-decked monster, gaily decorated with multi-colored lights. People huddled on an upper deck.

"So," said Jack. "Who's your friend and why're you here?"

Hoping he could help, and deciding to forego DeHorn's caution to keep this thing mum, I said, "Sid Hammersma."

He stepped back, as if ready to fight. From the slip to our right I heard mumbles and laughter. A large man in white stepped to the front to tie up. Two other men hopped off and hurried along the dock toward the exit.

"You're a cop?" Jack asked.

"No."

"Then what?"

"Someone asked to do a job," I said.

"By who?" he asked.

"Bradley DeHorn," I told him.

"What's he want you to do?"

"Gather some information."

"What kind?"

I didn't need to tell him everything. "He just wants me to ask some questions."

"About the professor?" he asked.

"That's right."

He stuck his arms on his hips again. He was suspicious.

"I was just hoping to get a feel for the place where it happened. Where Sid Hammersma left from."

Jack wiped a finger under his nose, stuck his hands on his hips. Webbed shadows wound across his suspicious face. "Back up, partner," he said. "Explain this to me again."

So I sketched the mission the seminary president had sent

me on. When I had finished, he leaned against a pole, fingering gum out of a wrapper. Circles of bugs swarmed around the purplish light atop the pole. A group of people had gathered on the foredeck of the large boat several slips over.

"You really a minister?" he asked, eyeing my T-shirt. On the front was a faded photo of the Rolling Stones. On my head I wore a University of Michigan baseball cap.

"I am," I said, realizing the way I dressed was sometimes more a problem than it was worth.

"What kind?"

"Christian Reformed."

He stuck the gum in his mouth and chewed slowly. He indicated the pack with a nod of his head. I declined. Apparently we were buddies again. "Can you beat that?" he said.

"What?"

"You don't look like a preacher," he said.

I felt myself blush, even in the night. Sometimes that was good, I thought. Sometimes not.

We were silent a moment. A breeze brought in a fish smell. "So," he said finally, "how can I help?"

We both then looked at the people coming off the yacht. "About the professor," I tried. "What do you know about that?"

He started to walk back down the dock. I followed. Halfway to the end, he stopped and jerked a thumb at a small, scoop-decked sailboat with a tarp covering the windows of what had to be the cabin. "This is it, by the way," he said. "The professor's boat."

I could barely make out the lettering on the side: The Wittenberg Door. An apt name for a boat that belonged to a man who often reminded me more of Luther than Calvin.

"Been back awhile now," said Jack, staring up at the sky, the inside of an umbrella filled with dangling, dancing stars. "Maybe four weeks or so. They hauled it in a week or so after the Fourth. Coast Guard and county guys went over it with a fine-toothed comb, then drug it back. Been sitting since." The boat dipped in the inky water. "His wife going to sell it?"

"She didn't say."

Jack faced me again, his chin bobbing. "You asked me a question."

"What do you know about the day the professor left."

"Not much. He liked to go out by himself. Like I told the police, I didn't talk to him that day. Saw him walking out here, carrying his gear, is about it."

"Which gear?"

He rubbed a hand over his face. "Overnight bag, something like that."

Jack pulled on his nose and spit again in the water. We continued down the dock. His back swayed as he walked. I asked, "What do you think happened?"

He craned around. "Not sure."

"His wife thinks it was an accident."

"Most everyone else does, too."

We had reached the end. "What about you?" I asked.

He shrugged. "I'm not paid to have theories. I fix boats."

"C'mon, Jack," I prodded. "You have to think something."

He grew serious; the Popeye arms folded over his chest. "This a formal interview?"

"I'm just wondering."

"Wonder all you want; you won't get it from me."

"Get what?"

"Whatever you're looking for."

"What am I looking for?" I asked.

"Beats me."

He seemed to know more than he was saying. I didn't press, though. "You mind if I hang around here awhile?" I asked.

He turned, waving a hand as he went. "Free country. Just don't bother the paying customers."

Once he'd stridden off, I let my eyes drift back down toward Hammersma's boat. Other than the people still milling around the deck of the craft on the other side of the marina, things were quiet. I touched the small flashlight I'd stuffed in my back pocket. Why not? I thought.

The Wittenberg Door swayed under my feet. I let the slender beam of my light flick across the foredeck. Nothing. Then, on impulse, I tried the door to the cabin. The hinged knob turned. The door stuck. I checked behind me and shoved. It opened, and in I went. I didn't think that I'd actually broken in. After all, the door was open — just a little hard to move. Inside, I searched the area. Found a couple life jackets. Realized I didn't know how many had been there in the first place. Even so, I kept looking. Sitting on a small sofa in what had to double as a living room and bedroom, I let the light idly scoot over a counter, a small bookshelf, a couple framed photos of Hammersma on this very boat. In one, his wife sat in her wheelchair. In another, a young man stood next to the professor, a loop of rope slung over his bare shoulder. I stood, examined the photo. The kid had curly hair, a full mouth, frightened and yet mean-looking eyes. Hammersma, next to him, seemed slightly embarrassed. Or maybe he was just squinting into the sun. A nephew? Friend? Student? I etched the photo in my mind, thinking it might be important. I then drifted through the boat, trying to smell, feel somehow the presence of Hammersma. Under me the boat rocked slightly, dreamy in its motion.

Back on the deck, I looked up at the jib stay, reaching up into the night. I tried to imagine Hammersma in the water, naked, alone. The image struck me as horrid. I saw him floating, his dead body bloated, hair splayed out like wings on the murky water. I shivered at the thought, let the flashlight beam bounce over the deck again. About 25 feet long, the boat seemed sturdy enough — and sleek. I thought of returning below, rifling through drawers and maybe pondering the picture again. Instead, the night seeming to close around me; I decided to leave. I could come back and snoop through the boat the next day. For now, I thought, The Wittenberg Door seemed a little haunted. The sails, strapped to the boom, struck me as lumpy and flesh-like. I left.

~ ~

I had nearly reached the exit to the marina when someone called my name. I immediately recognized the voice. It was Monica Smit, my former fiancee — or almost fiancee. We never actually made it formal. She was walking with others coming off the yacht that had pulled in a little while before. She stepped away from them and headed my way, blond hair bouncing. Her calves were bare and tanned, even in the greenish glow cast by the marina lights. She looked better than any minister had a right to look. The curve of her cheeks was so familiar; the mouth even more so.

"Hi," I said, trying to ignore the clamminess that came to my hands and wondering what the Lord had up his sleeve in this ritzy boat yard. I hadn't seen Monica in a few months. The way my heart snapped alive told me absence had healed no wounds.

"What are you doing here?" she asked brightly. She wore white shorts; a knit top showed a half-moon of skin at the throat. Draped over one arm was a sweater; held in the other was a large straw purse. A firm, intelligent woman, always in command of herself.

"Checking out the stars," was my lame response.

"Nice night to do that," she agreed. Her eyes flickered with more questions than she had asked. "We've been out on the boat."

Behind appeared her boss, the Rev. Richard Rhodes. "Turkstra," he said in his deep, sonorous voice, a voice that drew large crowds into his spacious sanctuary from all over West Michigan every Sunday. Thousands more tuned in to his weekly TV broadcast. In a time when most TV evangelists had fallen, he had remained. Low-key but sturdy, tried and true with what he called a practical theology for today. I'd been in his place a few times, and had abhorred what I'd seen.

"Richard," I said.

Monica, between us, shivered. She no doubt noticed the tension. I had followed Monica to West Michigan four months after she left Chicago. I didn't want to keep doing street ministry there without her. She'd been fed up with the drunks, dope addicts and idle homeless. She wanted to move on. I'd remained behind a month or so, then resigned my job. I'd loved the work, but decided it meant far less to me without her. Soon after I showed up, on her urging, at the church where she was so comfortable, our relationship ended. For many reasons it broke apart, not the least of which was our clash over her choice of career and the church in which she wanted to nurture that vocation. That I ended up staying in this part of the world had surprised both of us. I took the charge in Overisel, almost on a whim. I never thought I'd stay. I answered the call temporarily and it had taken root.

"Were you out on the water, too?" Monica asked.

"No," I said. Been on a boat, but not sailing. "How was it?"

"Beautiful," she said.

"We're out on a fund-raiser with folks from our fellowship. Raising money for the election," Rhodes told me without my asking.

"Election?" I wasn't much on local politics.

"For sheriff and others running for the county commission. Primary's coming up."

"The sunset was stupendous," interjected Monica. She was youth minister at the church. Reared in the Christian Reformed fold, she drifted off and attended seminary at Chicago Divinity School. Our denomination (and I agreed with them) did not ordain women. We had met in Chicago when she did an internship that turned into a full-time position at our Euclid Street Christian Center. We'd worked together until her urge to move on took her away. She had told me that God called her to Rhodes' church. If true, I wondered if God had lost his marbles.

"Sunset did look nice, what I saw of it," I said, anxious to go.

"Making a pastoral visit out here tonight?" Rhodes asked, not ready to dismiss me, a pink sweater around his neck.

Before I could think of something to say, Todd Engstrom, business manager of Rhodes' church, appeared. He was big-

boned, thick-jawed, and had the sharp, blunt features of someone whose good looks almost always look unreal. I recalled
once hearing Rhodes explain how he'd come across Engstrom
in prison, where the young man found Jesus. And, once
released, he came to work for Rhodes in a menial capacity.
Over time, he'd risen to handle the finances — a role I thought
well suited to a former felon. We both grumbled a greeting.

"So what brings you out here tonight?" Rhodes asked.

I looked down the dock, at starlight bouncing on water. I
felt trapped. "I'm thinking of buying a boat," I lied.

"You're kidding," Monica rejoined. She loved sailing, even
had a small craft out here someplace. I hated boating.

"No," I said rather proudly, as if saying I could change my
tastes whenever I wanted.

"What kind?" she asked.

"Sailboat."

"Which one?" wondered Todd, standing close to Monica,
his handsome face. His tan looked glossy in the dark.

I didn't want to get into the truth. So I expanded my lie.
"It's back out there." I waved a hand vaguely behind me.

"What kind?"

"A small one," I said.

"Anyone's we know?" asked Rhodes.

"Doubt it."

"Is it the Terraby boat?" said Engstrom to Rhodes.

"It's Sid Hammersma's," I finally said. I almost kicked
myself for doing so, but the lie was in flux and I had to fill it
with facts. Rhodes' eyebrows rose.

"It's not officially for sale yet," I said. "Someone in my
church knows Mrs. Hammersma, knew that she was thinking of selling and knew I was in the market."

"Truman, that's great," said Monica. "You're finally going
to get out on the water, instead of just looking at it."
Engstrom — the snip — smiled. Truman was my middle
name, given me by my mother, a Catholic Democrat, the
absolute antithesis of my Dutch Republican father. It was

their enduring warfare over religion that had made me the spiritual bastard I was. Serving as a CRC pastor, I sometimes prayed to Catholic saints at night.

"Well, you never know, do you?" I said seriously.

"How much is she asking?" questioned Rhodes.

I told him I had better not divulge that. I was the only one who had actually taken a look at it. Rhodes considered this. Tufts of wiry gray hair poked out of the neck of his polo shirt. "From what I know, she's a worthy vessel." He'd made what sounded almost like a biblical pronouncement.

"Anyway," I said, noticing Engstrom loop an arm around Monica's shoulders. To her credit, she seemed to stiffen, then slip to the side. "I'm making no decision tonight."

"I do hear, though," said Engstrom, acting possessive, "that Mrs. Hammersma is in a bad way."

Was he calling me a ghoul for swooping in on the woman as she awaited the life insurance? I suspected so. "I wouldn't know about that," I said, ready to leave, but not wanting to give him the pleasure of driving me off.

Staring down the row of boats, Rhodes shook his head. "Damned shame what happened to Sid."

"Did you know him?" I asked.

"Of course." Rhodes looked at me challengingly.

"You were friends?"

"For many years." Rhodes' ruddy face gleamed with sweat. His square chin pointed in my direction.

"Have you heard much about his accident?" I asked.

Rhodes didn't answer for a moment, checking me out — probably sensing more than just passing interest. Rhodes wasn't on my list. Still, he might know something. "Only what I read in the paper," he finally offered. His tone had grown far less expansive. His stance had become slightly defensive, a shoulder thrust forward, hands on hips.

"Truman," Monica broke in, slipping out from under Engstrom's grasp, "we're going down to the Schooner for coffee. Want to come?"

About as much as I really wanted to buy a sailboat. "No, thanks," I said. "Been a long day. I have to get back." A tremor of what had to be jealousy, bolstered by a strong dose of longing, moved through me. I recalled many nights walking with her along Chicago's lake front — sometimes followed by visits to her apartment.

"C'mon, Turkstra," urged Rhodes. "We could give you some pointers about your new ship."

"Thanks anyway."

"But," I then heard Engstrom say, "how can the boat be for sale with all of this life insurance up in the air?"

I leveled my eyes on his face. He was questioning my motives. "I don't know anything about that," I snapped, wanting to push him into the lake — dampen his tan.

Rhodes cut in, "That is a funny business."

"What?" I asked.

"That life insurance fiasco," Rhodes said.

I looked from Rhodes to Engstrom to Monica, then said, "Who knows?"

All four of us hung there a moment. "I certainly hope whatever happened to him comes to light soon," Rhodes said. "If for no other reason than to help that poor woman."

Monica was staring at her feet. Engstrom said, from behind a smirk, "Praise God, don't we all?" In my mind, I shoved a slab of rancid salami down his throat.

5

When I started my truck in the damp, dreary dawn, country and western music blasted in my ears — Garth Brooks crooning about having friends in low places. I wanted something soothing. But after switching a few stations and coming up mostly with corn prices and nauseating DJ blather, I settled instead for silence. A bottle of cold Diet Pepsi between my legs, I headed east along 124th Avenue, over and down silently rolling, misty hills — more humps in the landscape than hills — toward Grand Rapids. As I drove, I looked ahead to a day in which I had high hopes of wrapping up my work for DeHorn. Or at least the interview part. I wanted to stop first at Saint Mary's Hospital.

On my machine when I'd come home last night blinked a message from Sierd Westra. He said he'd heard that I wanted to talk to him. He'd been the source of the rumor about a second will. It made sense. He was a lawyer and a friend of Hammersma. Westra informed me he'd be at the hospital early with other members of his family, maintaining a vigil at the bedside of their sick mother. He informed me if I wanted to talk that would be the only time, since he had a big court case later.

After making that visit, I wanted to see the editor of The Outreach, a church magazine for which Sid Hammersma had been a regular columnist. Randy VanAntwerp, the pudgy editor, had been on DeHorn's list. He, too, had left a message, answering a call I'd made. He said he would be in his office and able to talk with me about 9. After that, I had a meeting with Benny Plasterman, a presiding elder in my church and a sergeant with the Ottawa County Sheriff's Department. In yet another late phone conversation, he had agreed to meet me and outline the police investigation — from the sheriff's department end — into the professor's disappearance. A full day on my plate. I shook my head and flipped the radio back on. I took a stiff drink of pop and rubbed the corners of my face. Putting myself on track, I sniffed moist, manure-scented air, and kept turning the dial for appropriate music. Finally, I landed on an early morning devotional show beamed from the Grand Rapids location of the Christian Reformed Bible Network, our denominational radio ministry perched on a hill overlooking — perhaps appropriately — the Kent County Jail on the eastern outskirts of West Michigan's largest city. Speaking in soft, pious tones this morning was the Rev. David Andrews Hoekstra, an elderly pastor whose approach to the faith was, if nothing else, appallingly orthodox. I usually found his droning about as stimulating as cold oatmeal. But this morning, as I neared the entrance to the U.S. 131 expressway, he was waxing on with some actual emotion about a topic close to my heart — guilt. He spoke about Peter, the rock of Christ's church, and how the sturdy apostle had berated himself on the night Christ was sentenced to death by denying his master three times.

"In Peter's denial there was weakness, great and grave human frailty," Hoekstra intoned to his early listeners. "But it was in the even greater and graver repudiation of himself that we find the seed of his salvation and actual superhuman strength. By realizing where he fell so short, the man Peter was able to rise in a glorious way toward God — through, of course, no help of his own." What I liked about this was the wonderful Reformed way we had of romanticizing our self-loathing — almost deifying our shortcomings. Masked in self-hatred, we all knew we were the chosen — as long as we never forgot, and continued to feel remorse for the fact that we were truly scum, dropped, dripping and whining, from the muck that was our lives without Christ.

Thinking these dour thoughts, imagining myself a lumpy swamp creature arising from some great marshy beyond, I began to feel much better. Somehow, through Hoekstra's frothing words, I was able to taste the commonness that I had with others. Knowing so many others fell short, including the blustery Peter, helped boost my spirits.

⌁ ⌁

It was all I could do to keep from stretching wide my jaw with a mouth-widening yawn as I stood at the foot of the bed and watched Marilyn Jean Westra struggle for life. Clasped firm, as if set in concrete in preparation for entry into the next world, were her lips. Her knobby, blue-veined hands were folded over the massive, slightly heaving belly. Two days before, they had unhooked her from the breathing machine, assuming she would in short order die. But right in character this woman, who had borne six staunch, blond children, held on, in the aftermath of her stroke and in the midst of her diabetes, defying all odds, a Calvinist to the core. I had hoped to meet her son in the lobby, but he'd left word there to come up to the room.

"Reverend?"

My eyes had to focus on the person who had spoken. It was Ellen Westra, one of the daughters-in-law. In recent days several members of Mrs. Westra's family had been keeping a watch at her side.

"Yes," I responded softly.

We were crowded around the bed at Saint Mary's. That their loved one was probably living out her last days in a Roman Catholic institution had caused a few in the Westra fold to grumble a week or so before, I would guess. But by now most had probably accepted this as their fate.

"Do you want some coffee?" Ellen asked.

On my right, through large windows, I saw the city waking up. Cars moving five stories below. The murky outline of downtown, the Amway Grand Plaza Hotel catching rays of the sun and reflecting them back through the dissipating haze.

"Sure," I said. "Black."

Three-quarters of the hovering contingent left. That so many of them were here this early was probably a surprise to nurses on the floor. To me it wasn't. This was a family with strong connections. Much that they did, they did en masse. Usually this was good, but not always. As they removed themselves from the room in careful, single-file shuffles, the woman on the bed stirred and groaned. Except for a turned head or two, none of the departing seemed to notice. They had played this scenario, or one close to it, out before at Holland Community Hospital in the spring. I had visited once. And at another Grand Rapids medical center last fall. Each time, though, this woman had been able to rally and bounce back, unwilling, even as her organs failed, to give up her fierce stranglehold on life. I suspected she might do the same now.

"I'm glad you stopped by," David Westra said to me, seriously and sadly when they had gone. He was a big man in overalls, an onion farmer from Vriesland, with hands as wide and nicked as shovels. His small wife, almost paltry in his shadow, clung to him. Both looked wizened and wrinkled in a way that seemed more careworn than depleted. I could almost taste their faith. If I compared it to my own, I knew I would be embarrassed. They stood on the other side of the bed from me. Other than Sierd, who stood next to me, the rest of the family probably figured I was here out of simple pastorly kindness — even if I was not their minister. Before going into a nursing home in Grand Rapids, Marilyn had been a member of my church.

"I'm glad I could come," I told him.

On the bed, the old woman breathed on. I thought of how we first met, years ago, while I was delivering the newspaper to their house. Pedaling by on my bike, I flung the wrapped newspaper up toward their porch. They lived in town then, and I made the four-mile trip in for a summer to do a paper route. At any rate, the paper flopped halfway up the walk. I was blithely riding on when the woman shoved open their front door and, half in Dutch, half in English, commanded me to return, pick up the newspaper, and place it in her open, outreached hand. Which, of course, I did. Grumbling the whole time, then holding the paper in one hand and tapping it like a hammer in the other, she demanded my name.

"You're Rita Turkstra's son?" she asked. I told her I was. "And what would she say about you doing your job in such a way?" she added.

I had hung my head, my ears burning. When I didn't answer, she asked if I wanted lemonade and a cookie, that afternoon long ago. I didn't say anything. She took my mute response as acceptance and told me to sit on the steps. She'd be right back. I sat, and she returned shortly. Many times after, she had fed me food and helped here and there with chastisements that were really her form of advice. After coming to the church, her insights into the church members, their silent struggles and infighting, had been invaluable. Watching her struggle for life now, I realized I would miss her and was starting into a prayer when Sierd edged over to me and said in a low voice, "Pastor, you wanted to talk?"

As we stepped into the hall, up and down the corridor I saw a flurry of white coats and uniforms. Sierd stuck his hands in his pockets and looked up at me with a quizzical half-smile on his face. His steely gray hair was brushed briskly back on his prominent, softly-lined forehead. "So?" he said, offering the opening I wanted.

I leaned in closer. "The two of you, Sid Hammersma and yourself, were good friends?"

He nodded curtly. "Were?"

"Are?"

He smiled more, showing teeth now. "Yes. From childhood." His eyes began to probe mine.

I examined his face, saw something that encouraged me to go on. "Did you see him much before the incident on the lake?" I asked.

He grew serious; his expression lost a degree or two of warmth. "I'm not sure what you're asking, Pastor."

Nurses bustled past; a man, his mouth gaping, rolled by on a gurney. An aide with frizzy hair and Cuban heels was at the helm, steering the patient somewhere.

"I think you know," I said.

The mouth opened and closed; the tongue poked out, exploring flesh. The lawyerly furrow in his eyebrows told me he'd begun calculating.

"I'm sorry if this is a bad time to ask questions," I added.

His eyes flicked back into the room, where I could see only the tent in the covers made by his mother's feet. "What is it you want to know?" he asked, not unkindly.

"Was Sid sick or depressed the last you saw him?"

He blinked, but took it without any more expression than that. He shook his head. He was a tax attorney, a mighty man with figures. "We were friends, but Sidney was also a very private man. Unless something like that was blatantly obvious, he wouldn't disclose it to me."

"From what you could tell, he was … OK?"

"All outward signs were normal."

"He didn't look sick to you? He didn't talk about his health?" I pressed.

He peered intensely up at me. "No."

"That has been a rumor, though," I said.

"Whose rumor?"

I shrugged again, this time with a little more vigor.

"Do you think it has any validity?" he asked.

"You tell me," I responded.

Sierd Westra's face collapsed into an expression of concern. A forefinger and thumb gently gripped his chin. I suspected he was holding back, that he wanted me to dig something out of him.

He shook his head and smiled grimly. "Sidney had a first-rate mind, a powerful pen, a prodigious ego, and was very much a baby when it came to physical or mental pain." I just stood there, not having to feign interest. "Sidney kept his ailments to himself, for certain. But once they were out, even a cold, he could whine and wail like nobody's business."

I was a little confused. First, he said Sidney Hammersma was a model of reserve and inner resolve. On the other hand, he was a crybaby. Also, Sierd seemed to be toying with me a little, almost setting me up.

"But if, as you're saying, he did tend to keep things to himself, he probably wouldn't have said anything if the problem was long-term. Maybe not so immediate, maybe not painful at the moment."

"Something like cancer, you mean?" he asked pointedly.

We stood there in silence a few seconds. "Have you spoken to Sid's wife about this?" he asked.

"I have, and she says her husband was fit as a fiddle before he went out that night in his boat."

Sierd Westra chuckled. "Funny way to describe Sidney."

I felt a little embarrassed. He was making fun of me. "From what she said, he was healthy," I amended.

His head bobbed in agreement, possibly a little ashamed at his own levity. "But he was very circumspect with her, particularly about matters such as this," the lawyer said.

"Oh?" I said with interest.

Perhaps noticing my curiosity, he stepped back. "Is this all you wanted to ask?" he wondered.

I checked my scuffed running shoes. "No," I replied. "I heard you might know something about another will."

A worm of interest squirmed in his temple, a blue vessel under white skin. His eyes flicked up and down the hall. "Before I get into that, I have a suggestion." I waited.

"I know who would know if there is anything to the business of Sidney's health." I said nothing. "Henry Baak, both Sidney's and my golfing partner and family doctor. I saw him in the hall earlier, on my way up here. If he's still around, you can ask a question or two. Would you like that? Would it help?"

We caught up with Henry Baak in the doctors' section of the parking lot, off Jefferson Avenue. In the lot, we exchanged greetings. As we did, the doctor eyed me suspiciously from under his bushy brow. He was leaning on the trunk of his shiny black Saturn. A Dutch doctor's Porsche. He wore oxblood loafers with tassels, shiny socks, a crisp gray suit and pinstriped shirt, set off by a delicately checked tie. He had the lined, impassive face of a patriarch in his prime. The doctor looked curiously at Sierd, folding his arms over his chest. In the murky morning air was the smell of exhaust fumes as well as the unmistakable nasal prick of midsummer pollen. Birds cackled overhead, darting in and out of the space between hospital additions. The three spires of St. Andrew's Cathedral towered across from us. My lungs, sometimes asthmatic, quivered slightly. I took in a few deep, steadying breaths.

"Reverend Turkstra here was asking me a question I thought you might answer."

"Oh?" The physician gazed at me serenely and with a smidgen of disdain. Being a doctor, he couldn't help it.

"He wants to know," Sierd Westra said, "if Sid Hammersma was sick." The doctor blinked. So did I. The lawyer cut no corners.

"And why is it you want to know that?" Baak wondered, not looking at the lawyer.

"I've been asked by the seminary to track down some rumors," I explained. "One of them is that Sid Hammersma was sick?"

We fell silent. A van pulled out of a spot down the line and moved past us. Loud music thumped so loudly within that I wondered if the driver was carrying a live rock band.

"And," Baak then asked, "you thought I would answer that even if it were true?"

"It's not true?" I asked.

He held up a hand. "I say nothing of the sort. I only wonder why you'd think I would violate the doctor-patient relationship." Saying this, he smirked. Maybe it was a wince. He seemed pleased with his own ethics.

I looked to Westra for help. He stared at a crack in the pavement.

"I had hoped you would help, sir," I said.

The "sir" softened him a little. If nearly seven years in the ministry had taught me anything, it was how to soothe bloated egos. "I'd like to help," said the doctor, patting a hand at the side of his wavy gray hair. "But there are serious constraints on what I can tell you."

Westra's shoe kicked a stone. "C'mon, Henry." The doctor stiffened, sitting on the trunk of his car. "Can't you help him out," Westra said.

The doctor stood, pulling down the back of his suit jacket. "Is that legal advice, Sierd?"

"Skip the details," the lawyer said. "Just tell Turkstra what you told me on the golf course Saturday."

The doctor looked at me carefully. "What did I say on the golf course Saturday?"

Westra looked at me, back at the doctor, and then at the ground again. "You said Sidney came to you in the spring with some worries."

Gazing in my direction, the doctor prodded, "What else?"

Westra's head bobbed up. It struck me that they were going to tell me what I wanted in a way that more or less protected the doctor.

"You said he'd been having trouble with his liver."

"Did I say that?" questioned the doctor, still gazing at me, as if trying to gauge my reaction.

"Yes, Henry, you did — and something about a blood test."

"I must've been talking in my sleep. Score I ended up with seemed to show I was dozing. What else did I tell you?"

Westra sighed, perhaps weary of this game. "That you referred Sidney to a specialist who came back with a report that was positive."

The doctor now looked at his friend. "I don't think I said

anything about a report coming back positive."

"No?" Westra asked. "Maybe I didn't have that part right."

"Maybe."

With that, the two golfing buddies stopped talking. It was my turn. "If Sid Hammersma had something wrong with him, how come no one knew it before this? Like his wife or the police?"

The doctor screwed his mouth to one side. I noticed that his skin was so closely shaven that it glowed. "Who says they don't know?" he asked.

"As for the police, I'm not sure. But I spoke to his wife last night. She was pretty clear — her husband was not sick."

"Virginia told you that?" asked Baak.

"She did."

Baak addressed his next question to Westra. "I wonder why she said that."

Westra shrugged. "She probably has some reasons."

"Or," added the doctor, "Sidney never told her."

"That," replied Westra, "I doubt."

Almost forcefully, the doctor then said, "I don't."

"Told her what?" I asked. Neither man said anything.

I wanted to know more, but I knew both men were getting restless, ready to continue their days.

"That all?" Baak asked, turning to me.

"Was his cancer terminal?"

Baak tilted his head. "I'm not sure, Reverend, I said anything about cancer."

We were still playing the game. I nodded, as if I liked this run-around way of reaching the truth. I pressed, "Then what was it?"

"At least theoretically," said the doctor, "I know liver cancer is never a hopeful diagnosis."

"Is that what he had?" The doctor didn't answer. "Whatever it was," I said, "did he know he was sick with something serious?" Neither the doctor nor the lawyer spoke.

Standing there, I wasn't exactly sure what they were giving

me. "Did Sid Hammersma have liver cancer or not?" I asked. They turned on me blank looks. "Was it cancer?"

The doctor sighed, looking at his tasseled shoes. "Only this I'll say ... Sid Hammersma had a blood test. And, cancer aside, the results came back very strange." The doctor then curtly dismissed himself, slipped into his car and backed out.

My mind reeled with possibilities as the doctor drove off to save lives and bolster his bank account. Blood test? Not cancer? A faint feeling of fear and anger passed through me.

As the yellow arm of the parking gate raised, allowing the doctor to pass out of the lot, I turned to Sierd. "What blood test," I demanded.

Westra blocked my question with a hand. "Hold on."

"To what? It's seems lots of people know a heck of a lot more than they are saying."

Westra checked his watch, turned, let his gaze wander up the side of the hospital, as if checking on his mother. "I really have to get to court," he said.

"But what about the blood test?"

Westra's eyes rolled over my face. "I really can't say any more about that."

"Can't?"

"Correct."

"Why?"

Westra's mouth trembled slightly. "I suspect you'll find out what you need to know soon enough."

"But not from you, Sierd?"

He nodded, a hint of embarrassment on his face.

I took in a few breaths, and decided not to push him. "One other thing, though."

"My time's running short, preacher."

"What about the other will?"

Westra ran a hand gently over the nearly hairless dome of his head, then buttoned his suit coat. "You'll tell DeHorn where you got this?"

"I'd prefer to."

The lawyer started walking down the aisle of cars. "If you absolutely have to, do. If not, keep my name out. Please."

My silence I'm sure he took as agreement.

Over the next couple minutes, Westra explained that Sid Hammersma and he had gone out to lunch in April. During that meeting, the professor took a document out of his pocket. A new last will and testament, he informed Westra. Spreading it out on the table, Hammersma asked his friend to serve as witness as he signed on the dotted line. When Westra tried to learn more about the will and the reason for it, Hammersma grew testy and asked if he would witness it or not. Westra reluctantly agreed. And as soon as he'd scribbled his name, Hammersma refolded it and slipped it in his pocket.

"You have no idea what was in it?" I asked.

"None."

"But how can you have …?"

"By Michigan law you need only have someone witness the signing. The witness need not know what is in it."

"That's crazy," I replied.

Hands in his pockets, Westra shrugged.

"So you have no idea what was in it, or why he wrote it?"

"That's right."

We stood by the gate through which the doctor's gleaming Saturn car had passed minutes before.

"Or," I added, "where it is now, or if there are other beneficiaries, or …"

Westra's mouth pinched into a pea-sized purse. "Or any of it, pastor. Any of it. All I know is that Sid Hammersma wanted a witness, and so the son-of-a-gun chose me."

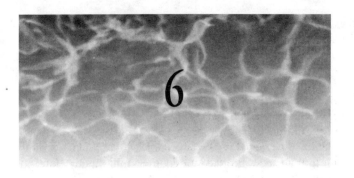

6

Down a tall, almost airless hallway which smelled like rat poison, I made my way to the office of The Outreach and its editor, Jay Randolph Van Antwerp. I'd been here a few times, bearing a piece or two of poetry I had wanted considered for publication. Besides hiking and reading and occasional spurts of running and biking, my hobby was scratching out poems. Sketches of life as I felt it, or saw it, or hoped it would be. Most of it was doggerel; some of it got published in various places. Although The Outreach office was less than palatial, and the publication itself was fairly drab and forbidding, the magazine had a solid reputation for probing, often in an entertaining and enlightening fashion, the issues facing our church. It was a publication full of divergent opinions always soundly based in the tenets of the Reformed faith, of which our 300,000-member denomination was a small part. Some obscure, somewhat marginal ministers such as myself occasionally found their way into the magazine's solidly gray pages, but a few long-time stalwarts were there month in and month out. These were the half dozen or so columnists, among them — perhaps the premier writer among them — Sidney Hammersma. Every three months when the magazine appeared, there he would be, expounding on matters of faith in his stimulating, sometimes pedantic way.

VanAntwerp, also known as "The Twerp," seemed almost as large as the bookcase taking up half the wall of his cluttered office overlooking the gritty intersection of Eastern Avenue and Wealthy Street. In looks and manner, he was nothing like his father, Daniel, founding editor of the publication.

"Sorry I'm late," I said.

"Turkstra," he replied, without turning. From the backside, with the white fabric of his shirt stretched tight across his shoulders, the large, boyish editor made me think of a drive-in movie screen. On his back I envisioned Laurel and Hardy dancing. He turned before I had even said anything. "How are you?" he asked, extending a milky, pudgy forearm and hand.

"Good, Randy," I said.

"Sit," he said, mopping his brow with a small, wadded towel.

Air conditioning of sorts churned through the room. Still, the old building was stuffy. I sat in a ragged armchair across from his desk, piled with books and reams of paper.

"Bring any poems?" he asked.

"Not this time."

His face sagged in mock disappointment. Or at least I assumed he was kidding until he said, "Turkstra, Houseman or Yeats you're not, but you do have things to say."

I looked away. Much of my poetry lately — I'm ashamed to say — had been born of the ambiguous feelings connected with Monica.

"I mean it," VanAntwerp said. "The ones you did last spring about the old barns, comparing them to God's handiwork, were superb."

I looked back, pleased, but suspicious. He hadn't mentioned the one about the bird that flew from the barn — Monica. "Why're you buttering me up?" I asked.

He mopped his brow and scowled. "Just handing you a compliment is all."

"Thanks."

As VanAntwerp adjusted himself, his chair creaked and moaned. If anything, he seemed bigger than the last time we met. "Before we leave this subject," he added, "I could use something for Christmas. Maybe a quartet, something about the season out in your neck of the woods."

I didn't want to write poetry on demand, even if I was the one doing the demanding. "I'll see what I can do," I grumbled.

"Good," he said, setting both hands atop his desk, making a few papers shake. Circles of sweat decorated his shirt around the underarms. "But it wasn't your literary endeavor you came here to talk about?"

I shook my head in agreement and crossed my legs. Leaning back in the chair, I thought momentarily of a boat drifting, unmanned, on the lake. From shore it was a faraway dot, its sails drooping. As it bobbed on the water, it got closer and closer to the horizon, from where it would drop off the edge of the earth. A sense of falling snapped me back to attention. "What can you tell me about Sid Hammersma, about the column you were telling me he wrote."

His face clouded, with dimples folded in on themselves. I noticed a rashy redness encircle his neck like a noose. "On the phone you said this is all confidential."

"More or less."

"Meaning …"

"That I'll have to at least report to Bradley DeHorn."

"Who," VanAntwerp said, " will blab it to the world."

"He'll probably inform the seminary board."

He sighed heavily, grabbed his towel and began mopping again.

"Why the reluctance if you know something, Randy?"

He made a face, as if he had just bitten into an apple filled with worms. "If you haven't noticed, the seminary board and our magazine have never been fast friends."

"What do friends have to do with it?"

His eyes flicked over me. "It's too complicated. Suffice it to say, telling you about the column puts me in a position I don't like to be in with any part of the hierarchy of our church."

I suspected it had to do with the fiercely independent

stance The Outreach had maintained. Always, especially with this man's father at the helm, the publication had steered clear of any link, formal or otherwise, with the church that quite often was the subject of its editorial fodder. Even so, the bulk of its readership and support came from the church.

In this way, it was odd but understandable. Ours was a conservative, evangelical church. Meaning we didn't go for all-out Bible-thumping and hell-fire preaching, at least in public. Plus, ours was a church with a rich intellectual heritage. Backward as some might see us, we thrived on well-founded, high-minded discussion — which is why The Outreach, liberal as it was, could catch a substantial following in our denomination. Small as we were, we took our traditional faith seriously. And focused as we were on the literal truth embedded in Scripture, we also paid heed to human intelligence. At least to a point, we revered the human mind. Sometimes, of course, the heart suffered.

"I'll do my best to involve you as minimally as possible," I told the pudgy editor.

He smiled. In the midst of his wide face, the grin looked like the split in a melon. The teeth were tiny seeds.

"Turkstra," he said, growing serious, "do you have any idea of the complications some of this might have?"

I uncrossed my legs and leaned forward. "No, not really."

"Reputations can be destroyed."

I was intrigued, but I kept calm. I scowled and insisted, "I'm listening."

His mouth made an O; he chuckled nervously and began rooting around on his desk. When he found what he was looking for, he set it down, smoothed it out with a hand and blinked. "Can I preface this with a few remarks?"

"Preface away."

In early May he had gone abroad to participate in two church meetings. One was in Amsterdam; the other in Prague. "Things are really opening up over there, like you wouldn't believe," he said. "Eastern Europe has become our onion."

I nodded, wondering how the better part of a continent could be a vegetable.

After Prague, he took a three-week tour of China. An old-time missionary in our church now ran tours of the country's central and northern provinces. I sensed VanAntwerp wanted to tell me much more about his trip, but, probably noticing my irritation, he brought himself quickly home and up to date.

"I returned last Wednesday. Thursday I sorted through copy for our fall issue. It's due at the printers," he said, checking his watch, "in two hours. Anyway, most of the stories were all edited and left for my final read and approval." As he spoke, his eyes drifted down to the papers in front of him on the desk. "Of all that I saw, only one caught my attention." The eyes looked into mine; a balled fist dropped gently onto the papers. "This," he said, still looking at me. "This column made me think twice."

"Hammersma's?"

"Yes."

"Why?"

"Because," he said, swinging the papers in my direction, "of the subject matter."

"And that is …?" I leaned forward, scanning the words.

"Dr. Death," he said.

"What?"

"Dr. Death."

"Who?"

"Jack Kevorkian."

"The guy in Detroit?"

"None other."

Kevorkian was a blabbermouth retired pathologist who had made a name for himself by helping terminally ill people kill themselves with a "suicide machine" he'd developed. As I understood it, it was a device that delivered carbon monoxide to the people, who strapped a mouthpiece to their faces and breathed in. Patients died quickly — and painlessly.

"What's this have to do with him?"

"Kevorkian's the subject of the piece."

I reached over, but VanAntwerp wasn't ready to let go yet. "Not only that," he said, "but the good Doctor Kevorkian is made out to be nothing less than a folk hero."

I just sat there, reading snatches of words on the computer print-out.

"Doesn't that strike you as a bit odd?" he asked.

"How so?"

"That Sid Hammersma, champion of life at almost any cost, would come down on the side of killing, of suicide."

I leaned back, folded my arms over my chest, not willing to beg for a full read of the column. "Sid Hammersma sometimes took positions just to get people thinking. Chances are he'd find Kevorkian thought-provoking."

VanAntwerp shook his head. "Well, the essay goes further than that. Near the end, it gets very personal, and Sid Hammersma as much as says that he wouldn't mind, if it came down to it for him, to be hooked up to Kevorkian's machine."

That part did surprise me. "He says that?"

"Pretty much."

"Does he ... does he mention that he was sick?"

VanAntwerp's thin eyebrows rose. "You heard he was sick?"

"I did," I said.

VanAntwerp's moon face took on an expression of pained consternation. "With what?" he almost croaked out.

"That I'm not sure," I said, a little surprised by his obvious concern. "Someone told me something about a blood test and a bad liver."

"Was it AIDS?" he asked. A flicker of embarrassment shone in his eyes. They shifted, lizard-like, from one side to the other.

"You know something I don't?" I asked.

"I thought that that's what I was asking you," he said.

I felt my stomach quake as if I'd ridden fast down the rickety slope of a roller coaster. Cancer was one thing; AIDS, absolutely another.

"I'm sorry," VanAntwerp said. "I had no basis for coming up with that. It's just, the world being what it is these days."

I didn't believe him. Something told me I'd turned a corner and was glimpsing a whole other part of the landscape.

"Is AIDS mentioned in that column?" I asked.

He placed his hands over it protectively. "No."

I tried to read through his hands. The image of AIDS came back to me with stunning clarity. Especially Danny O'Hara, a kid I'd worked with and watched die while I was in Chicago. It was an awful, vicious, relentless disease, a plague of nature worse than any we'd seen in years. I'd read up on it. I hated it. I knew it was an illness in which God was sometimes the only comfort. And even then, given the approach some of my Christian brethren took, even God was of no solace.

"So … sorry," Randy said. "What was he sick with?" I said nothing. "Cancer? The heart?"

"Does it matter?" VanAntwerp made a movement with his shoulder, as if shrugging off fleas. The notion of AIDS lay in my throat like a rock.

VanAntwerp said, "If it's cancer, from what I gather, the kind determines the prognosis. My dad had it in the lungs, you know."

My first time in this office, years before with a clutch of poems in my hands, I'd met his father hiding underneath a cloud of Pall-Mall smoke. "I'm not his doctor," I said testily. "I really don't know." VanAntwerp looked away, as if I'd hurt his feelings. AIDS? I asked myself again. I thought of Danny's gaunt, hollow, terrified face.

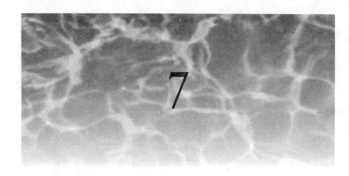

Noontime at Thrifty Acres in Jenison was a carnival of shoppers, gawkers, peddlers, and hangers around. It was the last category — old men on shiny benches by the shoe repair, a scrawny teen-age boy munching popcorn by the penny-a-ride bouncing plastic horse, the angry, bug-eyed woman protecting her massive purse with big-knuckled hands by the Lotto counter — it was these, the loiterers, that often grabbed my attention. They were the ones on the periphery, the idle few who didn't have to be here but were. These were the ones who had glimpses into the supernatural in a way denied the busy rest of us — those of us who bustled so maniacally in and out of this store and back into our pell-mell, too often pointless lives. It was in Thrifty Acres, a triple-barn-size store full of nearly every commercial item imaginable that the masses mulled and gathered. Down aisle upon aisle most of us wandered, full of purpose, seeking canned goods, canary cages, toothbrushes, and mushroom soup to carry with us back out into the world beyond. But on the edge of it all, this grand marketplace for grazing, sat the pale, possibly penniless wanderers. Occasionally, hoping to see beyond the surface of all this buying, I plopped on a bench and joined the outsiders. Once or twice, by shutting my eyes and just letting the huge place sink into me, I came close. I sensed the wonder of all God made, cereal and soap and tennis shoes included.

Today, I didn't stop. With hardly time to spare, I skirted

the loitering souls along the entrance walls and made my way upstairs past the barber shop, the quick-fix dental clinic, a photo mart, and into the expansive, brightly lit cafeteria. Buckets of sunlight, mixed with flickering overhead fluorescence, made the eating area seem suddenly as bright as I imagined Heaven to be. A truly blinding place in which every flaw and piece of perfection, whether a knobbed nose or a curving neck, was drastically highlighted. I had to blink a moment as I stood by the refrigerated display case showing slices of pie. My eyes adjusted to the glare.

"Reverend," said Sgt. Benny Plasterman just before I reached his table in the corner by a row of drooping, fluffy, moist-looking ferns that had been set by a bank of tall windows, overlooking a sea of parked cars and Chicago Drive beyond.

"Benny," I said, shaking his hand.

"You look funny, Reverend," he said.

I blinked, my mind still fuzzy. "Been a busy day."

As I sat, he gazed at me and said, "You going to eat?"

I looked back over my shoulder at the counter I'd just left. Vaguely, I said, "Maybe a tuna sandwich and lemonade."

Before I could tell Benny I'd get it myself, he started off, stopped. "Almost forgot — Slade'll probably come soon."

"Bruce?" I asked. A man who, as a youth, had made my life miserable.

Benny's brow knit. "It is his case."

"I know."

"Why the woeful tone?"

I shrugged. "Let's say he's not one of my favorite people."

Benny pursed his lips, sniffed. "I thought you'd want to talk to him, too."

As I waited, I closed my eyes and saw a clearing in the woods, a strangely familiar spot. But I didn't want to probe the image or the place. I opened my eyes and realized the thought of Slade filled me with anxiety. Closing my eyes again, I saw a cot. In a basement in Chicago. Danny O'Hara lying there, surrounded by his friends. Combined voices reciting the Lord's Prayer. Then the scent of tuna fish. Opening my eyes, I saw Benny and a sandwich on a plate.

"They were out of lemonade, but I got you iced tea with lemon in it," said Benny, reclaiming his seat across from me.

"How much do I owe you?"

"My treat." Benny watched me from above, hands folded under his chin. Behind his glasses shone owlish green eyes. He wore the brown and khaki uniform of the sheriff's department. "Eat up," he said. "I got time."

I unwrapped the sandwich after taking a sip, then a gulp, of tea. I was thirsty.

"So you stopped by to see Jean Westra?" Benny asked as I tore into my sandwich. I nodded, eating. "How is she?"

"Same," I said through a mouthful of tuna.

Benny frowned. He was the chief elder in my church. Ever since I'd come to Overisel, he'd been a friend, a father figure, as well as a guide when it came to navigating the potentially dangerous political and entangled personal waters of our congregation. In a small rural church such as ours, the intrigues numbered many. The same was true elsewhere, at bigger churches. It's just that the resentment seemed to run deep in a small-town church such as ours.

"You think this is it for her?" he asked solemnly.

I wiped my mouth with a napkin, drank tea, then said, "Truthfully, Benny, I don't know. She's been through a lot and looks awful, but something tells me she's probably still strong as a horse. But ... poor woman can't go on forever."

In short order, I finished the sandwich, the pickle wedges along with it, and wished I had another. My spirits were lifting; the cafeteria was once again ordinary.

"So," said Benny, "you don't like Mr. Slade?"

I rubbed my chin, as if ridding it of a foreign facial expression. "That obvious?"

"Clear as Jacob's ass," he said. I smiled. "How about you?"

It was then his turn to smile, showing blunt, gapped teeth. He seemed pleased with himself, but then grew serious. "Let's just say the detective leaves something to be desired in my book, too."

"What problems do you have with him? Mine go back to childhood," I said.

"Mine are more recent. Still," he said, his head dipping toward me, "it's best to leave it at that if it makes no never mind to you."

"No," I said, swishing the dregs of my tea before taking a last swallow. "Doesn't matter to me." However, it did. I wanted to know. "I do hear he wants to close this investigation on the professor," I said.

"In a big way."

"Why?"

Benny sat back, folded his hands on the table. The expression on his face fell asleep. "Politics, pastor, pure and simple."

Benny, as I knew, pulled double duty as a road patrol sergeant working out of the Holland office and as a community relations officer, for which he often dealt with inquiries from the media. I wasn't the media, but I had some questions and he was gracious enough to do what he could to oblige.

"Politics. In what way?"

"You do know he's thrown his hat in the ring for the primary," Benny said.

I remembered Rhodes mentioning his fundraiser the previous night. I rarely paid much attention to who was running for what office. "Pardon my ignorance, Benny, but what's he looking to get voted into?"

"Sheriff."

I nodded. "That has something to do with the Hammersma case."

Benny leaned forward, shoulders hunched, hands folded atop the table. "I think some of the heavy shooters in our church have put the pressure on."

"How so?"

"They would like this thing wrapped up. They just don't like it hanging out there. Given their power, Bruce would like to wrap this up for them, and then they can pat his back, too."

I tipped my empty plate side to side. "Is there something here to hide, Benny?" I wondered.

His eyes crossed, as if in perplexity. "Hide what, from who?"

"That's what I was wondering. I mean, if there's so much interest in figuring this out."

Ben sat back, right hand twiddling an ear. "I didn't say anything about figuring it out."

"You mean, folks just want the door closed without knowing what's inside?"

"Could be."

We sat in silence a few seconds. "But why?" I said.

"Best left alone," replied Ben.

"If it helps clear up …?"

Ben stared at me uncomfortably. "Pastor, I've said too much already."

I obliged him. Still, what was he holding back? Exactly why did Slade want the matter resolved? Or did he? And who was leaning on him? Was it just politics?

"I can do this," he said, taking folded papers out of his back pocket. "I thought you'd probably want to take a look." I smoothed the papers in front of me and gave him a quizzical glance. "It's the report we filed on the professor."

"Thanks," I said.

A slightly strained, official-seeming sound had entered his voice. He was backing up, being a cop now, not my father-figure elder. Without comment, I read what was in front of me.

"I'm afraid there's not much help there, though," he said, as if amending his faintly critical tone.

He was right. There was little in the report that wasn't already common knowledge. A French freighter carrying frozen sides of beef had been heading out of Chicago. Fourteen miles north and 3.6 miles west of South Haven, in an area called Flagman's Sluice, at 6:22 a.m. on a foggy morning — June 9 — a seaman had spotted The Wittenberg Door drifting about 300 yards off the starboard bow. At first he had been afraid and then angry, assuming the boat was manned and that the skipper of the vessel was below deck asleep, probably drunk. As the freighter passed through the fog, the sailor saw the sailboat continue a lazy pace directly toward the much larger ship. Fortunately, the two didn't meet — but barely — and the seaman's captain called in a report to the Coast Guard. The Coast Guard arrived less than 40 minutes later. Coast Guardsmen found an empty sailboat, with no signs of struggle or any kind of turmoil. Whoever had been guiding the ship had vanished. The report was simple and straightforward. The Coast Guard found an empty boat, intact and lolling in the water. It was an unanswered question in the middle of the lake.

"Anything in there of interest? Something maybe we can make a movie about?"

I looked up to see hairy red hands cupped over a crotch. A shiny half-moon belt buckle, a hard belly, plain striped tie, beard-stubbled neck, and Bruce Slade's square, unsmiling face.

Slade joined Benny on the other side of the table. I looked away, out the window at the parking lot, over which a blanket of heat wavered. A pudgy woman in pink shorts and a flower-patterned halter top strode firmly through the heat, a child tugging at each arm, en route to the store.

"So," I heard Slade say. When I looked back, he was staring at me with mild amusement in his pale blue eyes. "I'm trying to think of the last time I saw you," he added.

Slade was a year ahead of me at Holland High School. He'd been quite an athlete, especially on the ball diamond, where he had been a pitcher with amazing speed and ferocity. He also liked to hit home runs.

"I have no idea," I offered.

"I know," he then said brightly. I made no response. "A concert in Grand Rapids a couple years ago. You were just walking out. I tried to call you, but you didn't hear."

"Concert?"

"At DeVos Hall." Still I didn't remember. I rarely went out

socially. "When Willie Nelson was in town," Slade filled in, seeming a little disturbed that I was such a forgetful dunce.

I did recall. I'd gone a few months after returning here from Chicago. I loved old Willie. Monica didn't, but she'd come. It had been one of our last outings before the end. If Slade had called out to me and I didn't respond, it was no surprise. In those last times together with Monica, I had often felt stunned, broken, at loose ends to keep solid what was so quickly, painfully unraveling. Listening to Willie belt out "On the Road Again" and feeling so lonely because I knew that's where I'd soon be.

"Oh yeah," Slade said, "one other time, too, come to think of it. Last Christmas or so at the shooting range in Grand Rapids." He eyed me harshly, as if criticizing a preacher for playing with handguns. Every few weeks or so I carried the pistol I'd bought in Taiwan during my stint in the Navy to the range and blew off a few rounds — a powerful way to release tension. As I recall, I'd very much needed it last Christmas. "You were there?" I asked.

"A couple slots over." I nodded. "Still have the gun?" he asked.

I felt defensive and blurted, "I keep it safe in my dresser at home. I don't go waving it around church."

He shrugged. No longer did he care about my gun-toting habits. He then sat back, looped an arm around Benny's chair. "Didn't know the Reverend was such a secular culture hound or would-be marksman, did you, Plasterman?" He had spoken to Benny but was looking at me. His face was older but still carried in it a ruggedly sardonic look. A few strands of gray were mixed in with his curly, cross-cropped red hair. A moustache covered his upper lip. A package of cigarettes was outlined in his shirt pocket. Benny didn't respond.

In high school Slade also had played basketball, my sport. On the court, he didn't excel. I did, making honorable mention all-state my senior year. Even so, Slade was intense. Many times in practice we battled for the ball under the boards, his elbows flying. Once he flattened my nose. That time, I had shoved him down. He sprang up and we began wrestling, blood staining the glossy floor, until other players separated us.

"So," Slade went on, changing the subject, tapping the report with a blunt forefinger, "get what you want in there?"

"Nothing that hasn't been in the news."

Slade sat back and crossed his hairy forearms over his chest. "You expected something else?" Benny, I noticed, was staring into his coffee cup, as if searching for floating flies.

"I wasn't sure what to expect," I said.

I knew Slade had been a cop in Holland a few years back and then had moved over to the county department. He was a meaty slab of man who seemed to leak cynicism from every pore. A redness around his nose indicated to me too many after-work beers. As far as I knew, Slade's family name had once been "VerSluis." His father, John, a junkyard dealer, had, for some reason, changed it to "Slade."

"Tell me again, Turkstra, why you're doing this," said Slade, wiping a finger under his nose.

I looked to Benny, whose eyes rolled up at me. "I think I went over that with you earlier, Bruce," my own elder said.

"I want him to go through it again."

I sat back in my seat, shifted to the side and gazed again at the heat-shimmering parking lot. Cars and trucks rolled by on Chicago Drive. When I turned back, composing myself, I said, "Do you resent my nosing around?"

Slade smirked. "You might say that, yes."

"Why?"

"I think I'm asking the questions here."

"Just answer one of mine."

Slade slit his eyes, and said in a raspy voice, "Because I don't need any dipshit preacher getting in the way."

"I'm bumping into you?"

"That's what I'm trying to prevent."

"I thought this was Marlan Oosterbaan's case, when all is said and done," I retorted.

He blinked, as if I'd jabbed at him in the air. "He pushes the paper. Our guys have done all the work."

"But he has final say-so."

Slade chewed his lip, flexed his shoulders, glowered. "Looks like the preacher is playing peek-a-boo with the police, eh Ben?" Still, the dull eyes stuck on me. Fire spurted on inside me; anger clogged my throat.

I glanced down at the report, pushed it back to Benny. The knot in my neck and the heat in my cheeks told me to go easy. On impulse, I decided to leave. Why put up with this surly attitude? I thought. "Thanks for the help, Benny. I've got to go."

As I stood, Slade reached out and grabbed my wrist lightly. I froze, in anger or fear, I wasn't sure which. "Sit back down," he said softly.

"Let go of my wrist." I flexed my arm, tore it away.

His jaw jutted out. "Sit," he said.

"Fellas," said Benny, breaking in.

Slade relaxed, shook his head. "C'mon, Turkstra," he said. "Sit. Sorry. Been a crappy day. Just got my rear end wiped good in court. I'm probably taking it out on you."

Even as he apologized and I sat, I felt manipulated. One thing about this guy, his rage remained. Surprisingly it didn't cow me as it once had. Even so, I could feel trickles of sweat slither from under my arms. My hand still felt the pressure of his fingers. I wondered why a man of such temperament would want to be sheriff. Or, rather, how he expected to win.

"Just go back over for me why you're looking into this," he said wearily.

I told him. I didn't get into my conversations with the doctor or VanAntwerp. Not yet anyway.

But then he asked, "So what've you found out so far that is new?" He did look tired, his face lumpy and saggy.

"That the professor's family doctor believes he was sick. And that the editor of a church publication has a column in which Sid Hammersma talks very favorably, even personally, about suicide." Why I offered him most of what I had, I wasn't sure. None of it seemed to surprise him.

"You talk with Hammersma's wife?" he asked.

"She says her husband was neither sick nor came anywhere near killing himself."

Slade took in a deep lung full of air, let it out. "Very good, Turkstra. You get an A for effort." The sarcastic tone had returned. "Anything else?"

"Nothing."

"You're sure?" I nodded, not wanting to share with him VanAntwerp's speculation. I had read the column in his office, after which he had alluded to AIDS again.

Benny picked up and folded the report. He reached up as if to place it in his pocket, then held back. His eyes turned to Slade and flicked back at me. "Would you like this copy?"

"If I could."

Benny turned back to Slade, who shrugged. "No skin off my teeth."

Benny gave it to me with a nervous, conciliatory smile. As I stuck it in my back pocket, Slade cleared his throat and asked, "You've been through it then?" I wasn't sure what he was asking. "What you know," he said, with some irritation.

"I have." Slade nodded sagely, his chin moving side to side, as if he was sawing something in his mouth. "And?" I said.

"And?"

"Does what I have found add up?"

Slade jiggled change in his pockets, leaned back. He seemed to be making a production of appearing at ease. "I'd say you're on track. Wouldn't you, Benny?"

Benny sighed. "I wouldn't know."

Slade grinned. His chin rested on his upper chest. The eyes were those of an alligator. It struck me that what he lacked in political skill, he made up for in his intensity as a cop.

"You say I'm on track. But what else is there?"

"Paltry police details."

"Such as?"

"Nothing of consequence."

"Can you let me be the judge of that?" I asked.

Slade's eyes snapped to attention; he loosely clasped his hands in front of him on the table. "They paying you to be pushy?"

I took it as a compliment and told him, "No."

He stared at me intently a few moments. Beyond the over-bearing quality, I saw the confidence and competence. His approach from way back lacked proper manners, but I suspected he was good at what he did. He was the type of man who would use his broad, lumpy forehead to batter through a brick wall. He was really taking a read on me, giving me a true, official assessment, for the first time since he sat down.

"What's the biggest beef here?" he finally asked in a let's-get-down-to-business tone. "Why have the seminary yo-yos turned you loose?"

"Sid Hammersma's wife is in bad financial shape. She needs money that's coming to her."

"Don't we all?" said Slade, out of the side of his mouth.

"I think she's more deserving," I shot back.

He fended the remark with ease. "How bad off is she?"

"Don't you know?"

His eyes glittered. He breathed loudly through his nose. His teeth, stained yellow, looked moist. It suddenly struck me — he was like a wolf, hard to predict, intense in his tasks, a bit wild. "I never got into that with her."

"Maybe not," I said, "but that's the reason I'm here."

Slade shifted in his seat, twisted his head side to side, and faced me sideways. "Tell me," he then said, "how I can help?"

I was put off guard for a second by his accommodating remark. I had to wonder what it meant. If bait is what it was, I bit. "How come you've found no body?"

Benny was watching us both with interest. Slade pursed his lips and looked somewhere beyond me. "Ever hear the expression, 'The lake is slow to give up its secrets'?" I'd heard something like it. "Well," said Slade, "in this case, it's true."

"Bodies don't always wash up."

"About the size of it."

"So then," I said, pondering it out, "you think Sid Hammersma is still out there?" Slade nodded carefully, leaned forward on clasped hands. "You also think it was a suicide?"

"Did I say that?"

"I'm just trying to string together your inferences."

"It's best to never infer anything," he said.

"Then tell me what you know for fact."

"You're sitting on the edge, partner," he said. "Anything I'm telling you is out of the kindness of my heart."

"It's just anything you can tell me would help." I realized I had almost pleaded with him. I didn't like to beg. As for his heart, I doubted he had one.

Slade took in a deep breath, let it out slowly. His jaw sawed back and forth. "Benny," he said, "how about you get me a cup of coffee?" Benny frowned. "I need a few minutes here — alone."

Benny stood and walked over, his service revolver humped at his hip, his rear end ballooning inside his uniform pants.

"Benny's a straight arrow," Slade said to me. "I don't think he ought to hear this, though."

Slade leaned toward me, his eyes edging back and forth. I recalled seeing him as a kid, deep in the celery fields, standing among the migrants, shouting orders handed down from his father. That was before his dad went full time into selling junked cars. "Thing is," he said, "I have a person who talked to Hammersma the day he left. The professor came to him because he wanted help."

"Help?"

Slade nodded. "Seems the professor was at the end of his rope and didn't want to live. I'm not sure exactly if he came to this person to be talked out of it, but he went there. They talked. Hammersma told him what he had, what he wanted to do, and then he left. They were to talk again but never made it."

I took this in, wondering why he, a cop, had told me so much, noticing Benny hanging back, talking to a woman at another table. "What he had was what?"

Slade gnawed the inside of his mouth, flared his nostrils, squeezed his hands so hard that the knuckles grew white.

"He told this person he was sick, that he had cancer?" I asked.

Slade's eyes narrowed. "He was sick with something else?"

Slade nodded. The unreal sense of floating while still sitting in a chair went through me. Around the grave, Danny O'Hara's father and mother had remained impassive. I had cried. So had Danny's other friends, including Mike, his lover. AIDS.

"I heard something like that earlier," I said.

"Which was?"

"The crazy idea Sid Hammersma had AIDS."

Slade stared right through me, a look of something akin to compassion settling on his hard face. "I've heard things crazier."

"This isn't off the wall?" Slade shook his head.

I searched his face, the pores, the coarse skin, the weary eyes, the faint scar on one cheek. "He did ... have AIDS?"

He didn't exactly smirk, but the expression that emerged was not pleasant. Yet in it I saw hurt. A kind of hidden pain he probably never shared. "What it looks like."

I remembered he and his buddy, Marlan Oosterbaan, walking together down the dirt road to school. Always talking, shoving and laughing. Theirs was a friendship based on mutual brute strength, childhoods marred by parents whose demands were as many as they were fierce, and a gallows humor that seemed to believe that inflicting pain on others was funny. Given who they were and where they came from, I found it odd that both had become police officers.

"How sure are you of this?" I asked, only vaguely wondering what the ramifications of this would be if it got out. But if all of this were true, or even parts of it, I could see why the lid had been clamped tight.

"That part's privileged."

"You can't tell me?"

"Not going to."

My fingers tapped the table top. Did Slade get hold of the blood test results Baak talked about?

"Do you have something in writing about this?"

"Most of what we got is medical gobbledy-gook."

"Can I see it?"

A hand reached up, cupping air. "Look, I shouldn't have told you this much. But chances are, most of what I just said, or the most basic parts, will come out soon enough."

"In what way?"

"We'll probably, after more work, take this as quietly as possible to probate court for resolution."

"Resolution?"

"To have him legally declared dead, and with a cause. Then whoever deserves it gets his money."

"Can you do that without a body?" I asked.

He sighed, gazed at me, man to man, equals. "If you've been talking to Marlan, you probably know I'd close it up right now if it was up to me."

"You're that sure of ... his suicide?"

He said nothing for a few moments, gazed out the huge plate glass window at the sweltering parking lot. His fingers drummed the table. "I am."

"But how ... why?" He looked back, slowly, head tilted back. "As far as I'm hearing, everything you have is circumstantial."

He sighed heavily, leaned closer, rubbed his stubbled chin. "Guy we talked to saw your professor dragging a heavy bag of something down the dock the day he got in his boat and left."

"A bag of what?"

Slade shrugged. "I'm thinking rocks."

"Rocks?" He nodded, checking to see if Benny remained out of earshot. He did. "For what, for heaven's sake?" I asked.

"My guess is to pack his jacket full, just before he took his plunge." Saying this, Slade made a dipping, nose-diving motion with his hand.

"Sounds like science fiction," I said.

Slade sat back up. "Maybe."

"But that's your best guess?"

He remained silent a few moments, checking me over. I could hear a faint wheeze in his chest. "Coast Guard found his duffle bag. Couple rocks still in it."

I stared. Hard. Trying to read more deeply why he told me this. "If that's true, why hasn't it come out until now?"

"Like you say, Turkstra, what we're talking is circumstantial."

"But it has enough believability for you to agree to the suicide theory?"

"Not a theory. I'm convinced he did it." Slade's face showed no expression — a blank hunk of flesh.

"But it's not enough to convince Marlan?"

"Marlan Oosterbaan's a careful man."

"Too careful in this case?"

"You'd have to ask him."

I was silent a moment. A bitter, metallic taste filled my mouth. A rotten egg smell stuck in my nose. "So what's your suggestion on what I should tell DeHorn?"

"Nothing that I told you is foreign matter to him."

"He knows all of this?"

"As far as I can tell."

"You've told it to him?" I asked.

"The nuts and bolts, yes." I sank in my chair. What sort of shady trip had the seminary president sent me on? "The part about the rocks," he said, "is new."

"He doesn't know that?" Slade shook his head once — a gesture of finality. "Why'd you leave that part out?"

"He didn't pester me like you." He smiled, a half-baked grin, revealing impassive teeth.

"What about the AIDS? Does he know that, too?"

"As far as I know."

I twirled the plate that a few minutes before had contained the tuna sandwich. Another form of fish. A fish that swam in deep, deadly water. Down in black places, cold and dank, places which held, I wondered, a history professor with rocks stuffed in his clothes. A hellish, forgotten place.

"One other thing," I said. He waited, eyes registering the request. "Have you heard the rumor that there is a second will floating around?"

"I have."

"You put any credence in that?"

"Do you?"

"I'm not in a position to know," I replied.

"Neither am I."

"But," I pressed, "it makes sense?"

Slade rolled his neck, shook himself, as if awakening. "From what I hear," he said, "you don't get AIDS by eating too many cheeseburgers."

"So," I said, "if it was up to you, you'd put a cork on this case right now?"

He sighed, narrowed his eyes.

"If so, why don't you?"

"Ask Oosterbaan."

"Are you getting leaned on by people in our church to clear this up?"

The eyes snapped open. "Who told you that?"

I decided to lie. To protect Benny. And, maybe, pay the seminary president back for keeping me in the dark. "DeHorn."

He barked out a laugh.

"He says a few of the high-rollers in our denomination think the lack of a body will hurt you at the polls."

A flush bloomed in his cheek. His mouth bunched into an angry circle. "Bullshit!"

"Bullshit that people are pressuring you or that it will lose you votes?"

The flush turned into bright red splotches. "Turkstra, you're stepping into a swamp."

"But why would this be a problem at the ballot box?"

He leaned forward and pushed himself up. Just as I had done earlier. But I didn't grab his wrist. He tugged at a sleeve of his thin leather coat, a skin-like covering. "I gave you all I can, Turkstra. Report it back to your buddies. After this, I won't even answer the phone if I know it's you."

8

I spoke to the shoes poking out from under the car, a 1989, royal blue Buick Electra. In mint condition. "So you know all about the AIDS?"

After the meeting at Thrifty Acres, I'd stopped at my parsonage, retrieved messages, made a few calls, and driven into Holland to the seminary. Bradley DeHorn's secretary informed me he had left early to do some work on his car. I'd crossed the campus to the nearby neighborhood in which his solid brick home stood. He'd been tinkering with the engine as I walked up the drive. I'd started to sketch what I'd learned. He listened, and then crawled under the car.

"What's that, Turkstra?"

I squatted, closer to the shoes. Kept my emotions in check. It was bad enough to think he'd led me on a wild goose chase, and now a misfiring engine seemed more important than what I had to say.

"I said, did you already know that Sid Hammersma had AIDS?"

The shoes moved, followed by DeHorn, wriggling out from underneath. He blinked, fingered a shard of rust from the corner of his eye. He wore stained, pinstriped overalls. He sat, facing me. A series of wrenches were wedged in one hand. The other yanked a rag from a pocket. He dabbed his brow. "I had heard that," he said.

Parked on a slab of cement between the screened-in back

porch of his home and his garage, the car seemed to loom over us. He leaned against the front driver's door.

"Why didn't you offer me that piece of information?" I asked. "It didn't seem important to you?"

His mouth twitched. I suspected he didn't like my sarcastic tone. "Did you come here to complain, Turkstra?"

"I suppose I did."

"Then fire away."

A woman in the next yard watered her lawn. A few grackles flitted about on telephone wires. Heat from the driveway pavement beat up into my face. I hated it when people accommodated my anger. It took all the joy out of it — deflated my emotions. "I'm just wondering what else you've held back?"

He examined the wrenches, wiped one with the rag, stuck the rest in a back pocket. "Pretty much most of it."

I flopped onto my butt. "Then what in the devil is my role?"

"Confirmation." His brow crinkled. I noticed a white shirt and knotted tie underneath the denim material of his work outfit.

"But if you know the whole story, why do you need me?"

He tapped the wrench in the palm of his hand, let his eyes wander beyond me. A smudge of grease darkened a spot on his chin. "Because, Turkstra, I wanted someone to look at this mess with a fresh pair of glasses."

A dog yapped somewhere. A motor groaned; perhaps a garbage truck crunching refuse. "So you gave me the list, pretty much knowing what I'd find, and just wanted me to back up what you already know?"

The wrench stopped tapping. His chest rose and fell evenly. "I came back to fix my transmission leak so I can drive off to a meeting I have at 5 in Grand Rapids. So I really don't have the time to wrangle with you."

"Just tell me then, please, where all of what you're having me do is leading?"

He smiled. "Now that's the part I was leaving up to you."

I shook my head. Confused.

"The conclusion. If you can come to it. I'm well aware of the various parts of this thing. But I don't know what they all mean."

I propped my arms behind me in a cool cushion of grass. "Sounds like I just went from messenger boy to private detective."

He flipped the wrench a couple inches in the air, caught it. Twisted onto his back. Shoved himself back under. "I think you're starting to catch on, Calvin, I really do."

Calvin was my first name — a tag given by my father. Truman was the middle — a name conferred by my mother. I didn't know if she'd done it out of contrariness or not. But she named me after Harry S. Truman, a president who was not particularly popular in our highly Republican neck of the woods. I preferred Truman, and suspected my deepest leanings were in the liberal directions set by that man from Missouri. I lay on my back. Stuck my folded hands over my belly. Watched threads of white slide across the deep blue of the sky above. "I thought you said, sir, that I was not supposed to compile information, not dig up anything new."

I heard grunts come from under the car. Metal screeched. "I'm starting to change my mind."

"Why is that?" More groans of effort.

"Jesus Jenny!" he said.

I waited a minute or so, my mind in the clouds. The specter of AIDS remained. But somehow I didn't want to probe it too deeply yet.

Eventually the seminary president re-appeared. Speckles of dirt, or rust, on his face. His skin rosy with effort. A dab of blood leaking from a knuckle. "Fixed!" he said proudly.

He stood. So did I.

"You were saying, pastor?" he asked.

"You want me to do work that is really for the police?"

His eyes glazed over with a far-off expression. He wiped the back of a hand over his mouth. I noticed a coil of hose by his back steps. An air conditioner hummed in a back window. "You see, that's the thing," he said. "I'm not so sure any-more they are doing their job."

"You mean, Bruce Slade?"

"For one."

"And Marlan Oosterbaan?"

His face clouded. "I'm not so sure about him."

"But why are you suspicious of Slade?"

He stepped to the front of the car, bent into the engine block area, looked around, jiggled a few wires, tapped the battery. Angled his face toward me. "Again, I don't know."

"Or aren't saying?"

He gazed at his engine. "If you don't trust me, Turkstra, you can beg off right now."

The clipped tone told me I'd pushed him too far. I knew there was much more to what he wasn't telling me. I could drop out. But I didn't want to.

"Just one thing."

His arms raised toward the open hood. Hands rested there.

"Are there others who know ... that the professor was sick?"

His eyes rolled to me. "Not many."

"But some?"

"A few."

He slammed down the hood. The echo reverberated through his yard.

"How is it going to play if it goes public?"

DeHorn sighed. He slumped against the front of his car, staring at his garage door, on which was painted a large, fancy-lettered D. "I don't think that is too hard to imagine. Do you?"

Not really. Not well, I suspected. "Was learning it a sur-prise?" I asked him.

He stood, wrenches clinking in his deep front pocket. "Knowing Sidney and the demons that have driven him over the years, not really."

"But this demon," I said. "You were aware of it?"

His shoulders slumped. He suddenly looked unbearably sad. "Yes."

"Even when you tried to convince him to stay on after the offer from Harvard?"

"Especially then."

"But why?"

"Because, Turkstra, I was deathly afraid it would all come to this. And if it had to, I assumed, perhaps stupidly, it would be best to occur among friends."

"You're feeling bad now that it did — whatever it was that exactly happened."

DeHorn's right hand idly touched the fender of his well-kept car. "Why I'm feeling bad, Turkstra, is not totally because of what happened."

I waited.

The hand on the fender balled into a fist. Three knuckles, I noticed, were now smeared with blood. "I'm sad, disgusted actually, about something else — about the part about friends. I'm terribly afraid that it's Sidney's friends who have betrayed him in this. I really am."

"And you're hoping I can find out if that's true?"

A film of water covered his eyes. He smeared a hand over his forehead.

"Among other things, Turkstra, yes, I am."

9

From the vantage point of the third floor of the seminary's academic building, I let my mind roll through images of the place I had hoped to visit yet this summer. Maybe with my pulpit covered, I could do it soon. I'd like to go to Isle Royale, the rugged island in the middle of Lake Superior. I recalled the hills, the paths, the untouched beauty of the place. I'd gone there twice as a kid, once with friends and once with the Calvinist Cadet Corps, a kind of Christian Boy Scouts troop. The third, and so-far final, time had been two years before with Monica. The second day out, deep on the interior of the island, we had spotted a wolf, one of the few remaining in Michigan. The animal had darted across the edge of a meadow, on the track of a deer. I recall the gray-black ruff, the reddish eyes that turned in our direction before it vanished, through what looked from a distance like a welter of brambles. Two hours later, just before we made camp, we came across the remains of a doe in a bloody, pulpy pile by the trunk of a huge pine, not fifty yards from a fast-moving stream. Monica had been fascinated. She bent, examined, sniffed the worm-like remains. I'm not the scientist, nor even explorer, that she is. I had turned away, peering deep into the woods, and glimpsed, perhaps in my imagination, a pair of wary, watchful, reddish eyes. For that moment, I wondered if we were prey, too. Possibly something in the tension that had grown between us on that trip had brought to mind

77

those thoughts of danger. That night in our tent I slept fitfully. Several times I heard a terrible howl. Monica slept peacefully, dreamily, a bluish light glowing on her face. The next day, after lunch, as we started back to the docking area, when she told me it wouldn't work, that it would probably be best if I moved back to Chicago, I wasn't surprised.

I was brought out of my reverie by the phone on Sid Hammersma's large, polished desk. I reached over and answered it, as I had been expecting a call.

"Truman?" I heard on the other end.

"Hi, Jerry."

"What's up?" came the reply.

"I need some help."

"Who doesn't?"

I often wondered why journalists felt the need to wear their cynicism like armor. Hardly any that I'd ever met acted in any way compassionate, although their stories regularly showed powerful sympathies for the underdog.

"So," he said, "what're you looking for?"

Outside and below, the campus stretched, still sunny and mostly unpopulated. I glanced at my watch and noticed I'd been rooting through the history professor's effects in his large, book-lined office for nearly an hour. I'd been about to leave when I decided, a half hour before, to put in a call to Jerry VanderMolen, religion editor of The Press.

"What can you tell me about Sid Hammersma?"

I heard a nervous chuckle on the other end. "Have you become an investigative reporter?"

"Something like that."

Bradley DeHorn had given me the key to this office and permission to poke through the professor's things. There were books, papers, scraps of note pads on which were written Bible verses and article references. But nothing I'd come across had particularly helped. I'd especially searched for any sign of a second will. To no avail. And, given the mounds of paper in the office, I suspected I'd have to look for hours, maybe days, to determine if it was there. "What I want to know is …" I said.

"First," he cut in. "What are the ground rules here?"

"Ground rules?"

"If you're turning up some good dirt, do I get to put it on my shovel?"

Although a member of our denomination, Jerry had a strong bias — anything that even hinted at scandal in the Christian Reformed Church was often covered with almost pathological intensity. It was as if, because he was a believer, he made it his business to unmask, wherever he could, all wrongdoing and hypocrisy he could find. With that in mind, I said, "I'd prefer to let it stay as background for now."

"For now is how long?"

"Maybe forever."

"Forever is a long time. If it is juicy, I can't promise that."

"Can you promise a couple weeks, if I'm not your official source?"

"What is it, Turkstra? C'mon."

Above the trees outside the window hung a blank blue sky. The wolf in the woods had been looking and lurking. It struck me that Monica had always liked predators, which is probably why she was dating Engstrom. The very thought of one animal chasing down and tearing flesh from another made me uneasy. Somehow it challenged her.

"Jerry," I said, "I need your promise. Work with me, and I'll give whatever of the story I can to you."

"Ask your questions," he said. "I'll see if I can help."

"From what you know, was Sid Hammersma involved in sexual things?" I asked.

He laughed through the phone. "He wasn't a Catholic monk, for God's sake."

"I mean aberrations. Kinky stuff," I amended.

"Like what kind?" he asked. In his voice I noted rising curiosity. Aberrations were a journalist's stock and trade.

Before answering, I glanced around the office. It was large, messy, packed with Hammersma's books, plaques — boasting degrees earned, photos of the professor with academic and civic dignitaries, three large water colors of bright city scenes, and in one corner a large Japanese mask next to which was a sorrowful etching of Christ's crucified body. An Oriental carpet covered the floor; several file cabinets lined one wall. The desk top was covered with thick glass. Books were jammed into the floor-to-ceiling case. A portrait of Hammersma and his wife, she in her wheelchair, he looking especially hearty with his snowy hair and winning grin, stood before me by the phone. The photo looked as if it had been taken in Colorado; mountains massed behind them. Husband and wife, in the foreground, were almost diminished by the massive landscape. Yet even there, surrounded by icy peaks, Sid Hammersma was a clean-cut, well-fashioned character. In a room, in class, in church, on TV, at a lecture, he always drew attention. His bearing was such that it demanded notice. In the photo he wore a Panama hat, its shadow touching his forehead; his wife seemed hunched in, strained, but bravely facing the camera. Did this man's energies, his appetites, carry him beyond her and into what many in my church defined as aberrations?

Not wanting to get VanderMolen's mental wheels rolling too lasciviously, I answered, "I just wondered if you had heard if monogamy was his strong suit."

"Is it anybody's?"

"Well," I said, "was it his?"

"I'm not Ann Landers."

"Jerry, I need some help."

"What is it you want?"

I couldn't bring myself to offer him the AIDS rumor. "Just hoping for your general assessment of Sid Hammersma. Of his sexual inclinations?"

"Then I don't have much."

My eyes wandered out the window to the campus. Dusk was not far off. An hour or so yet. Still, the sky had taken on a tired, washed-out flavor; shadows lengthened. The heat, I hoped, was starting to ease.

"Could you ask around?"

"You just want me to dig up a few rumors?" he asked.

"If you don't have any on the tip of your tongue."

"I'm doing you a favor?" he asked.

"If you want to put it that way."

"I suppose I owe you a couple." I didn't dispute that, given the help I'd provided him on a few stories. "Can't you tell me what type of rumor I'm to track down?"

I preferred not to, hoping he would either confirm or dispute independently what I'd learned. "Just if you can see what type of after-hours reputation he had." I gazed at the healthy grin coming up at me from in front of the mountains. I noticed something I had missed before. His right hand was at his side. His wife's hand was raised from her chair and clasping his, in love, need, or fear. I wasn't sure.

"Can you give me until tomorrow to make a few calls?" he asked.

"Sure."

"But if this leads to the Pulitzer, Turkstra," he said, "will I have to share it?"

"If it does, I'll buy you dinner," I said. "You keep the prize."

10

I lapsed back into thought after hanging up, and my mind turned to poems. Words formed in my head as I watched the way the wisps of trailing white clouds gathered in puffy swirls. I imagined the clouds talking, massed on the horizon, sorting through their day. Nothing came of such paltry mental meanderings. The triteness of the images that formed made me realize it was dinner and some rest I wanted, not poem-making. I was relieved of the burden of my own thoughts when I heard, "Oh, I'm sorry."

Standing there, willowy and blond, eyes pale, was Sandra, the history department secretary who had directed me here awhile before. "I didn't realize you were still here," she said.

"I was getting ready to go," I responded.

She leaned into the doorway, a pencil poking out of her hair in back. "You find anything that might help?"

"Actually not."

"Too bad," she said.

Sandra had wide eyes and a firm, upturned mouth. Her petite prettiness reminded me of the celibate lifestyle I'd developed. A lifestyle that was turning me into a sexual snob. That Monica and I hadn't married as we'd hoped and as local church busybodies had expected, had left me as something of a social oddity. Many weren't quite sure what to make of my singleness. Monica, being in a fairly urbanized church known for its ministry to the young and even divorced, was more praised than ostracized, and probably even better accepted for it. I noticed the ring on Sandra's left hand.

"Do you have a second?" I asked.

"Sure."

"Could you tell me," I said, "had Dr. Hammersma seemed troubled to you?"

Sandra's eyes swept the room, as if searching for an answer among the books, papers and pictures. "Not more than usual."

"Dr. Hammersma was," I said, "a normally troubled man?"

"I'd say that. Yes."

"How?"

"Oh," she said, eyes turned to the ceiling. She wore a white T-shirt, on the front of which was emblazoned a blue-green globe under which was written "It's Your Earth, Too." Faded blue jeans covered her legs. "You know, he was always thinking, kind of burdened down, I guess you'd say, by the world."

"But what about before he disappeared? Did he seem moodier?"

"No. Like I said, he was in his own head a lot."

I knew how that was. "Did he say anything about being sick?" I wondered.

She blinked, turned full into the room, crossed delicate arms over the Northern Hemisphere. "Was Dr. Hammersma ill?"

I stood up from the chair and sat on the edge of the historian's desk. "He might have been."

"How serious?"

"Could have been very."

Her eyes grew wide; she put a hand to her throat. I had no idea why, but I sensed Sandra could help. "His wife," I said. "Did he talk to her often?" She made a face. Confused probably by this turn in the conversation.

"I'm just wondering, were there many calls back and forth during work hours?" Most of the calls, going in and out of the department, came through her. DeHorn had mentioned that as he'd given me the key to this office.

"Once in awhile, but not much. Maybe the usual. Why?"

"I'm beginning to think she didn't know how sick he was."
I was also starting to wonder if somehow the irate wife — for
she had to be angry — had brought an end in some way to
her husband. With help from the lawyer in Grand Haven?

"She would've had to," Sandy said firmly. "I mean, she's
his wife."

"But she's a pretty sick woman herself."

"I heard that," she offered.

I stood from the desk, idly fingered through junk mail on
the top of a stack of slick magazines. I sensed she was rolling
thoughts over in her mind.

"You know," she said, "he was losing weight."

"Oh?"

She nodded. "Not a lot, but some. It was noticeable. I
mentioned it a couple times and he just said it was the
weather. He always lost his appetite in spring. Plus, he got
out and did more exercising."

"Anything else?"

She thought, examining the ceiling. "He kind of had a
cough, I guess."

That fit, I thought sadly. "How long have you worked in
this department?" I then asked, again sitting, moving the
conversation elsewhere.

"Three years."

"In all that time, did Dr. Hammersma ever have run-ins,
serious ones, with people that you know about?" The AIDS
theory did lead fairly easily to the suicide conclusion. Losing
weight fit in, too. Still, parts of it didn't add up. I continued
to wonder about some kind of foul play. That he was sick was
clear, but how he died — and why — was not.

"Run-ins?" she asked.

"I guess I'm wondering — is there anyone who you think
really disliked Dr. Hammersma? Someone who might have
wanted to hurt him in some way?"

Her eyes grew saucer-shaped, and even haughty. "Oh no,"
she retorted. "He was very, very well-liked around here. I

mean, he could keep to himself a lot, but then he was also really friendly, too. He was always asking about my kids."

"No one, then, that you know, was his enemy?"

She replied firmly, seeming even a little upset, "Not at all!"

I was surprised at her emotion, taken by her loyalty. "If anything," she added, "it went the other way. People were always coming by or calling. He was a real favorite. If he was deep into work on something, then maybe he was not approachable. But otherwise, he left this door open. Always."

She closed her eyes a moment. Her neck was a gentle curve; a vein pulsed above her collarbone, indents from which shone underneath her T-shirt. Her eyes opened and fixed on me. She looked to be about 22. "I saw him last on the afternoon it happened."

"What was he doing in here?"

"Writing and making calls. Friday afternoons were generally a time for correspondence."

"What kind?"

"Letters. Catch up on things."

"Did you ever type for him?"

"Not that day."

"Do you know," I said, "did he write his column for The Outreach in this office?"

"Outreach?"

I picked up a copy from the desk and showed it to her.

"Oh, that," she said. "Not that I know of."

I tried to sense the presence of the man in this room, of him moving around, paging through these books, talking on the phone. Years back, I had come in here with a research paper. We'd gone over it. I recall the respect I'd felt, even as a seminary student, being with him alone. I remembered his energy, his distractedness when I'd come in and the way he'd given me his complete attention once he'd begun his review of my paper. "Do you have any idea who he might've been calling that day?" I asked.

Slowly, after some thought, she shook her head.

Glancing down, I stared at the phone, a silent beige instrument. Next to it was a pile of scrap paper. Notes were scribbled on some of them. Who would want to kill him? And why? At this point, there seemed far more reason for suicide than homicide. I took a stab in the dark: "Is there any record of who he called that day?"

She shook her head. "Funny, but no one's asked that."

"There is!" I said.

"The computer logs them all, in and out. Kind of like a little Big Brother."

The cover of The Outreach in my lap showed a rendering of a bearded man atop whose shoulders and on whose head danced four angels. Beneath the man in a cave of sorts, were five other heavenly bodies. Each was praying. The man, the central figure, looked to be in a state of anguish. It was Job. The powerful spokesman for woe. The ultimate victim. God's chosen scapegoat. It struck me now — I'd read this Outreach last year. Thoughts of Job had percolated since. I was beginning to have a different feeling for the man. For Job. Scourges perhaps weren't that clear-cut. Maybe there was pain, and awful disease we brought on ourselves. Maybe God wasn't always to blame, even if he was there to help. I asked, "How could I — or could I — get a list of the calls he made that afternoon?" From what I knew, Sid Hammersma left this office and headed straight for the marina, for his boat.

"Shouldn't be hard," she said. "I should be able to print it out in a flash."

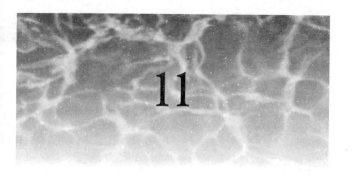

11

Easing my way down the swooping, carpeted staircase onto the basement floor of the Martin F. Kuhn Memorial Library, I experienced a kind of reverence. This library was a Reformed fortress full of a past whose richness helped shape my life and that of my father and of his father before him and so on. The result of a huge bequest by Kuhn, a deceased furniture company founder, the library rivaled, or surpassed, any in West Michigan. With original Flemish oil paintings on the walls and artifacts from different eras of the Dutch past displayed behind glass, the building was as much a showpiece as a center for research. At the bottom of the stairs, I nearly bumped into the man who helped to maintain this palace of learning.

"Reverend Turkstra," said Albert Rozek, a wispy, dark-eyed man who was head librarian and chief curator and had been while I was attending seminary here a decade before. "Can I help you with something?"

"The city directories?"

He stepped over and pointed a bent finger under his chin to the area behind the corkscrewing staircase. "Next to the medical and business dictionaries." I nodded my thanks, about to rush on. "How are you, Turkstra?" he added, pulling me back with his words. "What brings you down here on a stuffy summer night?"

Rozek was a small man, dressed in a white and blue seersucker suit. His pink shirt was open at the collar.

"I'm fine," I said. "I just have to look up some phone numbers." I suddenly recalled that Rozek, among other things, was a noted scholar in a technical area in which he was often asked to determine whether manuscripts were actually written by a certain author. Awhile back, he had been able to authenticate that several chapters of an unearthed book had actually been written by John Calvin. The subject of the chapters escaped me. Another time he had been one of a few scholars who concluded that a short story dug out of an attic in Baltimore or someplace had not, as had been suspected, been written by Mark Twain.

Albert came from Romania. He'd been imprisoned in a Nazi concentration camp and came to this country shortly after the war. On his face was a fixed, hollow expression that always reminded me of the chaos out of which he had risen. Poverty, hunger, repression. His father, a Reformed minister, had also come out of the Nazi camp alive — and was then put to death in the early '50s by the Communists.

"Why're you looking up phone numbers on such a hot night?" asked Rozek.

The library was nearly empty. His eyebrows, half-moon slices, flickered up. "You are having problems?" he asked seriously. He stood there, dapper in his suit, eyes moist.

I looked around, saw no one. It struck me that he could help. "No problem, really, but," I said. His eyes followed mine. "I'm wondering if you could do me a favor."

"That's what we are here for," Albert said.

I reached in my back pocket, slipped out the folded column written by Sid Hammersma for The Outreach.

"What I've got," I said, "is confidential for right now." I felt moistness that had seeped into the paper from being in my pocket all day.

"Confidential?" he asked.

"For the time being."

Rozek nodded, eyes on the paper. "You want me to …?"

"This is a column supposedly written by Sid Hammersma that was to run in September, in their fall issue." I handed it to him. He unfolded it and, holding it end to end diagonally with four fingers, started to read. "I'm wondering," I said, "if you could examine it, maybe compare it to a few of his other pieces, and see what you think. If he's really the one who wrote this."

The half-moon brows flickered like wings atop the furthermost bridge of his nose. "You have reason to suspect it is fraudulent?"

I sighed, gazing down at a nearby table, and noticed a rare volume with Dutch scribbling on the cover. I thought of those millions of words, many written carefully and probably passionately, contained within this library. Between the covers of each book was a world, a point of view, someone took the time, often years, to construct. Among the books in this place were no doubt those written by Sid Hammersma.

"I don't know why," I said. "I'm no expert. Maybe it's the subject matter."

He nodded as he read. "This man, Kevorkian, is in the news. But who is this for? Just for you?" he asked.

"Do you really need to know?" I asked.

"I would — if I agree to do it."

I told him, "Bradley DeHorn."

He gazed curiously at me, as if waiting for me to say more.

"It would be helpful," he said finally, "if the request came formally from him."

"Could you give it a quick read, say by tomorrow? If you turn up something, I'll ask DeHorn."

He examined my face, checked the words in the column again. "That much I can do."

The relief I felt surprised me. I thanked him. Just as I was about to leave, he asked, "Those numbers you are looking up, is that part of this, too?"

"It is."

He turned, started to stride away. "For this you need no formal request."

89

12

Outside, in a dusk that came on sultry with little hint of cooling, I walked across the campus toward my truck. Years before, I had made this journey at this time of day often. Back in school at the age of 30, studying for a ministry in a church I had forsaken, I had been filled with energy, joy and hope. I loved going to school, filling my mind and world with often obscure writers, thinkers and artists. The Bible was the source, the bedrock on which I stood and from which I learned. But there was much beyond that book I found enriching, stirring and useful. In those days, hustling from studying in the library to an evening job as a security guard at a Holland shopping mall, I had never dreamed of returning for good to the neighborhood of my youth. I planned to finish my studies and go West, with an ultimate aim of serving as a missionary in Central America. The years I'd spent in Chicago were satisfying. But being back here, a country church dominie, was surprising. I was caught back, and liking it, in an area I had once found suffocating.

As I walked, my mind moved beyond the collegiate memories to the numbers Rozek had helped track down. One had been to Hammersma's own home; another to a department store in Grand Rapids. One was long-distance, probably to the Benton Harbor area. And the last was to an extension at Golgotha Undenominational Church, the congregation overseen by the Rev. Richard Rhodes. I was wondering about this connection, recalling that Rhodes had said they were friends, when coming toward me, not 10 feet away on the sidewalk, was Monica. I had to look twice, but there was no doubt about it.

"Hey!" I said. Globed lamps threw down an orangish glow between us.

She stopped. The liquid movement in her eyes, even the faint flowery scent, were achingly familiar. A smile appeared. "Twice in two nights." "It's fate," I said.

For nearly three hard years, we worked out of the storefront in Chicago, supervised by a blustering, fatherly old fool of a minister who eventually gave up the street ministry to go into investment banking in Milwaukee. In those years we thought we had created a fabric of life between us that we would sustain through her move up here and my coming after. That it unraveled so quickly and so thoroughly surprised us both.

"Working in the library?" she asked.

"I was checking a few things," I said. "How about you?"

"Teaching my class."

"Oh?"

"A beginning writing class."

"Composition?" I wondered.

"It has to do with journaling," she said. "You know that stuff you hate — trying to get in touch with your inner child through dreams and writing."

I didn't hate it — I just found pseudo-Christian pop psychology hard to stomach. The concepts weren't unappealing; the language in which they were presented was. Monica loved that stuff. In a strange way, I admired her for it.

"Is it going well?" I asked, I hoped, brightly.

"It's mostly women," she said, a bit defensively. "But, yes, it is."

"I'm glad," I replied.

"Glad?"

"I'm happy for you," I said by way of clarification. "I knew you wanted to teach." Her eyes flicked over me.

A tentative smile appeared on her face. "Thanks," she said. Standing in the dusk, I wondered why Hammersma had called her church. I asked if she wanted to get coffee.

"Can't," she said. "Tuesday night's my busiest night of the week. I've got an all-women's Bible study at a cafe in Grand Haven — which I'm close to late for already." I nodded, feeling a little selfish, pondering my own motives. "But, you know," she said, "the way things are going, we'll probably bump into each other tomorrow or something. And we could do it then."

I appreciated her offer. "So," I said, fishing for something, "why don't we even make a date?"

"A date?"

"Set a date, a time, when we could do it."

"Oh," she said, a catch in her voice. "Sure."

"I could give you a call." I could see questions form on her face. "I could catch you at the church, couldn't I?"

Beyond her and above the roof of the library, the sky was deep scarlet mixed with a blue turning quickly to black. In the air, chattering lazily, were birds preparing for bed. I thought of the lake, a great wash of water lapping the shore not far away, full of its secrets, as Slade called them.

Her gaze grew curious. "Is something up?" she wondered. "Why?"

"I sense ulterior motives."

I started down the sidewalk. "I'll walk you to your car."

She stepped in beside me. Monica was slightly overweight, a plumpness that served her well. Her breasts swelled and swayed slightly under the gauzy fabric of her blouse. Even in the near-dark, as we moved along, I could see an outline of purposefulness in her face. She always carried with her an intensity I found hard to resist and equally hard to accept.

"Am I right?" she asked, breaking the silence.

Huddled couples — three, one after the other — passed on our right. "About?" I asked.

"Ulterior motives?"

I still recalled painfully the boat ride back from Isle Royale, the deadly silence between us, the awful weight of knowing what we had was over. Looking out over the cold, rolling water of Lake Superior, I had for a few moments felt like diving in and falling down among the mossy bones of sunken ships.

"No," I said to her, "no ulterior motives, really."

She stopped and peered up. "Truman, what's going on?"

"Why?"

"I don't know. I'd never seen you there before is all. At the marina. Or here, either, for that matter."

I wondered if the coincidence of encountering one another twice in as many nights was no quirk of fate to her. Did she think I'd planned this, that my heart was still pining?

A tree threw down a lengthy cross-ribbed shadow in front of us. Its leaves were sparse; in the heat of mid-August it was dying. I heard crickets scrape their skinny, scratchy legs. I remembered Engstrom looping his arm possessively around her.

"Monica," I said, torn by what I knew were strong feelings for her and wanting an answer about the connection to her church. "As far as you know, were Sid Hammersma and Reverend Rhodes good friends?"

"The history professor?" she asked. I nodded. "Why do you ask?"

"It has to do with why I was there last night."

"At the marina?"

I nodded. We kept walking slowly. In sync, each of our steps touching the sidewalk in rhythm.

"Friends?" she then asked.

"Yes."

"Turkstra," she said, stopping, "what's this all about?"

"You asked why I was there."

"You weren't buying a boat?"

"No," I admitted.

"You were spying on Richard?"

"Not spying."

She examined me carefully, a hand settled on her right hip. "What on earth are you talking about then?"

"If I fill you in, you'll be late for your Bible study."

"I'm probably late already."

So I sketched why. She listened with interest, even avid interest, not interrupting once. When I finished, she said, "This is one of your investigations, then?"

This had been another source of tension between us. More than once, she had said my desire to serve the Lord too often took me in many, often opposite, directions at once. The midget Baptist preacher who was a cocaine dealer on the South Side of Chicago was only one example. Chasing him down at the request of a local missionary group had gotten both Monica and me nearly killed.

"I guess so," I said.

She flung her head back and laughed.

"What?" I asked.

"And I thought," she said, "you were following me around. Carrying your heart on your sleeve."

I looked at my shoulder, as if trying to spot my dripping, bloody heart. It wasn't there. But inside it was beating a little faster than normal. "Sorry," I said.

"Nothing to be sorry about, Turkstra." She sounded a little sad.

"I know you have to get going, but what about Rhodes?" I prodded.

She considered it a moment. "You think he's tied up in this?"

I told her now about finding the phone number, a part I'd left out before. Monica seemed lost in thought as a car with its radio blaring rap music — a thumping beat that moved through the sidewalk — passed on the street.

Again, she was quiet. Her eyes drifted beyond me. Her face looked puffy, but the nose and mouth were strongly shaped. She wore a blue denim skirt, sandals, the white blouse, and had tied a blue bandana through her hair. Looking at the sidewalk, her books cradled in her arms, she seemed to be reaching into herself for something.

"Did you ever see them together? Did they ever talk on

the phone that you know of?" I asked.

"I'm not that close to him, to Richard," she said.

"Did they run in some of the same social circles?"

"I don't know." Testy now.

"Anything?" I said. "Can you think of any way they might be connected?"

"You're probably making too much of the phone call."

"Maybe."

Her eyes fell to the ground. "I feel like this is an interrogation."

"But do you know something? Is there a reason Hammersma would call him?"

She gazed at me levelly. "I don't know!"

I knew I should back off. But I didn't. "Monica," I said, "is there something you're not saying?"

"Truman," she said, her voice flat, "you're going to have to ask Richard."

"But, if there was anything, you would tell me?"

Her eyes searched mine. "To be truthful, Truman, in this moment right now, I'm not sure I would."

13

Scattered couples with children and a group of migrant workers ate at tables and booths around me. But it was the middle-aged man and woman on the other side of the restaurant, and their son, who got my attention. A movement of the man's shoulders, a jutting of the woman's jaw, and the youngster's frightened face brought back a memory. More than 20 years before, in this same restaurant, I'd sat in a booth with my parents. Tonight I'd stopped at Russ' Restaurant in Holland, to eat a cheeseburger, salad, fries, and pie. That evening 20 years or so before, we'd made our routine visit to this place on the way to pick up my sister, Doris, from her Wednesday night church group. Sitting with the grownups and sipping a huge chocolate milkshake, I'd felt special.

Russ' was a gathering spot for friends of my family. It catered to a crowd of mostly rural, hard-working folks. Even now, as I wiped a fry in a puddle of ketchup, it held a staid, relatively unadorned atmosphere conducive to talk about the preacher's sermon on Sunday, the problems plaguing the public schools, and the need for Congress to start buckling down on the liberals who were working so hard to get something for nothing for their lazy constituents. Vastly Republican in nature, our ethnic group prided itself on hard work and clear-cut conservative thinking. And somehow Russ', with its waitresses in fluffy peasant dresses and bonnets, reflected that. In its entryway, it had a book rack of devotional literature that lifted one's spirits without challenging the soul. Even though the business fairly reeked of Americanized Dutchness, and offered a menu bustling with fatty, calorie-soaked fare, I found myself stopping once or twice a month. Normally, though, I ordered a take-out. But not on this night.

I ate quickly, then left. Outside in the parking lot, I stuck my fingers under the handle of my Ranger and started to get in when I heard the scrape of shoes on pavement behind me. I froze. A fuzzy electric feeling shot up and down my back as the feet stopped. A faint bluish light fell from a tall lamp secured to a pole at the back edge of the parking lot. A few other cars were wedged into spots around me.

"Turkstra?" I turned quickly. "Scare you?"

"A little." My heart had started to squeeze vast quantities of blood through my body so fast I felt light-headed.

"Sorry," said Marlan Oosterbaan. He wore slacks and a knit shirt on whose pocket the words Windmill Acres had been stenciled. He ran a hand through his wavy red hair. "I was passing by, saw you, and stopped."

I glanced around. "I didn't hear you pull up."

"Parked the car around front."

I nodded, leaned against the door of my truck. He looked a little nervous, scratched below an ear with his finger. "I'd like to talk a second," he said.

"Here?"

"It won't take long."

We were directly behind the restaurant, on the far corner of the lot. A dumpster stood nearby, smelling faintly of rotting food. A few flies circled above, darkish dots in the diminishing light.

I said nothing. Continued to wait.

"Seems you're rattling a few cages," he said, flicking steady, probing eyes — cop's eyes — in my direction.

I felt the ground shift between us. Now I had to explain myself. Or was being asked to. I defended my position by saying, "Oh?"

The ball back in his court; he turned to the side, examined the bumper of a Blazer parked next to my truck. "Got a visit today from the mayor. You know him?" I didn't. "Well, he's a real fine fellow. Staunch member of the church. Anyhow, in not so many words, the mayor's wondering just how come I haven't wrapped up this Hammersma case yet." I waited, watching him carefully. He seemed agitated, but I didn't think at me. "Got a call, too," he went on, "from Bruce Slade. Pretty much asking the same thing."

Curious. What pressure, though, if any, had I applied?

Marlan stepped closer. He fished in his Windmill Acres pocket, dug out a couple of toothpicks, offered me one. I declined. He slipped one in his mouth and returned the other to his pocket.

"How come you're telling me this?"

"Wondered if you had any idea why all the pressure all of a sudden." He picked his teeth, let the small stick stay in the corner of his mouth.

"Because," I ventured, "they want this resolved fast."

"Who's they?"

I shrugged. "Bigshots in the church."

He twirled the toothpick reflectively. He had a sandy shoe-polish smell to him. Even in the half-dark, his freckles showed clearly on his blocky, sober-seeming face. "You mean DeHorn?"

"Among others."

He nodded, staring across the lot toward the rear of the restaurant, where a large air conditioning unit, the size of a shed, churned out chilly air and pumped it inside. "Why all of a sudden?" he asked.

"Like I said yesterday, because the board meets next week and they want it figured out by then. Or at least enough so they can make a decision on money they might owe Hammersma's wife."

He laughed humorlessly. "Fat chance."

"That it'll be ... wrapped up?"

He faced me — stern, hard, convincing. "Unless you, my

pastor friend, have come up with anything to help bring the matter to a close."

"Can't say that has happened."

He didn't immediately reply. "Anything close to it?" he tried.

I stretched my arms over my head. Marlan looked up at my hands. The ground had shifted again.

"I've learned, more or less, the professor had AIDS."

Marlan showed no response, touched the toothpick in the side of his mouth. "That's your cause of death?" he asked.

"No, but I'm wondering if having it led to depression, which caused him to commit suicide."

Marlan nodded. "Reasonable line of thinking. But how? Out of his boat?"

I mentioned Slade's comment about the bag full of rocks, or something heavy. As I spoke, I tried to gauge if this came as news to the Holland police chief. I couldn't tell.

"Rocks?" he said.

"Hasn't he told you that?"

Marlan pulled out the toothpick. "Maybe I didn't make it clear, sneaking up on you like I did, but I wasn't planning on this being a two-way conversation," he said.

Then go tend your little putt-putt land, I thought. "You just want to grill me?"

"Call it what you want." He stood away from the truck. His body looked lumpy; the stomach sagged; the jowls drooped wearily. A deep furrow cut between his eyelids, effectively separating his brow in fleshy halves. "Anything else you've come across?" he asked.

"Nope."

His eyes settled on me a moment, as if trying to climb under my skin. "Nothing?"

I thought of the phone numbers. Despite my desire to clam up, I told him. As I did, he brightened, studied my face. "One to Rhodes?" he asked. "And the other ... where?"

"Somewhere in Benton Harbor."

"To what?"

"Don't know yet." I had called it from inside Russ'. Got no answer.

He thought this over, pinching his jaw with two fingers.

"So," I ventured, "the phone calls are new to you?"

Marlan grew edgy. Defensive again. "I'll check with Bruce."

"What about this second will business? You come across that, too?" he asked.

I wondered just how much Slade had kept of his investigation to himself. I found it very odd that Oosterbaan was pumping me for information he should already have. Especially since he was the man who eventually had to dispense of the matter. Or maybe he was just trying to figure out what I knew.

"Nothing," I said.

Marlan swatted something on the back of his neck. Rubbed the spot, no doubt squishing bug guts into his pores.

"Do you really think there is one?" I asked.

Marlan glowered, faced me square on. "Again, I'm not here to clue you in … except …" He waved a hand in front of his face, waving away more bugs. "Just this — if I was you I'd ease up a little. Sounds like you've got quite enough already to write your report for DeHorn." His face had grown deadly serious. "Why don't you do it up nice and call it quits?"

"What are you warning me about, Marlan?"

"Sounds like a warning?"

"It does."

"Just a word to the wise," he said then.

"Then make me smarter."

He scratched behind his neck again. "Smart's got nothing to do with it. Just be careful." His eyes examined mine again, as if trying to communicate something to me.

"I'm trying to," I replied. "It's just, in the end, I'm waiting on you." He gave me a questioning glance. "To sign off. Close the book."

He scowled. "You, too?"

"What?"

"Pushing me."

"But what else is there?" I asked, thinking about Hammersma's column. If it had been doctored, what did that mean? "Why hold it up?"

"Without a body, there are still too many questions."

"Like what?" I asked.

He stared at me silently, face pushed forward. Anger stiffened his stance. He dropped his hands in balls to his sides. He sniffed. "I've got to go, Turkstra." With that, he turned and walked away.

"Marlan?" I said. He stopped and turned. "Do you really want me to cash it in?"

He scuffed a shoe on pavement. Made his shoulders bounce inside the windbreaker. "This is no game, Calvin," he said.

"Tell me, then, what I'm up against."

His mouth moved a few moments; no words came out. Then he said, "I've already said it. Just type up what you got, give it to DeHorn, and leave the rest to Slade."

"And you?"

He hesitated for a second before answering. "Right — and me."

"But," I said, "why wait, Marlan? Don't you have enough to close the case?"

"I just told you, no body, no case," he retorted.

"Simple as that?"

He scratched the back of his neck. Started off again. "I wish to hell it was," he said, more to himself than to me.

I sank back against my truck. The rocks in the bag, I thought. The rocks in the bag had surprised him. I thought of someone else to ask about that as well. For the first time, it struck me that Sid Hammersma's disappearance may not have been a suicide. Maybe that's what Marlan was trying to tell me. And if that was true, I knew just as Oosterbaan had warned, I'd better be damned careful.

DEADLY WATERS

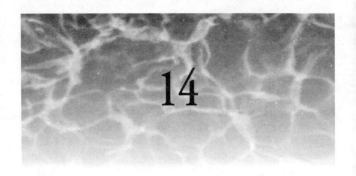

14

The ringing continued, nibbling into the atmosphere of the apartment on the other end of the line. With a finger crooked in one ear and the receiver jammed into the other, I watched traffic move through sluggish, tar-smelling heat on U.S. 31, heading north toward the woods and lakes. For a moment I thought of the vastness of a forest, of sunlight slanting through branches, of a river rolling to the lake. Of eyes peering through brambles.

"Hello," I finally heard in an angry, muffled tone.

"Sorry to bother you so late, Randy," I said.

"Who is this?" the editor of The Outreach grumbled.

"Calvin Turkstra."

"Who?" I told him again.

"Oh," was his only response.

Since leaving his office much earlier in the day, I'd come up with a couple more questions to ask. I explained this to him. What he said was, "What devil time is it?"

"Almost 10."

On my way out of town, trying to make sense out of Oosterbaan's warning, I'd stopped at a Shell station to use the pay phone. The garish glow from the shell-shaped service station sign that twirled directly above me made me think, for some reason, of the Roman Catholic notion of purgatory — a dim and dreary waiting room for those hoping the next stop was heaven. It was a concept first taught to me by my

Catholic mother, then later refuted by my Calvinist father. This yellow half-light, falling down on me from above, made me feel as if I was in some mid-point netherworld, grasping for a destination. Patience had never been one of my virtues. I was having to employ it now with VanAntwerp.

"You woke me up," the editor nearly whined.

"Sorry." He groaned. "But this is important." This was the time to push, not back off. Even if Oosterbaan had warned me off, I had to go on. Stubborn, bullish, like my father.

"It can't wait?" he asked.

"I'd rather not."

"What is it then?" asked VanAntwerp.

I shifted my weight and looked over to the gas pumps. Pulling into the station, just barely fitting under a stationary overhang, was a white semi truck-trailer.

"I wanted to know two things. First, do you have a hard copy — not a Xerox — somewhere, of Sid Hammersma's column?"

"The suicide one?"

"Right."

"Why?"

"Just do you?" I asked, trying to remain patient, noticing a halo of gnats spinning in a sphere above the sign.

"I suppose … Can you wait a second? My dog is at the bedroom door."

I imagined the editor, a stubborn rump roast of a man, heaving his bulk, clad in tent-size pajamas, onto the floor of his Heritage Hill apartment. In the dark of his room, he padded over, opened the door and stood aside as his dog lapped at his feet. VanAntwerp would be a poodle man, I thought.

"I'm back." I heard yapping in the background. "So what is your second question?" he asked.

"You haven't answered my first."

"I said 'suppose.'"

"Does that mean you do?"

"Probably."

"Could you take a look for me?"

"I don't have it here."

"I mean tomorrow."

"And look for what — if I have it?"

I asked him to compare if it was in any way different from other columns the historian had submitted.

"Different in what way?" he asked.

"Any way. The typeface, kind of paper, signature if there is one…. You do keep other hard copies of his columns?"

"I'm not sure, Turkstra. I'll check. What is this, nit-picking? You think Hammersma didn't write the column?"

"I'm not sure."

"What would make you think that?"

"I'm not sure."

"You're not sure of much."

"I am of one thing," I said. "You aren't being much help."

"Hush, Fritzy," I heard him say on the other end. To me, he replied, "I'm sorry. I had a pounding headache tonight. That's why I went to bed early. What's your other question?"

"From who or where did you hear the rumor about AIDS?"

"That?" His voice was far-off sounding and wary.

"Yes."

"From no one. It just came into my mind."

"You're sure of that?"

Silence, except for his exasperated breathing, a bellowing intake and outtake of air..

"From what I remember, you dismissed the rumor this morning," he said.

That wasn't true. But I didn't feel like arguing the point. "Things have happened to change my mind."

"Like what?"

"Just things — people I talked to." I said.

"What people?" he wondered.

"People who should know."

"Like who?"

My patience was slipping away. "I called to ask the questions."

"Don't like it when the tables are turned?"

"Look, Randy," I said. "I'm trying to find out what happened to Sid Hammersma. Not fight with you."

"Then you've taken on more of a burden than they've asked you to bear."

"What do you mean?"

"Trying to solve this thing," he said.

I felt weary and a little hopeless. I didn't want to wheedle or plead or even talk to him any more. But he was right; I'd gone beyond my mandate. "I probably have," I admitted. He mumbled something soothing to his dog. "Look, Randy, if you'll feel more up to it, I'll call you tomorrow."

"Tomorrow's not good. I've got to be in Kalamazoo." He paused, made a soft humming sound in his throat, then added, "What is it you want to know?"

"Who told you this? And where did they hear it?"

"You want to know both?"

"If possible."

The dog snapped in the background. Randy hushed it again, then said, "If I have to tell you anything, I'd rather only say where."

"Fine," I said, trying to sound more kind and understanding than I felt.

"If I tell you this, who else is going to know?" he asked.

"Just me for now."

"I'd ask you to promise that it is just you for good."

"I wish I could, but I'm working for someone else."

"Then, Turkstra, I don't know."

I sighed. If I were going to make headway, I was going to have to start striking bargains on my own.

"This is not just to protect the source, Turkstra. It's to protect me as well." Something in his voice told me that he wanted to help and that he was holding back for good reason.

"All right," I said. "You have my word it doesn't go beyond me."

"You're sure?"

"I just said I was."

"Turkstra," he said, "I hope I can trust you."

"You can."

"Then I also hope you can take what I'm going to tell you with a grain of understanding."

"I'll try."

"I heard it," he said, "at church."

"Church? What church?"

"My church," he said.

"At …?"

"Hope Community Reformed."

I understood immediately his concern. This was a primarily gay Christian Reformed congregation in Saugatuck. Our church took a strong stance against homosexuality. Even so, it was willing to allow Hope to exist. Quietly, of course, off the beaten path. It met in a former boathouse along the shore area in Saugatuck, a vacation community on Lake Michigan. Learning that, many other possibilities surfaced.

"Sid Hammersma went there?" I felt my pulse quicken, my interest grow keen.

"Sometimes," he said, almost weakly.

"Sometimes? Often? Regularly?"

"Occasionally. I saw him there maybe four or five times."

My mind swirled with notions. I looked up and saw the gnats still spinning above. "I'm not sure what you're saying." I said.

"I was answering your question."

"You're saying Sid Hammersma was … a homosexual?"

"I didn't say that."

"You implied it."

"I'll leave it to you to decide my implications. But not everyone who goes to Hope is gay, myself included."

Although this said some things about Sid Hammersma, it also opened the door on a side of VanAntwerp I hadn't known was there. He said he wasn't gay; I had to take him at his word. As for Sid Hammersma, it was another story. It wasn't a door opening; it was more like a floor falling through.

"Someone at the church told you Sid Hammersma was sick with AIDS?"

"Something like that."

"Can you be more specific?"

"I can, but won't."

"Even if I promise to keep it between us."

"I've told you too much already," he said morosely.

"Can you just tell me this," I persisted. "How reliable is your source?"

"Very."

"You're sure?"

"I just said I was."

"And this person told you Sid Hammersma had AIDS?"

"That person did."

"Why didn't you tell me this earlier?" I asked.

"If you think back, I more or less did."

After a few more moments of fruitless conversation, I replaced the receiver slowly and turned and walked to my truck. Behind the wheel, I sat watching the purgatory sign twirl. Oddly, I didn't feel as lost as before. Things were taking shape. The problem was I didn't seem to be moving toward heaven. The chain of events seemed to be leading in another direction altogether. And the road seemed to be forking — suicide or foul play? Or both? Weary as I was, I had other questions to ask. I wasn't ready to call it a night.

15

Rippling bands of light extended like fingers from the end of the dock. Encircling the lake stood tall, silent, sparsely lit cottages, summer homes and permanent residences. Under the sky, rich with stars, I tried to unwind. A breeze, a welcome respite from the mucky heat, came in off the big lake, which washed and rolled beyond the last line of cottages and homes that rimmed the far edge of this inland lake, Lake Macatawa. In the sky streaks of fast-fading white were all that was left of the sun that had gone down maybe 45 minutes before. The midsummer days stretched and light lasted longer than normal on the Lake Michigan coast. Next to me, lolling lazily in the calm water, were the docked boats, many of them tarped and taut.

I sat at the end of the dock, dangled my feet over, a yard or so above the electric blue water. I tried a chronology. Sid Hammersma was doing research of some kind on Hope Community Church. He met someone, a man. They grew close. Hammersma took him sailing with him. Hammersma got AIDS. He learned of it and, more distraught than he could handle, he killed himself. But how? Maybe he filled his jacket with rocks and dove in. Maybe his lover helped. This scenario made some sense. But barely. For one thing, I still didn't believe Sid Hammersma, even in the face of that fatal disease, would commit suicide. I didn't think that shame would motivate him to take such desperate action. What about the calls to Rhodes' church, to Benton Harbor? And what about the second will?

I stared at the water, envisioned a body entangled, several feet below, caught in strands of weed, floating with the fish, alone and cold and forgotten. I saw eyes, bugged open, waving hair, puckered, purplish skin. The mental picture came on me so strongly that I had to stand, turn away from the water. I'd recovered, had gazed out over the water again and was trying to picture the final Friday, the afternoon that Sid Hammersma pulled out of here for the last time, when I heard behind, "We meet again."

I turned to see Jack. Holding a lantern at his side, dressed in a sweat-stained T-shirt and baseball cap with the bill turned up, he scowled what looked to be a greeting. An unlit cigar stub poked from the corner of his mouth.

"You scared me," I said.

"Sort of meant to."

"That was nice of you." He squinted up at me.

"What are you doing out here — again?" he asked.

"Thinking."

He laughed, a sound that echoed down the dock.

"I'm hoping you're not going to give me a hard time again." I wanted to ask him questions, but wasn't sure how to begin. He removed the cigar stub. "Actually, preach, I was hoping for some help." He looked beyond me at the lake and pointed with his chin. In the light from his lantern, I saw that sun-baked skin stretched tight on his beard-stubbled face. I caught a whiff of whiskey. "One of the channel markers went out. Coast Guard's job to fix it, but it'll take them weeks to get off their duffs. And we need light tonight."

I gazed across the water, the slow pitch of movement, a silky curtain of liquid black, stretched out and ruffling. I detected a few pinpoints of red out there, marking the way in, or the way out.

"Won't take long," he said. "I know it's late, but …"

"I can help," I said. "My ballet lesson isn't until after midnight anyway."

It took about 10 minutes to reach the darkened buoy. As

we moved through the water, we didn't talk. After dropping the anchor, Jack reached out and drew the upper rim of the bobbing buoy to him. Bent over, grunting, he said, "Shine the light over my right shoulder, will ya?"

As I moved, he warned, "Careful." On my knees I edged toward him on the damp floor of the small, motorized skiff. I stretched out my arm. "Good, thanks."

I watched Jack jerk and yank on the buoy casing. I switched arms; the weight of the lamp was straining my left hand. Jack shifted his weight, making the boat tip, but not dangerously. I let my eyes wander along the far northern shore, where outlined in pale, peachy moonlight were the proud homes and cottages. In them warm lamps glowed; faint rosy flickering from within told me many people were forsaking the true night for the mostly made-up renderings on TV.

"There," said Jack finally.

Suddenly red light glowed, bathing us in a scarlet glow. I checked the skin on my arms, noticing the fiery tone. Jack turned back to me, his face touched with an otherworldly illumination, and asked, "How's it look?"

"Like we're on the outskirts of hell," I said.

Jack shook his head. "Jeez," he said. "Lighten up."

Not a bad idea, I thought. So, I sat back on my haunches, set the lantern next to me. Inside the glass case, the light burned like an orange eye. "Now what?" I asked.

"We head back."

Jack bent and pulled the cord to the motor. It quickly hummed to life, giving off smoke. Behind him the tilting buoy diminished. "Jack," I said. "Can I ask something?"

He had one arm draped over a knee; the other guided the motor. "Fire away," he said.

"The night Sid Hammersma came out here. The last night?"

Jack craned back, as if surveying the line of red lights moving out toward Lake Michigan. Or maybe he was recalling the history professor's last trip.

"So," said Jack, "what about it?"

"That Friday afternoon — can you remember what he was wearing?"

"Wearing?"

"Yes."

"Why?"

"It might be important."

"Why?"

"I'm grabbing at straws."

He cocked his head heavenward, turned his neck to the side. "I can't really say. I never pay attention to that stuff. Could've worn a suit of armor for all I know."

I sat up on the back bench of his boat. "Is there anything at all unusual that you can remember about that day?"

He sniffed. "You're not going to let this go, are you?"

"I can't. Not now."

He eased up on the throttle, let the skiff drift a few moments. He sat back, linked his hands behind his head. "Well," he said, "can't say that there was much out of the ordinary that day. No, not really." He leaned over and spit in the water. Then he coughed, rubbed his upper arms.

I shifted on the seat, heard water lap, the motor putter. "That day, you said you saw him walking to his boat?"

Jack shook his head.

"Caught a glimpse of him on the dock."

"You said before he was carrying something? Did it look heavy?"

Jack scratched his face,

"Can't say for sure. Only glimpsed him that time."

"Was there another time?"

The skiff moved up and down, the lake around us quiet. I thought that, 150 years before, Odawa Indians had lived along these shores, trapping, farming, living a way of life about to be destroyed by my white ancestors.

"C'mon, Jack," I cajoled. "Was there?"

"I guess this isn't really privileged information," he said, sighing.

I waited, anxious, trying to pull information out of him with my eyes. In the sky, beyond the clouds, I heard a motorized moan. A jet coming in or going out. I had no idea. People way above were encased in steel and going places.

"May not amount to a hill of beans," he said. I leaned forward a little, my chin reaching out over the lantern at my feet. "Must've been about 4 or so that day. I'd come around front there to check the mail. I'd got what we had and was walking back when I looked over, by the side of the building at the end of the parking lot, and there was the professor. Leaning in the window of a car and talking to some guy."

"A guy?"

Jack nodded. "Guy was in a green Plymouth — a Horizon, I think."

"They were talking?"

"Right. Don't know why I think this, but it was like the professor was giving him directions. You know, how you lean in, lean back, point this way and that?"

"You get a look at the guy he was talking to?"

Jack sighed. "See, the situation was I thought at first I recognized the guy — which is why I gave it a double take. An old buddy of mine drove a car like that. But wasn't him. The guy was younger, almost a kid. He had dark, frizzy hair, and seemed a little worried, from what I could tell."

I had to catch my breath; a bubble of air wedged in my throat.

"Was there anything else about the driver that seemed distinguishing?"

"He had a parking sticker from the college on the window."

"From which college?"

"The one in town."

"It wasn't from the seminary?"

"Could've been."

Had it been one of Hammersma's students? I knew the professor also taught classes at the college.

"This kid — what did he look like besides the frizzy hair?"

Jack shrugged. "Can't remember much. Maybe you could

say good-looking. I don't know." Jack scowled, looking down at his arms folded over his chest. His mouth dour.

"Oh, he had some kind of gold chain around his neck."

"Sounds like you got a good look at him."

"As I say, I thought for a second it was someone I knew."

On the way back in, I asked Jack if he'd mind taking a look at something. When I told him what it was, he agreed. Once he docked his skiff, we walked along the dock to the berth that held Hammersma's boat. Once on board, Jack knew how to work the lights to The Wittenberg Door. Standing side by side in the cabin area, we faced the photos, one of Virginia Hammersma; the other of the young man with the rope. The floor tipped slightly underneath us. Jack scratched his neck. He smelled ripely of sweat. "Look familiar?" I asked.

He glanced at me, then back at the photo. Again, it struck me that Hammersma seemed uncomfortable, his body slightly tense and angled away from the young man. Not more than 25, the young man looked almost haughty, the eyes lively and liquid. He was slender, slightly muscled, the shoulders well rounded. Hair curly, wind-blown. They seemed to be standing on a beach somewhere; blue water stretched behind them.

"How'd you know this was here?" he asked.

"I checked it out last night."

He scowled, wiped a hand over his mouth. "You know," said Jack, "this is trespassing."

"I know," I replied simply.

He smiled. "So," he said, "you're one of those preachers who kind of follows his own rules."

"Sometimes."

Jack seemed to like that — glanced back at the photo, squinted hard. "Well, yeah," he said. "Could be."

"Did the police ask you about this?" I wondered.

Jack sniffed, shook his head. "I wasn't here when they came by. I just talked on the phone once or twice, I think it was to the detective."

"Slade?"

"Think that's his name."

"So you don't know if he has made this connection — between the photo and the man you saw?"

"Don't know."

I looked around. A couch built into the wall; a bookcase containing mostly broken-backed best sellers. A bar area; four crystal glasses; a few bottles of expensive booze; a sheath of maps folded neatly inside a large plastic envelope; a radio; an empty ashtray rimmed with seashells.

"But this kid, the driver, didn't go out with him on the boat that day?"

"Not that I know of."

"Did he ever?"

Jack shook his head. "Never saw him before."

My spirits waffled. What if Sid Hammersma, if he was gay, just liked the same sort of person? Or maybe he was just being a nice guy and giving directions. Maybe the fellow in the photo was a student, an innocuous enough relationship.

"But what's your best guess?" I asked.

Jack examined the photo again. Leaned close, hands on his hips, chin jutted out. He squinted, licked his lips. "Don't hold me to it, but could be the same guy."

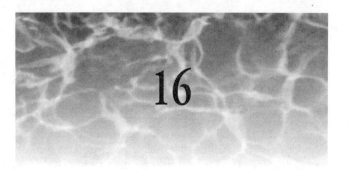

16

Already, not long after dawn, sunlight lay heavy on the fields. Rolling away on either side of my truck were half-grown rows of corn, stretching for hundreds of yards in each direction. To my left, flicking silver wands of water into the air, was a large, above-ground irrigation machine that made me think of a gaunt, long-necked dinosaur. Here and there on my fairly aimless route were sturdy brick and shingle-sided farmhouses behind or next to which stood mostly red-painted barns. As I drove, I could tick off the names of the families who once lived — and in many cases still lived — in these homes. Nearly every one of Dutch stock, diluted (some said polluted) by an occasional intermarriage with Poles, Germans and Irish. In these homes, and on these fields, resided a great pre-ordained force. As God's chosen, they labored hard, prayed fervently and stayed to themselves. They were not the Amish, easily recognizable by their garb, but they were bonded by many of the same ethnic ties — to religion, to the earth, to a common culture that stretched back to Europe. This enclave from which I had risen was walled in by beliefs that made the people feel special, if only by their rigid separation. As part of the cause, emerging from this Calvinist system of belief was a fierce commitment to the work ethic, which made many of these people prosperous.

Up ahead ran the yellow line, cutting in half 46th Avenue, that once clearly defined my days. Often now, I took this road in the morning, wandering alongside fields in which I once worked, played, daydreamed. This morning, having been awakened by the phone and unable to go back to sleep, I climbed in my truck and decided to take the long way back into Holland to continue my inquiries.

Taking a curve at 40 mph and feeling the warmth of the sun fall through the windshield onto my face and upper chest, I remembered the call I'd gotten this morning from Jerry VanderMolen at The Press. He'd left a message on my recorder last night. Since I hadn't returned until after 1 a.m., I didn't call him back. Once I'd swallowed the sleep that filled my mouth like cotton balls, I had asked Jerry what he'd found out. He did not sound happy, but he was to the point. He'd asked around yesterday, trying to delicately probe Sid Hammersma's personal life. To his surprise, he said he'd sensed right off there was something. No one, however, had been very forthcoming. But there were hints of sexual indiscretion. Finally, after one call had led to the next and so on, VanderMolen had spoken with Warren Roelofs, pastor of Hope Community Church in Saugatuck. The church that VanAntwerp, The Outreach editor, attended and the church, at which VanAntwerp had seen Hammersma. My ears pricked up when I heard this. I found it curious and encouraging that VanderMolen's path led there. Apparently, the Press reporter and Roelofs were friends and had spoken before. In the past, Roelofs had always been willing to talk, especially about his denomination's backward stance regarding homosexuality. Yesterday, though, he had no comment to make, none whatsoever, on anything related to Hammersma. VanderMolen then had, point-blank, asked if Roelofs thought Sid Hammersma might have been gay or bisexual, if the history professor may have been leading the double life to which at least two other of VanderMolen's sources had alluded. The pastor then had said sternly he had no comment and hung up. To me, VanderMolen said, "Turkstra, I touched a hot wire. I have no idea, but whatever it is, he wasn't about to tell me. You may be onto something."

VanderMolen told me he'd call around some more, but he was leaving town today to cover some Episcopalians in Lansing. He said he wouldn't be back until the weekend. I thanked him for his help. I told him I'd talk to him later.

At the corner of 46th Avenue and 56th Street, I slowed to a stop and gazed at the peaked roof and sandblasted red brick of what had been my schoolhouse. Surrounding it now was a well-tended garden, a neatly trimmed lawn, swing set, and boat tautly covered with a blue tarp. Noticing at one corner of the back yard a woman hanging sheets on a clothesline, I turned up 56th toward Drenthe.

Sometimes I rode through Pleasant Valley Acres — the subdivision built on land once owned by my father and mother. The old farmhouse, constructed by my great-grand-father and his son, stood on the far eastern fringe of the development. Drifting through some mornings, I stopped and walked the edge of the field surrounding the farmhouse and subdivision beyond. But I drove past this morning. I didn't want to bother with thoughts of how my father, out of spite and encroaching poverty, had sold off prime farm land as plots for bland tract houses.

Up ahead at the intersection of 74th Avenue and Perry Street I saw old Clarence Venema camped out, as always this time of year, at his fruit stand. To the right, the road wound deeper into the muck fields toward Zutphen. To the left was a dead end.

A Detroit Tigers cap pulled down over his brow, Venema sat in the shade of an overarching apple tree. In front of him was a long wooden bench piled with fruit. A short-sleeved plaid shirt hung from his bony frame. Poking out from his ears, like black buttons, were what looked to be earphones to a Walkman. His eyes, behind thick lenses, swam in a milky blueness into which, even years back, very little sight entered. Nearly blind, he still wore the glasses. I suspected it was some form of farmer's pride — a stance he took to show that, no matter how blurry things were, he was still trying to make out the shape of the world. For many years, from the early season when strawberries and zucchini were ripe, to late fall when apples and squash were for sale, Clarence sat out here. His ramshackle but sturdy farmhouse hulked behind him. His wife, who tended a huge garden, and his offspring, who ran farms throughout the area, supplied the produce. I stood before him and tapped the table gently. He was nodding. A crackling sound came from his earphones. I rapped with a knuckle. Clarence smiled before he spoke. "Hallo?" he said.

"Hi, Clarence," I replied.

With rosy, large-fingered hands, he unplugged the foam-rubber covered earphones. In front of him was a coffee cup on which was stenciled "The Boss Is Coming Soon." Next to that was a stack of tapes. Arranged on the table and in bushel baskets on the ground were peaches, pears, potatoes, a few tomatoes, some corn, and two heads of rusty lettuce.

"Turkstra?" he asked, squinting behind his glasses and tilting up his bony chin.

"How you doing, Clarence?"

He waved a hand in front of his face, as if shooing flies. "Hot," he said. "You?"

"The same, but hungry."

"Want peaches?"

"Sounds good."

"Got Elgin plums, too," he said, looking vaguely to his left. "And a few early Empires." I stepped over and examined the plums, pressed the skin of one. Too firm for my taste. "What brings you out so early?" he asked.

"Enjoying the morning before it gets too muggy."

"Already too muggy," he groused. He slipped the buttons back in his ears.

At the far end of the table, on the lip where sunlight beat past the edge of the tree, sat the peaches. I hefted one in my palm, took a bite. Juice dribbled down my chin. Flies made a circle around me.

"Find one?" Clarence asked loudly. Munching, I nodded.

"Say what?" he asked, pulling one button from an ear.

"These are good." I picked up a tray containing three more.

"Try the plums?"

I set the tray in front of him. "These'll do."

His shaking hand reached out and touched the peaches, fingers flicking over the fuzzy fruit as if they were small skulls. "You like peaches, don't you?"

"I do," I said.

He smiled, lips parting in a watery way. "I remember your mother does, too. Remember the pies she baked? She'd always bring me by a piece or two." I did remember. "How is she, anyway?"

"Tough as ever."

He peered sightlessly up at me, eyes pinched shut behind the glasses. "Give her my regards."

"I will."

He fiddled with the peaches, as if checking their sizes. "How about some Empires?" he asked. "Son Fred grows them."

"Not today," I said.

"Be a buck, then," he said.

"I've only got a five," I said.

He reached out a palm, whose skin was crossed with lines as deep as smiles. "I got change."

As he rooted through a cigar box, I asked, "What're you listening to?"

He had draped the earphones around his neck. "One of them TV preachers. Talking about Corinthians, about love and that," he said.

"I'm not so much into the TV preachers," I told him, for no good reason.

"I can't see them much, of course, but some of them have good things to say."

I folded the money and put it away. I picked my half-eaten peach from the edge of the table.

"Really," he said, "farmers over there in Overisel could probably use a few new ideas." I laughed, a little too loudly.

"What?" he said, sounding offended.

"Clarence, I never knew you were a liberal."

His expression fell; he was offended. "You can't keep your mind buttoned up."

I felt guilty. "Well," I said, looking at his stack of tapes, "who do you have there?"

"Take a look."

I licked peach juice off my hand, then glanced through. They were names familiar to me, but one more familiar than most. I stopped halfway through and examined it: Stories of the Reformed Saints, the label read. The narrator was Dr. Sidney J. Hammersma.

"You find one?"

I noticed Clarence's wife standing on the large, pillared front porch. I waved. She stared back and poured water into a blooming pot of geraniums. The yellow flowers spread out below her like candle flames.

"Well, this," I said, twisting the tape around, peering at the serious expression on Hammersma's face. The professor was pictured standing in front of a large church organ — it looked like the one in the chapel of the seminary.

"Which?"

"By Dr. Hammersma."

"Sid?"

"Yes."

"You can borrow it."

"What's it about?" I asked.

"Not just Calvin and those guys, but Martin Luther King and Gandhi and some of them, too."

"Not all of them are Reformed."

"Got that right," is all Venema said. I flipped it over in my hand again. "Main message in it," he went on, "is there is saints all over the place. Not just in our church. I guess a bunch of us believe the same things."

"Does sound interesting," I said.

"Like I say, Luther's in there, too. Some of it's kind of racy."

"Oh?"

Clarence Venema nodded vigorously. "Luther liked his ale," he said, almost proudly.

"I've heard that," I said.

Venema nodded some more. His eyes drifted off a moment, then marginally back to me. "Hear anything more about that?" he said.

I stared at Hammersma's face, trying to see something — perhaps the shades of a hidden life — in it. But it wasn't there. He looked placid, proper, and fatherly on the cassette. The historian who was taking us on an informative trip through our religious past.

"About Hammersma?" I said.

"Right."

"Not really," I said.

Venema stared at me a little sourly. "Pretty strange deal, though, don't you think?" I agreed. Venema's face was turned up, as if he was staring off into the distance. "But know something even more strange?" he asked.

His eyes behind the glasses were vacant but dreamy. "What's that?" I prodded, noticing the way his fingers, splayed out in front of him, twitched, as if in time to some inner music. Just behind him appeared his wife, Flora, scowling.

Venema bent his head back and said, "You remember Turkstra here, don't you?" It seemed as if he'd addressed her as much to let her know he knew she was here as to introduce her to me.

"Certainly," she said, giving me a quick, defensive smile. She placed her hands on his shoulders.

"What were you saying, Turkstra?"

"You mentioned something that you thought was strange."

His wife had a wary expression in her eyes. Hard to read. Even as children, we had thought she was a little odd — a perfect mate for the blind fruit vendor.

One of his hands reached up and disengaged his wife's from his shoulder. He did it gently, but the message was there. She stepped off to the side and fiddled with the hard plums.

"I was saying," said Venema in a low, conspiratorial voice. His eyes shifted side to side. I leaned a little closer, aware that his wife was doing her best to act like she wasn't listening. "It was that same day — had to be," he said. "Or right around there. But he was here."

I stopped eating my peach, flicked a glance at his wife. She was rearranging corn. Until now, I had been more or less accommodating the old man's ramblings, if that's what they were. "Here?" I asked, my interest more than piqued; at the same time I wondered if he was crazy, if some of his wife's "oddness" had rubbed off.

"Yup," said Venema, eyes still gazing off at some distance only he could discern. "About dinner time. Stopped to ask directions."

Flora Venema made a sound in her throat, a cluck of disgust about it.

"To where?" I wondered, trying to keep the curiosity out of my voice.

"Down the road."

"Which way?"

"To the left. Down Perry. To the little park by the stream at the dead end. By the graveyard."

"The graveyard?" Venema nodded seriously. "For what? Why?"

His wife moved close again, arms stuffed in the front pockets of her house dress. She had a harrowed, heartless expression on her face. I wondered if her husband was making this up. Had his blindness caused him to see and hear things that weren't there?

"That I don't know," said Venema.

I turned and gazed down the road. "What time you say he came by?"

His wife cut in: "You're very interested in this little story of my husband's, Reverend?"

I felt warmth come to my cheeks. "People have been wondering what happened to the professor for weeks. Did you tell the police about this?"

"I called," said Venema. His wife was staring at me —

hard. "Actually Flora called," he amended. I gazed at her, encouraging a response. She had none.

"Police said they'd call back," he said.

"Did they?"

"Did they, Flora?"

"They did," she said tersely. "They told me they wrote down what you said."

"But they didn't come out to talk to you?" I asked them both.

Glancing at the back of her husband's head, Flora replied. "We're not so sure there was anything to report in the first place."

Clarence Venema's shoulders slumped, his hands clasped in front of him like two dead birds. "Flora thinks I'm woozy in the head," he said.

She stepped forward, touched his shoulder. "Clarence, that is not true." She gave me a look that made me think of a child whose hand has been caught in the cookie jar.

"She says selling fruit alone out here all day makes me nuts. Says I make things up."

She scowled and squeezed his upper arm. He flinched but didn't pull away. "Clarence, Reverend Turkstra only stopped by to get some peaches," she said. "Didn't you?" she asked me.

"Clarence," I said softly.

He looked up, vaguely, in my direction. "When Sid Hammersma stopped, was he alone?" His wife's mouth grew even more stern. She released her hand and stepped back again. Her eyes narrowed; she looked frightened.

"I don't think so."

"No?" He shook his head. "Why not?"

"I heard him say something to someone when he got back in the car."

"Was he driving?"

"I don't think so."

"Was this someone else male or female?"

"I don't know."

Flora Venema sniffed the air, as if detecting betrayal. She put a hand to the side of her neck and shook her head.

I stared down the road again; it curved off to the right. Tall trees stood on each side. "The car he was in — can you remember anything about that?"

"It was loud, like it had a hole in the muffler."

"Anything else?"

Venema shook his head three times. "I think the car came back a few minutes later, after they left. Going the other way down Perry, like it was circling around, and then just took off." His milky eyes were awash with something akin to sorrow. "Honest to Pete."

His wife was livid about something. Again, I played along.

"What about other cars? Did you hear them go in and out of there about the same time?"

"What are you thinking, Turkstra, something happened back there?" asked his wife.

"Do you?" She turned away. Clarence twisted around, as if looking for his wife. She started walking back to the house, slowly, as if marching.

"Were there any other cars?" I prodded.

Venema turned back to me. "Bitch," he hissed. "She probably saw it, too."

I stepped back, startled by his anger. "Saw what?"

"The whole thing," he said. "She never gives me a moment of peace. She's always standing on the porch looking out. But she thinks I'm lu-lu."

Now it seemed as if he were asking something of me. "Don't you think?" he said. "Don't you think she saw something, too?" The eyes behind the glasses were wide. Crazy-looking in their blankness.

17

The gate gave way slowly with a pull, almost flopping off its hinges. Knee-deep weeds stood in my way. Thick vines dropped from trees bordering the back side of the cemetery. I paused, hearing flies buzz and smelling the mossy scent of decay. I waved a hand in front of my face, licking dried peach juice from my lips. Directly in front of me, shaped in a cement cone, was a marker: "Frederick Clavenburg, 1801–1862." Words and numbers nearly worn smooth. I had been here a few times before, years ago, as a teen-ager. Alone, or with friends, I would fish Ottogan Creek, the stream that wound below at the base of the path that led to this family burial place. It was down there that Clavenberg Roadside Park had been built. Consisting of a picnic table, trash barrel and cement grill, the park mostly served fishermen who came here in the fall when salmon swam up-river and down small tributaries to spawn. The tiny park had not been there when my buddies and I waded through, trying to snag whatever fish we could with our mostly makeshift poles. Down there minutes before I had seen nothing of interest, only the small stream moving sluggishly, carrying with it a few leaves and twigs, moving toward the Grand, about 15 miles to the northwest. I came to poke around and try to figure why, or even if, Sid Hammersma had come here. It was quite possible that the disembodied voice asking directions was a figment of Venema's imagination. Maybe he and his wife made up stories, then denied them to keep themselves busy. They'd always

125   DEADLY WATERS

been an odd, aloof pair. Still, he mentioned the history professor had been with someone. Was it the person with whom Jack had seen Hammersma talking by the marina mailbox? The guy in the picture? Heat seeped through the graveyard grass; insects clacked and clambered everywhere. The stones were haphazardly placed, tilted and in a couple places toppled. They made me think of frozen slabs of time. Each slab marked the brutal end of life — because the ending of any life, no matter how it happened, was brutal. Something nibbled at my neck. I swatted at it and came up with slime.

Winding around a few plots, I stepped to the graveyard's northern edge. Just over the sagging fence was a large rock, veined with fine rivers of blue and red and orange, on which we had rested as kids. I stepped over the fence and climbed atop the rock, retrieved from the ground years before. Instead of sitting, I stood on the boulder. Moving in the distance, cars passed on I-196. Sunlight flashed as they moved in steady streams east to Grand Rapids and west to Holland. This side of the expressway was untended, clotted and lumpy land, a small haven for hawks, barn owls, deer and even some fox. I believe the Clavenburg family sold it off years before to an oil speculator, who dug deep for fuel and, despite the murky, marshy texture of the soil, found none. Here and there, almost hidden by brambles and bushes, were a half-dozen rusting derricks. Meandering around to the right and moving toward the expressway was the creek. Farther to the right, humped in the haze, was a field of hay, in which moved a John Deere baler, its bright green grasshopper body taking in a cutting. I breathed deeply the mushy, overheated air, pondering a moment God's great deeds and the way in which he so often hid himself from his people in the land over which they toiled. There was a peace to this part of Michigan; the rolling hills stretched to my left, moving down toward the lake. Feeling such ease even in the midst of decay, I decided to do what I'd done here in the past as a kid. I peed. A steady stream moved out of me. Following it down, I saw water disappear in a mound of dirt. Yellow jackets circled the pile. Apparently disturbed by my rain, a few swirled up, angry as jet fighters. I quickly zipped my pants and beat a retreat through the graves, down the path, hopped across the creek, stepped through the park and got into my truck. I was assaulted by a wave of heat that had been trapped when I had rolled up the windows before I made my curious trek through the cemetery on the hill. I turned on the engine and backed out. Then I stopped and looked at the graves mounded on the hill. My father was buried in a similar cemetery about a dozen miles southeast of there. I stared a few moments at the overgrowth, noticed a few flickers of sun on the stream. It didn't make sense. Why would Hammersma come here?

I stopped by the fruit stand again. Clarence sat alone, lost in the words pumping through his earphones. After I got his attention, I asked, "Clarence, when the man you think was Sid Hammersma came by, did you ask him who he was?"

Clarence stared up, as if I had interrupted a powerful daydream. "Didn't have time. Fact is, didn't think about his voice until I heard it later on the tape."

A car pulled up in the street, stopped. A woman behind the wheel combed fingers through her hair, preparing to get out to buy fruit.

Clarence peered around, squinting. "Turkstra, how come you're so interested?" Noticing that the woman held back, still fiddling with her hair, I said, "Folks at the seminary asked me to do some asking around." His chin moved up and down. He carefully adjusted his baseball cap on his head. Then he said forcefully, "Tell them this. That night, twice, I heard pops. Like gunshots. May not sound like much, because guys are back there hunting, poaching, a lot. But not usually this time of year. You talk to people, you tell them what I heard. Because what I heard is right. I'm not making it up."

DEADLY WATERS

18

Marlan Oosterbaan stood by a file cabinet in his office, sorting mail. He wore a dark business suit; the white shirt collar pinched his wide neck. The room was frigid. Sweat dried cold on my face. Beyond Marlan, through a window, I saw neighbor boys splashing in an above-ground pool. My mouth was parched.

"Lucky you caught me. I was heading out," Marlan said, leaning an arm on the file cabinet. He looked tired.

"Thanks for seeing me," I said.

He blinked and sat behind his desk. "You want coffee?"

"No, thanks."

He folded his hands in front of him and smiled slightly, a tad sadly, wiped a hand over his face, took a sip of the coffee which sat in front of him. "Long night," he said. "The 16th hole was flooded. The waterfall on the 13th had backed up and was sopping the whole shebang."

"You fixed it yourself?"

He had a wide, friendly face that held strength and a touch of churlishness I recalled as part of his personality, even in grade school. He leaned back, rolling his neck. "Sure you don't want a Coke or something? It's hot out there."

"I am."

"Then go on," he said. "I'm all yours for …" He checked his watch. "Fifteen minutes." I wasn't sure how to begin. "Is this about last night?" he asked when I said nothing.

I nodded carefully. "In part."

"Then sorry. I might have pushed you a little hard."

I found Marlan's graciousness a little baffling, yet reassuring. "The other part," I said, "is I need help." My eyes shifted. I tried to keep the worry I felt out of them, but failed.

"What kind?" he asked.

"Maybe just advice," I replied.

"Usually that goes for free."

"Maybe also an explanation?" I then added.

His eyebrows rose. "That's not always so easy." He tugged an ear. "So let's try that part first."

I told him where I had been an hour before, what Clarence Venema told me, both about talking to Sid Hammersma, or someone he thought was Hammersma, and the sounds he thought were shots. When I mentioned walking in the graveyard, his lips grew faintly white, but he listened intently to what I had to say. When I was done, he checked his watch, scratched his wrist above it. "Old man Venema has bats in his barnyard, you know?" he told me.

"That's what his wife says."

"She's no Sunday picnic, either."

"You think what he said is bull?"

He thought a moment, mouth twisted. "Most likely."

"He's just making it up?"

"Strong possibility." The hands went behind his neck again. The white shirt stretched over his belly.

Having caught something in the way he had answered, I asked, "He said his wife called the police. Did she call here?"

"Called twice, and the county four times. But that's just on the Hammersma deal. He calls pretty regular with clues on everything from auto theft to pig rustling. She calls, too." My spirits sank.

"Don't take it personal, Turkstra. That old coot and his wife aren't always off base."

"No?"

"Once he did tip us off on a kid who was stealing gas from

129   DEADLY WATERS

farmers' homes. He stayed up night after night for weeks. Finally heard something in his yard. Sure enough, it was the culprit. A 15-year-old kid. We got him walking down the road with a bucket of gas in his hands. Problem was," he said, "kid doing it was his nephew."

The room felt even chillier than before. I thought, what about the car, someone else being there? That agreed with what Jack had told me. I tried this out on Oosterbaan. Told him about the kid at the marina. The chief's face grew serious, less smug. "Who told you that?"

"Can't say."

"This person reliable."

"As far as I can tell," I said.

"Venema said it?"

"Not about the marina, but about someone being in the car."

I told him as well about the photo on the boat matching the description of the person in the car, the one to whom Hammersma seemed to be giving directions.

Oosterbaan slipped a note pad out of the top drawer of his desk. As he wrote, he asked, "You tell Slade this?"

"Not yet."

He glanced at me, blue eyes serious. "Are you going to?"

"Can you?"

Oosterbaan looked as if he wanted to ask something, but he didn't. He made a couple more notes. "What other tidbits do you have?"

"That, as far as I can tell, Slade was right."

"About what?"

"Sid Hammersma had AIDS or the virus that comes before it." I watched his expression; he scowled, tapped his chin with the pen. "Turkstra, you really think you're plowing new ground here?" he said.

I thought I was, but said, "No."

He stuck the pen in his mouth, took it out. "Police work is mostly busy work. When you think you've got something, you're probably wrong." I didn't say anything.

"How come you don't like Slade?" he then asked.

"I didn't say that."

"You just as well as did." I didn't reply. "He's not going to be happy, me being your messenger service."

"Then don't tell him. I'll write him a letter."

Oosterbaan smiled. "I'm sure he'd like that."

"That's what I was thinking."

He sat back, hands over the pad, considered me a few moments like I was a suspect in a crime. "So why didn't you tell me all this last night?"

"Didn't know it all then."

His mouth pinched in a gesture of distaste. He snapped off the paper on which he'd been writing, folded and stuck it in his shirt pocket. "Look," he said, "I'll pass it on. But I'm betting you'll hear from him real soon."

"One thing else," I said.

"What's that?"

I gazed back out the window and saw a rainbow splash of water, flapping arms, a boy's soaked head. Cool water, baptismally bathing, I thought. When my gaze returned to Marlan, I noticed he'd corkscrewed his mouth into an expression of impatience. His fingers drummed the desk.

"Do you think it could have been murder?" I asked. The fingers kept moving; the mouth shifted.

"If so, who did it?" he retorted, twisting his head side to side, as if working out a knot.

"Is that why you haven't closed the case yet," I wondered.

He looked into his cup. He seemed to be considering something. He then sighed, nodded, leaned forward an inch. "Turkstra," he said, "I really don't know."

"Do you suspect it?"

He gazed beyond me. "Remember what I said to you last night about being careful?"

"Of course."

"Then I'd continue to proceed in that vein."

"But …"

He cut me off by holding up a hand. "Truthfully, Calvin, you're getting in way out of your depth."

I didn't like what he said. A twinge of condescension mixed with a little arrogance hung in his voice. "If you know something, Marlan, shouldn't you …"

Again he jumped in. "Ease up, Turkstra. Give it a break."

"So whoever did what can go free?"

"No," he replied, "so you can go on preaching."

"Meaning?"

"Take it however you want." We exchanged a long, tense glance. Finally, he blinked. Then he stood. So did I.

"My advice is just let this be. Tell your friends at the seminary to back off." I detected a plaintive note in his words.

I wanted to know more. What was he holding back — and why? I sensed beneath his warning a desire on his part to help out. But I also saw a flickering of fear. But he ushered me out, walked me to the front lobby. Checking his watch, he said, "But you're not going to do it, are you?"

"What's that?"

"Leave well enough alone."

"If it was well enough, I might. But since I know it's not, no."

He shook his head. "Just like your old man. Frisian to the core — and hard as nails to boot."

19

The Rev. Richard Rhodes was an expansive man. He had a gift for saying in many upbeat words what could have been condensed into a simple sentence. And besides his wordy way and sonorous voice, he had a good tan. Store-bought, gotten in a booth, but sturdy, serviceable and glossy — it made him look healthier-looking and younger than he was. He always came across as a sincere, direct-gazing man; he pumped your hand with extreme authority and enthusiasm. He had just released my hand now and beckoned me to sit in the soft leather chair positioned across the rich carpet from an even softer-looking chair in which he arranged himself with nearly feminine delicacy. He scissored one leg over the other and brushed something off the leg of his well-pressed, dark green pants. "So, Calvin, to what do I owe this pleasure?"

"Sid Hammersma," I replied simply, looking hard for a crack in the sublimely self-satisfied face.

"Reverend Smit said you might be stopping by for that." I had paused, on my way up, at Monica's office and we chatted. She was in the midst of planning her Sunday service with the children. We made no mention about a date for coffee. I couldn't help but notice, however, the shape of her legs below the cuffs of her white shorts. The dimple below her right eye.

"Did she say why I wanted to talk about that?"

His silver-black hair was combed back from a high, rather square forehead. "That she didn't mention."

Staring across at him, I realized he carried a powerful presence that was somehow able to put you at ease, even as you thought he was full of fluff. Several times I'd watched his service, carried live on Sunday evenings on local cable. Under the focus of TV cameras, he could speak in a way that drew you into what he was saying. The God he promoted lived clearly in his words, especially when he started into his pitch for souls, his rap about the need for salvation now. As if speaking from the clouds, he asked that the faithful lay down their doubts then and there and embrace Jesus. Certainly a solid and necessary part of believing. But the grace on demand, give your life over this very second, approach left me skeptical and empty. Nonetheless, there was no doubt he was a powerful salesman for the gospel.

"What I'm wondering," I said, "is if you remember having a conversation with Sid Hammersma on the day he disappeared, or at least if he talked to anyone in this church."

The brow wrinkled; the thin mouth pursed. Shiny theological tomes stood on shelves built into the walls around us. "Before I answer your question, I have one of my own." I waited. Politely, he asked, "May I ask it?"

"Sure."

"Are you putting me, this church, under suspicion?"

"Do I look like the suspicious type?"

A grin flowered on his mouth, showing perfect white teeth. Tufts of gray hair puffed at the open collar of his mauve polo shirt. "Calvin," he chuckled, "I would say yes, if it weren't for the fact you are so tall."

I had to laugh. "That part I can't help."

Even as we sat, the man exuded confidence and calm. He was one of the Lord's own serenity-filled sentries — so sure of who he was and what he did. On the tube, he moved with animal grace, playing to the cameras, his entire body emanating the calm certainty that came with a narrow-minded, self-serving reading of scripture. A stance assumed by those able to follow a rigid path supposedly set down by a Christ whose message was more rules than redemption. Or so I cynically thought. And since his church and his boastful approach to believing had usurped the relationship I had with Monica, I probably was a terribly biased, short-sighted observer.

"But," said Rhodes, "you came to ask me a question."

I took a sheet of paper out of my pocket. "I've got a record that states Sid Hammersma called the church twice on the afternoon he disappeared."

Rhodes' brow furrowed. He crossed and uncrossed his legs. "You said something in the outer office about why you are involved in this. Can you explain yourself further?"

I sketched my role, told him about what DeHorn wanted of me. Mentioned a little, but by far not all, of what I'd come across. When I was finished, he shook his head. "Pardon my asking, but aren't you stepping a little outside of bounds?"

"How so?"

"If you're just gathering information, why come here with a phone number you've gone to some trouble to obtain?"

"One thing has led to another."

His eyes fell on the paper in my hand.

"I'm not trying to be obtuse, Turkstra, but where in the dickens would you get information like that?"

"Does it matter, really?"

"Not if you're the police, but if you're a fellow pastor with a simple job to do, it does to me, yes."

I wasn't sure why, but I answered. Told him about obtaining the computerized list from the history department secretary.

"That is clever," he said, smiling gently.

I handed him the slip on which the same number was listed twice. "My understanding is that this is Todd Engstrom's extension." I'd learned that this morning when I called and got him. I hung up before talking. Last night, when I mentioned the number to Monica, I had assumed, it was the church office. On a hunch, I dialed it before heading over here. Rhodes examined it. He ran a hand over the side of his face. On his feet were alligator-skin loafers, slipped on over black, ribbed socks. "I won't ask how you know that, too, but, yes, it is." I nodded, hoping he would go on.

"Whatever do you think happened to Sid Hammersma, Turkstra?" he asked mildly.

"I suppose that's the million-dollar question."

"Given what I read in the paper Sunday about the life insurance and so on, I'd say the answer is worth a quarter of that."

Rhodes was a tough character. In his church, he offered a glib, feel-good theology for his Bible-believing members. Yet, there remained in him much of the darker, not nearly so pleasant, Reformed outlook on the world. I'd often thought his theology was not markedly different; only his approach varied from the norm. In a way, I found it odd: a fundamentalist who offered worldly hope and comfort.

"So, Engstrom never said anything?"

I thought suddenly of the Sunday morning I'd actually visited Rhodes' church, soon after I arrived in West Michigan from Chicago. I'd slipped in the back of the large, bowl-shaped sanctuary — they called it an auditorium — just as a hymn, some modern number, was reaching a crescendo. My eyes had swept the swaying crowd, squeezed shoulder to shoulder in the bench seats. I'd immediately felt energy and power, a muted kind of frenzy. My attention had been quickly drawn to the front, where Rhodes smiled out at the people, clapping his hands, his blue double-breasted suit resplendent in the bright lights beamed on the pulpit area. To the left, I'd seen Monica, amid a group of children on the stage. Dressed in a white silk blouse, open at the throat, a fairly tight blue skirt, and moderate heels, she, too, had been clapping, swaying, her face aglow with religious intensity. But I saw something else there that had slammed me with powerful force. A sheen of sexuality. As the music built, the church's small symphony played, the voices rose, and Rhodes swelled. As all of this grew, I sensed Monica losing control, entering a realm of physical vulnerability I thought only the two of us shared. Watching her and noticing the way in which Rhodes orchestrated the movement of the service, I'd known at some deep level that I faced a rival. In Rhodes, to be sure. But even more importantly in the highly sensuous, mildly risque manner in which this type of prayer wrenched open the emotions and allowed sin to run amuck in the name of a higher good. Surrounded by leafy potted plants, colored windows and other swooning congregants, Monica had looked that day to be in another world. A richer, happier, more loving world that was described by Rhodes later in the service during his sermon. In his stirring, manly voice, he had assured his followers of their salvation and their secure place in the world as long as they followed the teachings of Jesus Christ — teachings laid out in blithely twisted form by the breakaway preacher.

Monica had seemed mildly transported even an hour later at breakfast. I recalled how she had looked at me with dreamy, almost uncomprehending eyes. In the service when that first song ended, she had seemed to deflate inside herself, as if sated. At breakfast she wondered if I ever thought of breaking from the Christian Reformed faith myself.

"So," I said, removing my mind from the disturbing recollections, "he did call?"

He touched the paper with a finger. "You have the evidence right here."

"What did they talk about?"

His lips pursed; the eyes danced. He stood, went to his door, leaned out and asked, "Jenny, could you see if Todd is in his office. Ask him to come down here a moment."

Moments later, Engstrom arrived, dipping his head in greeting as he entered the room. We shook hands, half-heartedly.

"Todd," said Rhodes, once Engstrom had taken a chair on my right. "Turkstra here has a record, a telephone call printout, that indicates Sid Hammersma called the church here on June 8, in the late afternoon. He asked me if the two of you had talked. I held off answering until you were here."

Engstrom was also dressed casually, in white pants and a

short-sleeved, button-down-collar shirt. On his sockless feet were brown Dockers — updated, pretend moccasins. I recalled how he occasionally appeared on Rhodes' TV show to tell the audience of his formerly wicked ways and how Rhodes and Christ had put him on the straight and narrow.

"So," said Rhodes, "could you tell him what you told me?"

Engstrom turned to me, his face blandly serious. How much of this was set up? How much had Monica told these two?

"Both times Dr. Hammersma called looking for Reverend Rhodes," he said. I felt as if there had been a long, involved wind-up for a quick, wimpy pitch. I looked at Rhodes, who seemed to be examining his lap.

"The second time we talked, Reverend Rhodes took the call in my office."

This opened the door on more questions. Why hadn't Hammersma called Rhodes directly? As if reading my mind, Rhodes put up a crossing guard's hand. "Turkstra, I hope you don't feel manipulated, but Todd knew you were here and why. I could easily have answered your questions, but I wanted you to hear the first part from him."

"Why?"

"Because of the extreme delicacy of this matter."

Engstrom leaned back in his chair, stretching his legs. Around his neck was a thin silver chain bearing a small cross. Rhodes looked blithe and innocent, but serious. Engstrom looked slightly worried.

"What's so delicate?" I asked.

Rhodes crossed a leg, made praying hands under his chin. "Understand, Turkstra, that what I'm about to tell you is in the strictest confidence."

All I said was, "I understand this is a complicated matter."

"Not complicated, Turkstra," he said. "Painful."

I granted him that. Engstrom wiped a hand over his left thigh and winced, as if to underscore the pain. We were all silent a good half-minute.

"That day," said Rhodes finally, "I was returning from a

round of golf. It's not on your records, but Dr. Hammersma — Sid — had called here a couple other times earlier in the day, wanting to talk to me. He'd called my office. I wasn't here, which is why he tried Todd."

Engstrom sank deeper into his leather chair. It struck me that he was moody.

"He called to ask …?" I said.

The hand rose again. "Todd," he asked, "do you want to sit in on the rest of this?"

Engstrom's eyes slid over in my direction. "If he doesn't mind." I said I didn't care. I just wanted them to get on with it.

"Let me back up a second," said Rhodes. He told me that I might have heard that Sid Hammersma and he were friends — fairly good friends — from way back.

"Bottom line," said Rhodes, "is that Sid and I were confidants, even, in a way. You may not remember, but when my father started this church, Sid Hammersma was an ardent backer. Said we were bringing fresh air into a stuffy, ethnic church."

This wasn't so wild; it did make sense that Sid Hammersma would go outside the fold, but not too far, to make his points. In addition, he was often a champion for self-determination.

"When I say confidants, I don't mean best friends, always unburdening ourselves to one another," he clarified for me. I had a vague idea where this was leading. "Todd knows," said Rhodes. "The three of us golfed several times over the last few years. We had things in common."

Engstrom nodded, his hands linked as if he were wiggling an imaginary putter — or strangling a snake.

"Anyhow," said Rhodes, "Sid called that day several times, tracking me down, wanting to talk."

Rhodes leaned forward, glanced at Engstrom, back at me. "Unfortunately, I never learned exactly what it was that was on his mind," said Rhodes.

Engstrom sat up, turned to me as well. Ready to drop the ball in the hole.

139

"Sid finally reached me, as I say, as I was coming back from a game. In Todd's office. He sounded terrible — distraught. I transferred him down here. We talked. Just a few minutes. Sid said he was despondent He said …," Rhodes paused, as if for effect. "He said, for the first time in his life, he was thinking of killing himself. It was that bad."

"What was that bad?" I asked. This sounded like strong evidence for that theory, the road that led to his suicide.

"He never got the chance to say."

I stopped him there. "You've told all this to the police?" I asked.

"They know."

This had to be Slade's source.

Rhodes' face finally showed cracks of emotion. The color had dimmed in his tan. The mouth was drawn tight. It was the face that showed on TV when he spoke of sin and pain in the world, the need for more money to fund his church. "There's not much else to say. I told Sid certainly we could talk."

"You didn't ask him why he was feeling suicidal?"

Rhodes shook his head sadly, held up a hand a third time, as if in defeat. "I thought he'd get into that later."

"Later?"

If I wasn't mistaken, something akin to tears glistened in his eyes. "Right, Turkstra. We made an appointment to meet at my home, about 8. I told him I would be there by then. I was. But Sidney never showed."

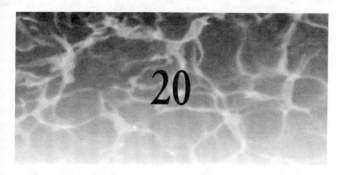

20

Standing in the lobby of the Oval Beach Health Club, I checked my reflection in the mirror next to the doorway that led into the heat. The T-shirt was loose; stenciled on the chest were three large Xs. The gym shorts also gave me room. My socks were white; my Reeboks slightly scuffed. I stretched this way and that, noting the wary glint in my eye, the scar on my chin left there from an altercation in Chicago with a wino who wouldn't leave a restaurant. It wasn't the wino who put it there. It was a police officer who, in his earnest attempt to help, slapped me with his nightstick. As experiences would have it, a very minor occurrence given the nature of what went on in my time there. Also in the mirror, coming up behind me, I noticed Warren Roelofs. He was rubbing his hands together. His running attire was a little more colorful than mine, but not much: blue T-shirt with the face of a Mohawk Indian on the front, rose-colored nylon running shorts and gray-black Brooks shoes. He wore sock booties that left room for his bony ankles to show. "Ready?" he asked.

We pushed through the door into a blanket of heat. We ran in place a few moments on the sidewalk. Roelofs checked his wristwatch. "How does six miles sound?"

"Awful." He glanced at me to see how serious I was. I smiled. He nodded, and we were off.

"I'll take it easy on you," he said.

The athletic club was named after the nearby beach that

fronted Lake Michigan. But the club itself was on the outskirts of Saugatuck, on the corner of Tacken and Allegan streets. We looped through downtown, a collection of upscale jewelry, luggage, music, clothing and souvenir shops mixed with delis, bars and fern-draped, glitzy-sounding streetside restaurants. Saugatuck and nearby Douglas were pockets of rich plenty amid the blueberry, peach and apple orchards of northern Allegan County. Both towns existed largely to serve the tastes of upper-class tourists, many from Chicago. Visitors had seasoned, artistic tastes. The sweat already breaking through my shirt, we passed several galleries behind whose windows hung original paintings, etchings, and sculpture. Large, turret-fronted homes with lacy wooden porches and peaked roofs filled in the neighborhood surrounding downtown. The sidewalks were crowded with shoppers — men, women and children in gaudy summer clothes. I followed Roelofs as he wove his way through them. Almost to the docks that were built out onto the Kalamazoo River, which separated half of Saugatuck from the big lake beyond, Roelofs looked back over his shoulder and asked, "How are you doing?" I blew sweat from my upper lip and nodded. Swinging an arm up, he pointed left.

Twenty-four hours before, I'd stepped out of Rhodes' office to find my truck unresponsive to both the turn of my key and the series of names, some profane, I used to describe the engine's lack of performance. As luck, providence, or the various winds of fate would have it, Monica had walked out of the church — just as I was about to beat my hands silly on the steering wheel. Saving me from a tantrum, she offered to give me a ride. I actually had not made many plans for the rest of the day. I asked if she would wait while I called a tow truck. She agreed. The truck came and hauled my truck away. Monica then dropped me off at home. She'd been on her way into Grand Rapids for something. We'd said little about my visit to Rhodes' church. As I got out of her car, she offered to drive me elsewhere later if necessary. I declined. I spent the rest of the day puttering around my study, catching up on church-related work. Sorting through a few bills. I also telephoned a few people related to the Hammersma business, and set things up for today. As the sun began to dip over the trees in my back yard, Monica called. Wondered about my truck. I told her it would be in the shop for a couple days and learned she, too, had to be in Saugatuck on this day. She offered to take me, and I accepted. As I ran with Roelofs, she visited with a nearby church member undergoing some crisis. We agreed to meet after I finished jogging.

Roelofs and I now ran along Lake Street, heading south to the U.S. 31 bridge that crossed the river. Ahead I saw the blue water glimmer. Boats dipped in and skimmed the surface. Sails of many colors, nearly still and unruffled in the windless afternoon, stretched from one side of the concrete bridge to the other. It felt good to be out, even if the heat felt like a sauna.

"How long've you been in town here?" I asked, coming alongside Roelofs as the sidewalk grew less dense with shoppers the further we moved from the business district.

He glanced over. He had a brow that poked out over his owlish eyes. The beaked nose and large mouth added to the bird-of-prey effect. On his left hand was a wedding ring. His ministry was mainly, but not entirely, to gays. He had been a year ahead of me in seminary. "Seven years," he said, sounding slightly winded, which made me feel good.

We reached the bridge and were following traffic out of town. Cars hauling boats; motor homes filled with families; vans bearing overloaded roof-top carriers moved on our left.

"You started the gay ministry right away?"

He glanced sidelong at me, shook sweat from his nose. "That's right," he almost snapped.

He sped up, crossing the bridge and making an immediate right. Afloat in the water as we ran was an abandoned ocean liner. It had been towed in here years before and used in one form or another as a stationary tourist attraction. Once, awhile back, I had eaten dinner on it. It looked empty today, but well maintained, out there in the water.

"Turkstra," Roelofs said as he ran, "you want to make it up to the beach by the state park, then head back? Might be a little more than six miles, round trip."

I told him OK. My legs and lungs, however, were starting to burn. But I would keep up.

"We'll take Perry up. Just watch for cars," he said.

Monica had dropped me off near Roelofs' church — actually the refurbished warehouse in which he held his services — about an hour before. I knew what a trial it had been for Roelofs to begin and maintain a church-affiliated ministry to gays, who lived year-round in Saugatuck and Douglas. His church, to keep ties with the denomination, had to walk a very thin line between adhering to the church's professed anti-homosexuality stance and offering spiritual services to those who openly embraced a lifestyle many in our fold viewed as aberrant, if not downright evil. He had told me the day before that he had a meeting today at 1:30 p.m. with business people, to discuss continuing plans for a new church he hoped to build. As if picking up on my thoughts, he said, "Up here." He pointed through a grove of pines. "Where we're hoping to put the new church."

I squinted. It looked like an empty farm field. "I heard you already started to build and then had to stop," I said.

"Right."

"Why?"

"Financing fell through."

"Why's that?"

"You tell me."

That was a strange thing to say, I thought. "How would I know?"

"Could be just as simple as asking Bradley DeHorn." We huffed along, keeping pace with one another.

"I'm confused," I said.

"How do you think we feel?"

We started up an incline. On the other side of the road two men on separate mountain bikes, their heads covered with plastic domes, pedaled downhill. They waved. Roelofs waved back. We were silent as we made our way up. At the top, I caught a glimpse through the trees on our left of a swatch of Lake Michigan.

"Nearly there," said Roelofs, arms rolling as he ran.

"But DeHorn," I said. "How would he be blocking your new church?"

"Maybe not him, but people he knows."

"But why?"

"I think," he said, "that's what you've come to ask."

⁓ ⁓

Less than a half-hour later, we stood on the far end of the Oval Beach parking lot and I took in welcome gulps of breath. Frothy waves washed the shore 50 yards away. Up and down the strip of sand were swimmers, sunbathers and children with buckets, shovels and balls. I heard loud music blare, saw two teens dancing in the sand. This was an eternal spot for West Michigan young. A volleyball game was in progress to our left. The lake stretched for miles, a heaving mass moving this way from Wisconsin. Clouds rode the sky in great white bunches. More boats bounced in the moderate waves a few hundred feet beyond the swimmers. I bent, set my hands on my knees and swallowed hard. The ongoing summer fun was a disturbing counterpoint to what I was trying to discover. My ears filled with the erratic sound of shouts, laughter, conversation, music and water breaking the shore. I looked up when a volleyball rolled to a stop near my feet. Roelofs scooped it up and flung it to a girl in a pink bikini with a necklace of tiger teeth around her throat.

"Got a little bit of everything out here," I observed, eyeing the tiger teeth. Roelofs gave me an irritated glance. I realized then how sensitive he probably was to comments criticizing the appearance or actions of others. I figured he heard things like that a lot. I thought of apologizing, but didn't.

We started down a path that wound through dune grass, across a road and up a wooden staircase to an observation deck looking out on the lake. Roelofs held on to a rail and stretched. I sat on a bench, gazing far out on the water. Thinking again about the unmanned sailboat, The Wittenberg Door, and a man swamped by waves or his own despair.

"You know," said Roelofs, grabbing both ankles with his hand, "you'll get cramps on the way back if you don't do this."

"I'll die on the way back if I don't do this."

He smiled and continued his exercises. I stood and did some minor, very minor, leg jiggling and hand flopping. Finally, checking his watch, Roelofs said, "We've got a few minutes. What is it you want to know?"

"I'm still wondering about DeHorn," I said.

"Nothing to wonder about there. He's a part of the loop. He's got his fingers in most of the pies."

"You think he threw a roadblock in front of your building program?"

"Maybe not him, but somebody like him." Hands over his head, Roelofs twisted back and forth from the waist.

"Now you're sounding like I did down there," I said.

He glanced at the beach. From here the scene was less busy. "How do you mean?" he asked. His brow knit.

"I was making fun of the girl with the teeth. You're lumping everyone in the denomination into the same bag."

"Not everyone."

"Almost."

"Not you." I wasn't sure what to make of that. I took it as a compliment.

He turned and faced the lake. I sat on the bench again. He spoke to the water. I directed my sodden underarms into the slight breeze.

"Turkstra, the only reason I'm willing to talk to you is because it's you." He glanced back.

"Why?" I asked.

"Because," he said, "you're a straight shooter. Pardon the cliche. But first," he said, facing me again, "tell me what you know. Like why you sicced VanderMolen on me."

"I didn't tell him to call you."

Roelofs shrugged. "Just fill me in some before I spill my guts."

I went over it for him, the brief version. Mentioning the AIDS. The possibility of Hammersma's meeting up with a young man the day he disappeared. Even telling him about Rhodes. The phone call.

He listened with interest and without interrupting. When I was done, he said, "A lot of that computes, but not the part about Rhodes."

"Why?"

"I didn't know they were such good friends."

"You think he was lying?"

"Probably not. I'm just surprised is all. I don't know why."

Roelofs looked at the people heading up our way on the wooden steps. "This kid you're talking about, the one Hammersma had met — what did he look like?" I told him, mentioned the picture on the boat. I thought I really should have taken it to show around. "He had frizzy hair?" asked Roelofs, placing both hands on his head. I nodded.

He was quiet a moment. "And what kind of car was it?" I told him.

He grew serious. "Sounds like Kenneth."

"Who?"

"Kenneth."

"You know him?"

"I'm afraid so."

The breeze dropped for a moment. I heard a man and woman climbing the steps to our left. Roelofs looked down and back at me. "Let's start back."

As we ran, Warren Roelofs told me that over the years Sid Hammersma had been a friend of his church. Every so often, he attended Sunday services. Roelofs said this was normally in the summer, and he assumed this was when Hammersma was out on his boat and docked nearby to catch weekend worship. About two years before, Hammersma started attending services more frequently. And a year ago Hammersma agreed to

147   DEADLY WATERS

quietly begin work with a few others on a document that was to be presented to next year's Christian Reformed Synod, the denomination's annual business meeting. The document was to be a thoroughly researched paper, based on biblical teaching, that called for the church to review its stance opposing homosexuality. This was surprising to me, to think someone of Hammersma's theological caliber would be thinking along these lines. It wasn't entirely that I thought such reasoning was terribly off target, but the reality of how fiercely our church hierarchy would fight such a proposal.

Roelofs told me that some change had come over Hammersma in the last year or so that had encouraged him to become more deeply involved. Not only that, but there had been another change, too. A half dozen times, this in recent months, Hammersma had come to church with Kenny Fortunato. However he wanted to view it, Roelofs said he suspected the relationship was more than casual. He knew the two met a few years back in class. Fortunato had enrolled in a semester at seminary, but had not lasted long. Roelofs told me that Kenny was trouble. He was unpredictable and prone to outbursts. He had just gotten out of the Kent County Jail in January, after having served a sentence on a drunken driving conviction. Roelofs added that he was concerned, and had been since Hammersma turned up missing, that Fortunato was somehow involved. In what way, I asked. Roelofs had just waved me off. He didn't know, or wouldn't say.

As we neared downtown Saugatuck, I asked Roelofs about the rumor of AIDS. His answer, after a poignant few moments of silence, was that he wouldn't be surprised if Sid Hammersma had been sick with the virus. As for where he had gotten it, that was all speculation. Perhaps Fortunato. But Sid Hammersma, he told me, had been no saint. He didn't come right out and say it, but Roelofs implied there had been others.

When we closed in on the health club and a welcome shower, I asked Roelofs why he hadn't gone to the police with what he knew. He grew cagey. But after I pressed, he said it wasn't two days after Sid Hammersma was reported missing that financing for the new church suddenly and mysteriously dried up. The message wasn't hard to read: Keep quiet about Hammersma. Higher-ups in the church did not want to be embarrassed by revelations that their star historian and one of the most popular defenders of the faith had been living in a dark closet. Let the police uncover what they might, but don't help them. Manipulative as that was and illegal as I assumed any judge would find it, it made sense given the workings of my church. But then why had Bradley DeHorn turned me loose on a path that would probably bring shame on many people anyhow? As to that, Roelofs didn't know. But he did know — and he couldn't explain why — that money sanctions were starting to lift from his church. In recent days word had filtered through that work could recommence soon. All of which, he said, led him to believe that there were those who now wanted him to talk, or at least mention what he knew to someone, perhaps because they believed talking about it was now more important than silence. As for taking this information to the police, Roelofs wasn't so sure. Not yet. What he knew only put Fortunato and Sid Hammersma together; it explained little more than that. Or that's what he thought. I was starting to think it explained a great deal more, and told him so. I asked him to agree to bring this information to the police, who, I suspected, knew it already. Reluctantly, Roelofs agreed.

After our shower, as we toweled off, Roelofs faced a full-length mirror. His eyes found mine in the reflecting glass. He rubbed the towel through his hair. "How about this, Turkstra?" he said. I waited. "Our good friend, Bradley DeHorn, knows exactly what happened to the professor. Maybe, given his homophobic inclinations, played some role for some reason in the disappearance. And now, with Hammersma's wife pressing, wants you to bite, hook, line and sinker, into the suicide theory, that way giving him more ammunition to bolster his case when he talks with the board." Our eyes remained linked in the mirror.

"But why would he have a hand in something like murder?" As for his homophobia, I didn't know about that either, I thought.

Roelofs shrugged. "Don't know. But he's a strange fish."

"Anyone else come to mind who might have had it in for the professor?"

Roelofs looped the towel over his neck, tugged on the ends. His face grew wan, slightly stricken. "Maybe Kenny."

"But why?"

Roelofs turned from the mirror and faced me directly. "Who knows, but Kenny was a loaded cannon. His background, his family, was pretty screwed up. From what I can tell, he was lucky to get out of that home alive."

I nodded. "His home?" I asked. "Where is that?"

Wrapping the towel around his belly, Roelofs gazed at the ceiling. "Benton Harbor or someplace like that."

Damn, I thought. I'd called the other number I'd gotten from the history department secretary the day before. A woman at a church of some kind in Benton Harbor had answered. "You know where in Benton Harbor?"

"I don't know, except his father, from what I recall, was one of us. A preacher. But I'm thinking of an entirely different ilk."

21

I slid into the Toyota Tercel beside Monica as she waited by the curb in front of the brightly painted cinder-block warehouse that served as the home of Roelofs' church. "Been waiting long?" I asked.

"Not long."

She stared at me. "You look pooped." I was. I told her about the run.

"And on a day like this."

"Tell me about it," I said.

"Are you hungry?" she then asked.

I was, but I had another idea. "Are you up for driving to Benton Harbor?" I asked.

"Why Benton Harbor?"

Inside Roelofs' church, I'd called the number again. This time I spoke to a woman who informed me that the pastor, the man I wanted to talk to, would be there about 3 p.m. I said I'd like to stop by to speak with him. She responded that was up to me and hung up. I explained to Monica what I had learned from Roelofs.

"You have to go there in person?" she asked.

"I'd like to."

She stared out her windshield. Tapped her fingernails on the steering wheel.

"Do you have the time?" I asked. She'd already mentioned she had the afternoon off. "I'll pay for gas and buy lunch," I said.

151   DEADLY WATERS

She sighed, pushed hair out of her face. "You'll have to drive, too." Her eyes got shifty. She turned down the flute music that had been pouring sweetly from the radio. It bugged me.

I stopped at McDonald's, on the outskirts of Douglas. She got a fish sandwich and a salad, which she placed in her lap and ate as I drove. I got two Big Macs and iced tea. Heading south on U.S. 31, we ate in silence. Munching, swallowing and sipping, I mulled over what Roelofs had told me. I had a sense of things further spreading out, like a stain. Sid Hammersma, I was beginning to see, had several sides, not all of them wholesome.

"Who're we going to see again?" asked Monica.

"We're trying to find a kid named Kenny Fortunato."

Finishing a bite of salad, she asked, "Who's he?"

"Sounds like a very good friend of Sid Hammersma's." I felt her eyes on me but gazed out the window, trying to look placid.

"Meaning?" she asked.

I didn't answer that. Instead, I asked, "How well do you know Warren Roelofs?"

"Changing the subject won't get you off the hook," she said.

"I'll get back to that."

"You know him better than I do," she said, eyes on the road.

"But he said you've been doing some work together." He'd mentioned that after I'd called Benton Harbor from his office.

She blinked, as if caught in something. "You mean on the board of the Hospice thing?"

"I think that's what he said." Besides building a new church, Roelofs was in the middle of trying to raise money to build a center at which persons dying of AIDS could live out their final days. That project also had run into snags. Snags that his silence on the matter of Hammersma's disappearance had started to free.

"I'm on the board with him, if that's what you're asking." Her tone had grown chilly and distant, a tad irritated.

"Is there something about working with him that you don't like?"

Her blond hair moved with the whiffs of wind coming in her window. Her skin was pink, face scrubbed. Half-moons of dull polish decorated her nails. She wore a tan and green blouse and dark skirt. The fabric of the blouse also moved with the breeze. I saw a faint design of flowers in it. She glanced at me, then back at the road. "Not really, no."

"You reluctant to talk about it?"

"Not about that. But about this whole thing." Now she seemed angry.

"What bothers you?"

She sighed with exasperation. Either that or additional anger, or both. "Truman," she said, "you've got everyone in an uproar."

I sort of liked that. "Who's everyone?" I wondered.

"Are you blind?"

"You're losing me."

She fixed her eyes on the road ahead, chewed her lower lip. "Yesterday you came barreling into the church, accusing Todd and Reverend Rhodes of who knows what. You ask me to be your taxi service and then you start pumping me with questions like I'm some kind of suspect." Her face was flushed. In her eyes was heat. Her hands gripped together tightly. I wanted to touch them.

"Pardon me, ma'am, but I believe you offered the ride."

"After you begged me."

"You could have said no," I responded.

She blew out her cheeks, a child-like gesture. Small studded stones shone in the lobe of her left ear. She said nothing for a few moments, her face riveted to the windshield, salad half-eaten in her lap. Finally, she said "Could you do me the courtesy of just telling me clearly, step by step, what this is all about."

I told her the story, start to finish, as I knew it so far. When I'd finished, neither of us spoke for awhile. I kept driving and noticed the expressway unwind ahead, rising up a slight incline, cutting through apple orchards filled with tortured-looking trees. Bent branches, twisted limbs, lumpy trunks all poked up out of the ground to bear fruit. To the left, standing alone and sagging, was a red barn.

"Tell me this again." Monica said finally. "You think Professor Hammersma was not only gay but that he had a lover who was once one of his students and now lives in Benton Harbor and that he's involved in the disappearance?"

"It's one theory."

"And you also say the poor man was sick with AIDS, which he may have gotten from this kid, and that you wonder if this kid may have killed him for some life insurance money?"

"About the size of it."

"Do you really think Sidney Hammersma would mix himself up with some weirdo who would kill him for life insurance money?" asked Monica.

"Stranger things have happened."

"I think you're stretching it," Monica said.

"Why?"

"First, is this character a beneficiary on the policy?"

"I don't know. I'm trying to find the second will, to see if it names him."

"You should. That would be important."

I didn't like her bossy, although familiar, tone. "Thanks for the advice," I almost said, but kept quiet. Monica had turned to me. In the past, we had loved to play cribbage, setting down blocks, plotting strategies. Bickering. Struggling. Making plans. Debating.

"Any idea where that will is?" she asked.

"None."

"Or if it really exists?" she wondered.

"My suspicion is it does."

"Why?"

"Just a hunch."

"OK, then," she said, "what do you make of his call to Reverend Rhodes?" Of that I wasn't so sure. I wondered what she knew — if it was more than Rhodes had told me. "From what you said, Sid Hammersma was distraught. He was at the end of his rope and wanted to die. Maybe this kid from Benton Harbor had dumped him," Monica said.

"Dumping him, if that's what happened, wouldn't cause him to want to die." My words sounded hollow in my ears.

"Some people put their most intimate relationship right on the top of their list, Truman. When that breaks, so do they," she said. Seemed to me she was preaching. Either that or criticizing me. Or maybe she was telling me about herself, which I doubted. "Really, Truman, sometimes you're so dense."

I felt as if I had been slapped. The odd remaining connection between us, the unwillingness to truly break the bond, I found baffling. "Sometimes you're not so nice yourself," I said, feeling snotty.

"Who said anything about nice?" She put a finger to her temple. "I said thick. As in the noggin. You can't see your nose in front of you."

"What part of this is so obvious to you, Miss Marple"? I asked.

She shifted around even more, holding a fan of hair out of her face. The blue in her eyes made me think of sun on clear water, showing shifting shadows underneath.

"Look at it this way," she said. "Sid Hammersma, God forgive him, got AIDS. From where or who, we don't know. May never know. This kid somehow finds out. Probably Hammersma tells him. Maybe they are in love. Lord, maybe Sid Hammersma passes this on to him. Who knows? Maybe this kid gave it to him. I don't know. But," she said, "Sid Hammersma takes a hard look at himself. Doesn't like what he sees. Decides he can't take it anymore. He debates what to do, even cries out for help, maybe to Dr. Rhodes. But then, he can't take it. He asks his friend, this kid, for help. Who knows how, but Sid Hammersma dies. Probably does it himself. Maybe gets Kenny to play a role in hiding it. Who knows? You've been living with this longer than me, Truman, but I think it fits."

Cresting another small rise, I saw spread around us a landscape of blueberry farms, a bog, thatches of black bramble, and a row of ranch-style houses fronting the Blue Star Highway that ran parallel to the expressway.

"So you've got it all figured?"

"It's just a thought," she said.

"Most of it I can buy," I said after a moment, glad she'd taken interest in the case.

"What part don't you accept?"

"What about the meeting in the graveyard?"

"You told me the police think your fruit seller made that up."

Barely moving on the far side of a corn field was a green tractor. A white farmhouse, squared in by trees, stood beyond the machine. The country normally comforted me. Not today. I thought of some deadly virus living out there in the land on which I was reared, only inches below the soil, growing stronger, trying to destroy life as we knew it. Like AIDS.

"How about Todd?" I asked. "How does he play into this?"

"Todd?" I nodded. "Why?" she asked, a little defensively.

It struck me I was asking two things at once. "Was he a friend of Sid Hammersma's, too?"

"You've got me there."

I drove on, hands clammy on the wheel, wondering if there was any kind of pesticide that could kill what was starting to ail so many of us. I thought of hell. It really wasn't flames. It was what we did to one another. Without Christ's intervention, we were indeed sunk. Dumb dupes without hope.

Somehow the notion of Hammersma having AIDS deeply disturbed me. Even though I'd ministered to people suffering from it, the terrible, wasting disease had still been beyond me. The pain, the sorrow, the sickness had been someone else's. In the few cases with which I was acquainted, the persons with AIDS had come from entirely different worlds than me. I had offered them help, but had felt as if I was secure in my church, my domain. But the likelihood that this awful sickness had infected one of our own, and one of our best minds, shook me at the core. Exactly why I couldn't say, but the encroachment of AIDS, the interference of this horrible occurrence of nature, turned my thoughts to Engstrom. He was another invader, bringing with him pestilence. I knew I was overreacting emotionally, but didn't care.

"Are you involved with Engstrom?"

She looked out the window on her right. Her body was still; she seemed to be hardly breathing. I saw the back of her neck through the hair. Curved. A light blue vein carrying blood. I wanted to touch it and feel its flow. I knew that I was getting carried away. The worm, the infection, seemed to be in me as well. She asked the window, "Why?"

"Because," I said, nervous at what I'd started to wonder, "I want to know if you are protecting him, or your church."

I was surprised by how quickly she turned and by the sorrow on her face. "What if I am?" she asked.

"But from what?" I asked.

"From hurt or lies."

"Which lies?"

She didn't respond. Face drained of color, gnawing her lower lip, she gazed in her lap. "Just what if I am protecting my church? Would that be so wrong?"

"I just want to know if it ties in to Sid Hammersma's disappearance." My eyes kept flicking from the road ahead to her and back.

"What's it?" she asked.

"Todd's involvement. Or Rhodes', for that matter."

"I know Todd's not involved."

"Not involved?"

"Right."

"How about Rhodes?"

"Him either."

"You're sure."

She turned to me and said heatedly, "Yes!"

I stared at her for longer than was probably safe. I was drawn back by a bump in the road. "What in your opinion is it that we're saying?"

"You're saying," she said.

"And that is?"

She faced the windshield, hands in her lap. Softly she said, "Jealousy. I think that's what you're saying."

"That's outrageous," I replied halfheartedly.

Her gaze scorched my skin. "I don't think it is."

I watched the road ahead, sorting through my emotions. I felt a little dirty. Like I'd been dumping some of my fear and confusion on her. Beyond that, in truth, I did feel jealous. It did matter to me who she was dating, exactly who she loved and whose side she was on.

22

I parked across the barren street from a ramshackle row of buildings bearing scars of age and neglect. Slumping along the sidewalk on our side of the street was a man in a tattered, flapping overcoat. He shivered, even in the heat, his rheumy eyes locked on some spot in front of him. His lips moved, mouthing some message to the grimy air around him.

"Welcome to Benton Harbor," I said, watching him pass, a huge bent fish out of some odd waters.

"Does it remind you of some place?" Monica asked.

Our South Chicago storefront. The place in which we met, nearly married — and moved on. A haven for lost souls, not all of whom stumbled in off the street. The place where I first came face to face with AIDS. So did Monica.

Up and down the desolate street, I sensed lethargy and loss. Signs hanging from the few open stores were worn, droopy, had letters missing. Two blocks over, on the main drag, efforts were under way to rebuild this dying town.

"Do you miss it?" Monica asked.

"Wacker Street and the rest?" She nodded, arms huddled over her chest. "Sometimes. Do you?"

"Not the storefront work," she said.

The wreckage that we'd both encountered at the mission remained with us still. Monica had come to West Michigan, seeking comfort, safety, and a career in a new type of religion. I returned to keep from going crazy in a city filled with sores and sorrow and blood on morning doorsteps. The only worse place I could think of was Detroit.

"I think I'd only go back now if they paid me, say, a million dollars in unmarked bills," I said.

The last half hour on the way to Benton Harbor we'd been silent. Neither of us mentioned the matter of jealousy again. We simply let it sit between us like a wound.

"Do you remember Danny?"

She turned to me. "Oh God, I'd forgotten him."

Together we'd talked to him, helped him find an apartment, visited him in the hospital. I'd been closer to Danny than Monica, but she'd been there, too.

"This has made me think of him again."

Monica stared beyond me, a far-off expression in her eyes. "Remember how awful it was?"

I did. The huge eyes, sallow skin, the spots on his arms, the swollen tongue, the bony chest, the psychosis that overtook him in his last days. Dying in the hospital, he had more than once called his friends, myself included, demons.

Monica shifted in her seat, leaned her head against the passenger door and slumped. "Might sound silly, but I'm thinking of moving back."

"To Chicago? For what?"

"For school. Get a Ph.D in psychology."

"Stop preaching to the kids?" I asked.

"There are so many needs out there, Truman," she said, not really answering my question.

"You want to be a psychologist?"

"As a minister and a counselor, I could do a lot."

I saw she was serious. "But what about working in the church with kids?" I asked. "You were so set on that."

Her mouth turned down. "I could still do that, but I'm not so sure anymore that's exactly my calling."

I thought of the fierce battles we'd had over this. Now, she was just going to chuck it? I wondered if she planned to return there alone. "What kind of counselor?" I asked.

She blinked and spoke to the windshield. "Sexual abuse."

Somehow that struck me as brave. But I didn't tell her that. "You mean incest?" She nodded.

For a moment I wanted to tell her if she left the area I'd miss her. Instead, I was silent.

"How about you?" she asked. "Are you happy where you are?"

The Harbor Light Church of Christ Risen was almost directly across the street from us. The windows to the place were frosted with what looked like soap.

"Me," I said. "I'm thinking of joining the rodeo."

She frowned and sat back in the seat. "How long will this take?" she asked.

"Not long," I said. I looked at her; she was still as a statue. I turned off the car, got out and stretched, watching two guys on bikes wind slowly toward us down the sidewalk. A skinny, yellow dog with floppy, shovel-shaped ears panted between them. The few trees, poking spindly, skinny trunks through pavement, looked dirty and ragged. I could hear the buzz of electricity grinding through overhead wires. The virus is everywhere, I thought, shuddered, and then told myself to lighten up. "Are you coming in?" I asked, peering in the car. She said nothing. "Monica?"

She didn't move; she was mulling something in her mind. "Can you tell me one thing?" Her face swiveled toward me.

"You can ask."

"Are Todd and Richard caught up in this?"

"That's what I'd asked you."

"Don't toy with me."

Monica had a full, firmly formed face, cheekbones that stood out and begged to be noticed. A mouth that could be sultry and churlish and strong at the same time. In her eyes was that deep blue fire, a determination that made me quake with regret, even when we were together. Next to her and her aspirations, not to mention her abilities and questing heart, I shrank. But even with all of her many strengths, she had one soaring shortcoming. She'd never been a good judge of people, myself included.

A car passed on my left, slowed but kept going. I didn't look. I said to Monica, "I don't have much to go on, but, yes, my sense is they are. Somehow."

"How deep?"

"That I don't know."

"Speculate."

"I can't until I know more."

"Try," she said. "Help me out."

"How?"

"By telling me that what I suspect isn't true."

"What do you suspect?" I squatted, facing her.

"I can't say."

"Can't or won't?"

"Won't."

What she was holding back was causing her obvious pain. I wasn't sure how or why, but she had apparently decided to tell me the truth, or part of it. "I'm just really hoping you're wrong, Truman," she added. She seemed near tears.

"Why?"

"Because both men, not just Todd, are decent." I stared at her, trying to see if she really meant it.

"So," I said, after a moment, "are you coming?"

"Just promise me one thing," she said. "Whatever you do, be fair. Don't slam someone just because you don't like them."

"You mean Engstrom?"

"He and Richard both. Give them the benefit of telling you their side of the story."

She turned slowly to me. "If you find out more, then ask them again."

∞

23

The woman, a grim, bulky matron with a ponytail told us we would have to talk with Reverend Blanton Swarthout. He was the pastor; he answered all questions. I figured she was the one I'd spoken to on the phone. She said he would arrive shortly, at 3 p.m. The woman said it was his job to supervise the day-care center from then until 5. So we sat for a few minutes in straight-back chairs, not talking, and waited. The door on our left opened and, sharply at 3, a man strode in. Almost immediately the woman glared in our direction, grabbed a large purse and started to go. "They want to see you," she said, pointing at us.

Monica and I had stood up soon after the preacher came in. "Everything is in order, Sister Marge?" he said, as she made for the door. Monica stood to my right, smiling down at two children building a block castle near her feet. I stepped out of the way of the woman.

"Far as I can tell, pastor."

"Kids've had their snack?"

"Yes," she responded. She gave me a glance again, fearful, almost withering.

"What time till Michael's mother comes?" asked Swarthout. One of the boys on the floor looked up curiously.

"Three-forty-five." And she was gone.

Swarthout had not acknowledged us. He was a square-shaped man with a soft belly pushing out the cloth of his plaid shirt, open at the collar and revealing a ruddy neck.

"Hello," I said.

His greyish eyes appraised me. Baggy black pants, belted below his waist, hung under the lump of stomach. He had black eyebrows that puffed from above his eyes like plump caterpillars. "I'm Blanton Swarthout," he said, stretching out a hand.

I told him who I was, then introduced Monica, who had lowered herself to her knees to help the boys build a wobbly tower. In a corner I noticed a girl about the age of 3. Arms outstretched, in a simple dress, she spun, a human merry-go-round. Two other girls slept on cots in a corner.

"Two reverends," Swarthout said. "From which church?"

I told Swarthout our denominational affiliations, actually in Monica's case it was just the church. It was no denomination. Swarthout picked up on hers. "That's the one on TV? Rhodes is the name?" He was looking down at Monica.

She glanced up and said, "That's right."

"You like it there?" Swarthout had his hands on his hips. His gray-black hair was wet, not from sweat. It looked as though he'd just taken a shower. His hands were rough and chafed; the fingernails rimmed with black. I wondered if he worked the night shift somewhere and pastored this storefront during the day.

"I like it fine," Monica said, turning back to the boys. The children in the room, I thought, seemed slightly off, muted. Two boxy fans, one behind me, the other by the dancing girl, cut through the heat of the room.

"They let you preach there?" he asked.

A blotch of color showed on one of her cheeks. "They do," she replied stonily.

"Your church," I said, drawing Swarthout's attention back to me, "is part of some larger group?"

"Just us. Started it myself 19 years ago next month. Been in this same place the whole time."

The day-care was in a tall, wide room, with walls painted bright yellow. Chairs were stacked in a far corner on a large movable tray. To my left I spotted a small stage. A spindly lectern stuck at the back. On the wall a faded poster showed the famous side view of a long-haired, bearded Christ with milky-white skin and burning eyes. Another comely Christ of our fanciful creation.

"What brings you here?" Swarthout asked.

"I understand," I said, "you are Kenneth Fortunato's father." Roelofs had told me this.

Swarthout winced, as if I had moved to punch him in the guts. I saw pain, or something worse, leap in his eyes. Something caged stalked; he blinked it away. He said, "That why you're here?"

"You're not his father?" I asked.

"I didn't say that."

"You are?"

"Just state your business."

"I understand that a man named Sid Hammersma called here on June 8, the same day that he left for a ride in his sail-boat and never came back."

"What's that got to do with us?"

"Not you necessarily. Just Kenny."

Swarthout looked to the floor, scuffed a shoe at a crack in the wood. "Kenny," he said softly, " is my son. From my first marriage."

Someone walked through the room behind us into another room, an office. I handed Swarthout a copy of the calls made from Hammersma's office. He squinted. Lines in his face told me he was older than the coal-black hair, combed straight back, indicated. The muscles in his arms came from other work than preaching.

"You say this was to Kenny?"

"That's what I'm thinking." He handed the paper back and stared at me.

A fan made the dancing girl's hair and dress move in gentle, slow-motion waves. In the doorway behind me appeared a wiry man with small eyes and a haphazard moustache. "Hello, Brother Leonard," Swarthout said, without looking.

"Got the prayer books you ordered, Preacher."

"Put them in the back, Brother."

Leonard started to leave, but Swarthout asked, "Brother, can you check something on the schedule? On June 8, in the afternoon, was Kenneth working? Painting that back room?'

"Schedule?"

"The calendar in the office. It'll be marked on the day."

Swarthout continued to stare hard at me after Brother Leonard left. Then, "Did you ever talk to a Sid Hammersma?" I asked.

"Don't know the name," he responded. We waited. Leonard returned with an open book in his hand. He paged through. "June 8, you say?"

"That's right."

There was a vast chilly distance in Swarthout. He had an immobile posture, the type of rock face that held everything in. Damnation preaching, a Jesus with blood flowing from every pore, would be his approach on Sunday. Try as hard as he might to be kind, he would always come up mean as a stepped-on snake.

"Looks like here," said Brother Leonard, "that, yeah, he was. And a couple days before it. You got it down."

"Thank you." Dismissed, Brother Leonard left.

"That answer your question?"

Monica still sat on the floor. She and the boys had dismantled the castle and were starting something else. Both boys had now turned their interest to the blocks.

"Where can I find him now?" I asked. Swarthout's head shook side to side, once and back. "He's not in town any longer?"

"Far as I know, no."

The little girl still spun slowly. On her face shone a bland, beatific expression. I wondered if the afternoon snack included doses of Ritalin. But this was the type of church where Swarthout was boss, not God. Given that, high-tech drugs seemed out of place.

"Do you know where he is?" I asked.

"Boy could be anywhere."

"You say he comes and goes?"

"Worse than the wind." I detected a kind of humor in that statement. Or maybe it was just resignation. Or, worse, indifference.

"You have any idea where I could reach him?"

"Someone think he's tied in to this other man?" he asked.

Brother Leonard rattled on in the room behind us, carrying in prayer books. The girl still spun. Monica brushed a wisp of hair out of one boy's eyes.

"A possibility," I said. "Do you know if your son and Sid Hammersma were friends?"

Swarthout scowled. "How do you mean that?" If I wasn't mistaken, his chin trembled.

"Did they know each other? Was Sid Hammersma ever here?"

Swarthout turned slowly and gazed behind him at Brother Leonard, who gave him a funny, lopsided grin.

"Told you I never heard of Hammersma." His balled-up hand rose to a spot below one eye as he added, "Kenneth had a lot of friends."

"You didn't read in the papers about Hammersma, his sailboat turning up empty? Or hear it on the news?"

"We don't watch TV or read the papers," he said simply. Brother Leonard, behind him, nodded as if to back him up.

"So all of this comes as a surprise?"

"With that boy nothing comes as a surprise."

"He was in trouble?"

"Trouble's not the word," Swarthout said. "Like his mother, it's devastation. That boy causes devastation." Everyone in the room seemed to pause, struck by the intensity of his words.

"You have no idea where he is, then?" I asked lamely.

"I don't."

"Do you know anyone who does?"

"Are you asking for the police?" he wondered.

"For my church."

"Your church?"

"The police haven't come up with much, and I've been asked to look into it." Not exactly true, but I was trying to play on his allegiance to powers beyond this room.

"Who's Hammersma?" he asked.

I told him. Gave him the church connection.

"And he went sailing and didn't come back?" I nodded. "Was Kenneth with him?"

"Not that we know. But we do suspect they were talking at the marina beforehand."

"Why's your church so interested?" I gave him a condensed version of the financial plight Hammersma's wife faced. "He was married?" Swarthout asked.

"For many years."

Swarthout folded his arms. "Is my son mixed up in the money end of things?"

"That I don't know. As I say, my church wants, as best it can, to resolve matters with Professor Hammersma's wife."

He considered this. The ecclesiastical and family connections seemed to make sense to him. Or at least it encouraged him to answer, "His sister, Carla, my daughter, might know where he is."

Monica's posture, even on the floor, was rigid. I knew her so well that I was sure she didn't like Swarthout. I found him to be hard-pressed, combative, angry. I had the image of him nearly drowning those he dunked in his baptismal font. He was probably the type that used some dank river to bring the fallen into the fold. A river slimy with muck, full of a swampy acid that would burn away skin.

"Carla?" I asked.

"That's right."

On the floor, I heard Monica say, "How about if we make a road?"

"Expressway," said one boy brightly.

"No," said the other boy. "A skyscraper."

"Jason," Swarthout snapped. The boy glanced up, a shadow of fear in his eyes. "Don't be difficult." Jason hung his head. Monica's back grew even more taut. The little girl's spinning had slowed. She flapped her arms like wings. Her eyes dropped. Her dress hung in folds.

"Where?" I asked, "can I find Carla?"

"She lives out in the country. Back up toward Kibbie."

"Kibbie?"

"Little place east of South Haven," he said.

"Does she have a phone?"

"Don't know."

"Have you talked to her lately?"

"We don't talk."

That didn't surprise me. "Could your son be living with her?"

"Could, but I doubt it."

"Why?"

"Because he hasn't been by in awhile for money."

"You mean looking for work?" I asked.

"That or borrowing — or if not that, just stealing." The pain was alive in his eyes again, no longer stalking. It was out of its cage.

"I'm sorry," I said to him.

He shook his head, trying to catch my train of thought.

"It must be very difficult, having a boy like that." As soon as I said it, though, I knew children don't spring wild-eyed from the womb.

"He's got his reasons," Swarthout, to his credit, allowed. "He grew up hard. Some of it, I was hard on him. Plus, his mother was a slut." Monica's face shot up. I hoped she wouldn't say anything. She didn't. I did my best to ignore his remark and the hatred it implied.

"My understanding," I went on, "is that your son was in jail until earlier this year."

"Wasn't the first time. Could be there again, for all I know."

"But you said you never heard him talk — or saw him meet up — with Sid Hammersma?"

"Never.

Now I detected self-pity. This man's compassion had limitations. I suspected he was the type who cried after administering the rod.

"Carla," I ventured. "Could you give me directions to her place?"

He said nothing for a few moments. Then he called, "Brother Leonard."

Leonard appeared in the doorway again. "You going up near Kibbie?"

"Can."

"Are you or not?"

"Wasn't planning on it."

The little girl had curled up in a ball on the floor, done dancing, thumb in her mouth, sleeping, a cherub in a devilish trance.

"But I can if you want," Brother Leonard interjected.

"These people want to go there," he said. Brother Leonard nodded. That was fine with him. "It's a complicated road out there. You mind taking him?"

Brother Leonard gawked at us both, mouth partly open. "This man here, and the woman," Swarthout said, "want to talk to Carla."

Leonard nodded. "Think she'll do that?"

"Not mine to know. They can ask."

Brother Leonard then turned from the door. "Sure enough, then. Just hope Webster's not around."

Swarthout examined me from under the bushy eyebrows. His jaw worked up and down. I saw blackheads, like dabs of pepper, wedged along the ridge of his chin. "Anyone think my boy went down in this boat, too?"

"Boat didn't sink. Coast Guard found it empty," I said.

"Whatever," he groused.

"About that, no one knows right now. Like I say, no bodies have washed ashore."

Swarthout pulled on his nose. "Think the two of them run away?"

"I don't know."

"Wouldn't put it past Kenneth. Just what his mother did before he could walk." His eyes burned with resentment; his voice simmered with rage. I didn't answer. Wondered if the anger, still so fresh after so many years, would engulf him. Monica got up from the floor. The boys looked glum. They had apparently enjoyed their playmate. I saw Monica's eyes settle a moment on the no-longer-dancing girl.

"Does she always dance like that?" she asked.

Swarthout seemed a little startled by the question. "Miss?"

"This girl," said Monica, bending and touching the back of the child's hand. "Does she always act so dreamy?"

Swarthout seemed uncomfortable. He gave me a look, as if asking me to answer the question. "That's Anna Parmelee. Her folks say she's not right."

"In what way?"

"That she's got some kind of disorder."

"She on medication?" Monica asked.

"No pills around here, just prayer," replied Swarthout.

24

I rode with Brother Leonard in his rattletrap station wagon. Monica followed at a discreet distance, as if giving the dark, smoke-belching vehicle in which I sat plenty of room to foul the two-lane road between us. Slightly hunch-backed, Brother Leonard drove with his gaze attached somewhere above the steering wheel. He had pulled a rolled-up stocking cap onto his head. Oblivious to the weather, he also wore a long-sleeved blue denim shirt and blue work pants, the waist of which were drawn to just below his sunken, wheezy chest. When he spoke, it was with a rabbit-like snarl. With Swarthout he had been accommodating, almost docile; with me in the car he was harsh, even cynical.

"I hope your wife doesn't drop too far back, else we could lose her in the dust," he said, glancing into the rear-view mirror around which was coiled a green garter belt.

"If she doesn't lose us in a cloud of exhaust fumes first," I said, smelling fuel through rusty floorboards.

He barked a laugh. "Don't like the transportation?"

"It does seem to be giving off gas."

The laugh intensified. "Tell the EPA."

Outside the storefront, Brother Leonard said the way there, since he'd be taking a back-roads shortcut, would be confusing. He offered to let one of us drive with him. Wondering if he could answer some of my questions, I climbed in his station wagon. Monica didn't seem to mind.

"She's not my wife, by the way."

He looked over. I shook my head. "Kind of like the way she got under the preacher's skin. Not too many people bring him up short," he remarked.

We bumped along. I checked the side mirror. Monica's car was a dot in the smoky dust. "Who's Webster?" I asked.

"My cousin. And Carla's husband."

"Why're you hoping he's not there?"

"Just do." He was silent a moment, then said, "You known the preacher long?"

"Just met him today."

Sided by trees, the road ahead looped and curved to the right, sweeping along the edge of a lake whose blue waters flashed here and there through dense vegetation.

"You seemed to get along with him all right," Brother Leonard said.

It hadn't seemed that way to me. "Doesn't Reverend Swarthout like many people?" I asked.

Brother Leonard smiled, showing small, sharp teeth. Bristles of hair grew in the folds of skin on his face. "You could say that. I been in his church five years now and sometimes he still treats me like shit. My missus says so anyway."

The statement didn't surprise me. I knew too well the sadistic dimensions of why we believed and worshipped as we did and with whom we did it. "So, why stay?"

He frowned behind the wheel, moving his mouth in munching motions, shrugged.

The station wagon jounced along, the air twinged with fumes. In the side mirror I saw the Tercel appear over the small rise we'd just descended. I knew I should leave it, but the minister in me wouldn't let go. "It doesn't sound like it bothers you too much, if you're staying," I said.

His arms moving slowly left as he followed a bend taking us along the far shore of the lake, he asked, "What church you say you belong to?" I told him. "They don't put the fear of God in you?" he added.

"They do, but they try not to treat you like crap."

"Oh no?"

I had to think about it, realizing both that I was starting to lose him and that maybe he was right. There was this Reformed sense we were all sinners, lost in brackish waters of our own making. That we were shit. "Well," I said, "the theory is that we try to treat each other with kindness."

"That's good, if you can get away with it," he agreed.

Discussion of theology had gotten us nowhere. I tried talking about what I wanted to anyway. "How well do you know Carla?"

He sniffed, his nose twitching, rabbit teeth moving under thin lips. "Like I say, she's my cousin's wife, but there's not much to know."

"How so?"

He grinned. "She can't hear and she don't talk much."

"What?"

"She's pretty much a mute."

I wondered if Swarthout had played a trick on me. "How're we going to communicate with her? If she's home."

"She'll be home. They never go anyplace. Leastways she don't."

"What's Webster do?"

"Drives truck."

The road ahead was a straight strip, dividing brownish fields of stunted-looking wheat, rye and a few limp sunflowers. Heat shimmered off the road ahead, a bulging black strip of patched asphalt.

"So we'll be able to have a conversation with her, you think?"

"She reads lips. Sign language, too, if you know it. I heard she taught it once in a church."

"Why is it best if her husband's not there?"

Brother Leonard made a twisting gesture with his hand, the fingers crimped down, long nails sharp. "Because he's mean. And he especially don't like us."

"Us?"

"From the church. Him and me used to at least be civil. Not no more."

We passed a small home. A woman raked a pile of leaves by the side door. A child swung on a tire hung from a tree branch. Two rusted cars, their roofs broken and bent, languished inside a sagging garage.

"Can't say as I blame him, though. Folks from our church can get pretty pluckersome sometimes."

"Pluckersome?"

"You know, keep plucking and won't let go." His pointed fingers picked imaginary feathers out of the air. I wanted to ask again why he went there, but didn't bother. We rode in silence awhile. Behind us on the road, Monica was keeping up. The heat coming in the car windows stuck to my face.

"Is her name Fortunato, too?" I asked. He gave me a quizzical look. "I think that's Kenny's last name."

He chuckled. "That what he's going by now?"

"He has aliases?"

"You could call them that. I always figured they're stage names, like. He wants to be an actor."

"Did he come by the church often?"

"Couple years back, maybe three or four, he did. I haven't seem him much since. He came by to do that painting awhile back. That's about all."

A swamp appeared on the right. Green water stretched for several hundred feet. Rotten tree trunks poked through the muck. Atop one, still as death, sat a red-tailed hawk. As we passed, it stretched and took to the air, large wings gracefully embracing flight. It moved off, a large slow-moving dot over the trees.

"You ever talk to Kenny much?" I asked.

"Him and me didn't hit it off anymore."

The bird reappeared and cut across the road ahead, casting a darting, dimpled shadow. I looked at Brother Leonard. "Why's that? Your not getting along?"

"Got in a fight."

"A fight?"

Leonard balled one hand. "Not with fists. An argument."

"Over what?"

"Don't matter."

The station wagon rolled up a hill. Dusty tree branches drooped on either side of the road. Through them, I saw more branches and tree trunks. Here and there, I spotted parts of mobile homes, set back, down winding drives.

"Thing is," said Brother Leonard after a bit, "He's a nice kid, whatever last name he's calling himself by these days."

"But?" I asked.

"He's got his problems."

"Like what?"

"Like he don't need us going on about him, too, picking through his laundry."

"Too?"

Brother Leonard looked like he'd just taken a bite out of a lemon. "Small towns like ours, everybody talks. When you figure how he is, he never had a chance."

"How he is?"

Brother Leonard gunned the engine as the station wagon bounced up and over a rusty metal bridge spanning a small creek. On my right opened a clearing in which stood a half dozen, stupid-looking cows. Their udders hung full; their eyes blank as a baby's brain.

"If you don't know, why're you so persistent in asking?" he inquired.

"Because he was gay?" I then ventured.

"Queer is what they call it around here."

"Is that what you call it? Is that why you argued with him that time?" I asked.

"Not like you might think. I told Kenny he didn't need to put up with all the guff. God made him like he was. If people didn't like it, that's their problem. Not his."

"And he got mad?"

Brother Leonard nodded fiercely, his hands tight on the wheel. "He told me God made him into a freak. Everyone who called him that was right. He told me to go to hell for butting in."

Crossing the road again was the hawk — or maybe another. I watched it bank and soar over a hill in the distance. It struck me you found strength and courage and true Christian caring in the strangest places. I never thought I'd find it in a station wagon that smelled like the inside of a parking garage, with a man the shape and size of Brother Leonard.

Nearing Kibbie — more a name than a place — Brother Leonard told me he would drop me off and leave. His presence, connected as he was to the church, was sure to make matters worse, whether or not Webster was there. Feeling the stickiness of the day mix in my pores with the dust from the roads and the fumes from the car, I asked, "These people have problems with religion?"

"With churches they do."

"Do they have any kids?" Behind us, Monica's Toyota swam in a swirl of dirt.

"May be one of the problems," Leonard said. He glanced over at me, as if checking to see if I wanted to know more. Of course, I did. "They had a daughter, Diane. Born in Grand Rapids when they were living up there — with a bad heart. So bad it never got better. They were hoping she'd have one of them transplants. Fact is, she was waiting for one when she died a couple years back. She was only 15. Was quite a deal. Her mom, Carla, came to church for a time before it all, maybe figuring prayer would help. But it didn't. Girl died anyway. Carla never come back."

Despite the heat and discomfort of this station wagon, I felt like riding in the seat for longer. My body was hardly recovered from the run in the sun of two hours before. "That's sad," I said.

"Sure is," Leonard nodded. It was like he was a guardian angel, come down to give me the low-down. A channel for gossip, he dished up some more. "Folks say the child was her curse."

A dark look came to his face; the lines on his forehead seemed to collapse on themselves. I knew, or suspected, for men like Leonard the devil was more than a bad guy in the

Bible, a tempting spirit, a fallen angel. He was a real person, who must be faced. "What was this curse?" I asked.

"Don't know. But it was when her child was born with these holes in her heart, like she just stopped speaking."

"She talked before?" I asked.

"Far as I know."

"She always deaf?"

"Think so."

As we made a circle up and over a small hill, I gazed over treetops toward a haze I suspected was South Haven and Lake Michigan. A murky soup of clouds gathered.

"They say she can talk but won't?" I asked.

"Right. But some say she just can't. That she drank Drano. Right after her baby was born."

"Drano? Seems like that would kill you," I said.

Brother Leonard said matter-of-factly. "Not sure she did it, but that's what they say."

"But what about this curse? She thought God was some-how to blame?"

Brother Leonard shot me a narrow-eyed glance. "Wouldn't you?"

"People are born with defects all the time."

Brother Leonard turned back to the road. I noticed again the hump outlined on the back of his shirt. I felt guilty. "I mean there are crosses we have to bear. Challenges God puts in front of us."

He held up a hand. "Save it."

"Just one more thing."

"What?"

"Why did she stop talking? Was it just that her baby was born with a hole in her heart?"

He eased back on the gas and glowered. "I think some of it came from how she got pregnant in the first place."

"You mean the baby wasn't Webster's?"

"Something like that."

∽

25

Monica slowed her car to a stop in front of the house. Brother Leonard had dropped me off at Webster and Carla's house, and now Leonard's station wagon was speeding off, shrouded in a cloud of dust. From the garage I saw Webster peer at me through welder's glasses. A rainstorm of sparks flew around him. Monica climbed out of her car and stared back down the road where Brother Leonard had disappeared around a bend by a rusty, green water tower. "He's in a hurry," she said.

Tongues of fire danced and spun, almost obscuring Webster's upper body.

"How was the ride over?" I asked.

"The Dust Bowl revisited. I don't like this neighborhood."

We walked slowly up the gravel driveway. "Does he know we're here?" Monica asked.

"Me he does."

The house itself was about 20 years old. Built of pinkish brick and green siding, it looked more like it belonged in a bland suburb than stuck in no-man's land. We stopped at the entry to the large garage. I saw small machines, puddles of oil, a pile of rags, a greasy hoist hanging from a cement rafter that spanned the length of Webster's repair shop. Through a large window on our right I spotted the side of his truck. "Webster Blanchard — Long or Short Haul Trucking."

The smell of seared metal moved out to us. We waited as

Webster flicked off his welding gun and began to beat a hammer on metal. He was a scrawny man, but strong. The arms rippled with ropy muscle as he slammed the hot steel. When he was good and done, he turned, wiping his forehead. "Help you?" He flipped up his glasses.

"Mr. Blanchard?"

"That's me."

"I'd like to talk to you a few minutes."

He stepped toward us, moving out of the smoky dimness, revealing a long, gaunt face with bugged-out eyes, topped by a shock of gray hair. Sweat stained his T-shirt. On his right arm was some sort of tattoo, blue whorls with tiny words. "You Jehovah Witnesses?" He wiped his face again with a wadded bandana, then stuck it in the back pocket of heavily stained brown pants. He wore scuffed black boots. I told him no. "What you want?"

"To talk to you and your wife, if she's home."

"About what?"

"Kenny."

He rubbed the back of his neck, the eyes making a circle around Monica. "He's not here."

"Is she?"

"We don't know where he is," he said, ignoring my question.

"That's not what I wanted to know."

"Who are you?" he asked.

A black Labrador retriever appeared from a doorway, sidled up to Webster, who shoved it away with his boot. Ears droopy, it moved over to us. Monica dropped to a knee and began rubbing its neck as it good-naturedly sniffed her.

I gave him our names. "You're from church?" he asked.

"Not one near here."

"From where?"

"Near Holland. I'm Reformed. Monica is undenominational."

Webster went back to his work bench. He touched the chunk of metal, some kind of handle, with a finger, drew it away.

"Why you want to talk with us?" he said, his back turned.

"It's about your wife's brother."

"Half-brother," he simply stated.

I wanted to step over, take him by the shoulders, spin him around and drive him through a wall. Instead, I watched as the dog left Monica and padded over to a door that led into the house. Behind the screen I saw a woman. Her eyes moved to us, down to the dog, over to Webster, and back to us.

"Hi, there," Monica said, a little too brightly. The door opened, but the woman remained inside. "Are you Mrs. Blanchard?" Monica asked. The woman didn't reply.

"Is it all right if we come in a moment?" Monica tried again.

"Monica?" I said, moving to her.

Webster's face shot around, hammer held in mid-strike. "Do your talking right here, preacher lady."

I stepped in. "This will take only a couple minutes."

"Who brought you here?" he asked. "That wino Leonard?"

Monica stood five feet away, glaring at Webster, the dog at her feet. Carla stepped back inside. "Mrs. Blanchard," Monica said, as if pleading with her to intervene.

"Monica," I said again, softly. "She doesn't talk."

Monica's brow knit, as if she didn't believe me. Then she looked at the bottom of one shoe, as if inspecting for oil. Standing in here, I saw Carla pull something from the pocket of her house dress — a note pad — and began scribbling. As she did, Webster stood there, angry and bored at the same time. Monica gave me a why-didn't-you-tell-me-that look. I felt guilty I hadn't sketched for her what we faced. When Carla was finished writing, she rapped a knuckle on the door.

Webster glared at her fiercely. "What?" She rapped again. "For Christ sake." He stepped over, snatched the paper. Read it, crumpled it and threw it away. "She says let you come in."

Moments later I gazed out an oval-shaped window that looked on a rolling field unfolding for about 200 yards before ending at a stand of scrawny Christmas trees. A shed, a swing set, a large pile of cut wood, and a tractor spread out on their fairly well-manicured back lawn. Flowers bloomed along one side; a garden in full progress of growth on the other.

Webster leaned against the refrigerator, beer in one hand, the other arm looped across the top of the appliance.

At the table, Carla faced us, sitting in a chair with the window behind. Stacked nearby on the floor near her chair were pieces of dolls — hands, arms, legs, heads. Piled in a box to the right were finished dolls, faces looking serenely our way. On the wall above the boxes hung a photograph of a teen-age girl, a school picture of some kind, her stern features peering from a plain yellow background. She had piercing eyes, blond hair, a firm mouth. I wondered if this was the daughter. I noticed that Monica, sitting next to me, stared intently into Carla's face. I scanned the room for a picture of Kenny. I saw none.

"So, talk," Webster said. The dog rustled near our feet.

"When," I said to Carla, "was the last time you saw Kenny?"

She nodded, her moon cheeks dabbed with a circle of red. I looked over at Webster.

"Answer the man, honey," he said softly, with some feeling. Her hand reached out for the pen.

"I know sign," Monica said gently.

Carla flapped her head yes. She almost reached out for Monica's hands, held back, but nodded vigorously.

Webster turned away and took a drink of beer. He held his head far back and chugged. "Hope to hell you're not the police," he groused.

Carla's face flew in his direction. Worry etched her eyes.

"Because anything you say," Webster said, "can come back. Big time. Always does."

Carla's hands made motions in Monica's direction. Webster shook his head angrily, swigged beer and left the room. But her fingers kept moving.

"I don't know why the hell you're even here," Webster said from the other room.

Monica watched the woman shape words out of air. It went on for half a minute. Then Monica spoke back, with her hands. "She wants to know if Kenny is in trouble," Monica asked me. From the other room Webster barked, "Punk's always in trouble."

I said, "Not that we know of. Ask her when was the last time she saw him."

Webster loomed in the doorway. "The day I kicked his butt out for stealing my coin collection." Carla gazed at him as if he were a bear with boils.

"Tell them, Carla, with your goddamned hands. Tell them what that shit has done to our home." His neck bulged with veins. He held the beer bottle by the long neck, as if trying to strangle it. "Tell them." Then he addressed me. "Who are you, anyhow, come poking around here?"

Slowly but clearly, Carla's face unraveled. She put her hands over her eyes. Monica moved over and reached out to comfort her. Webster stepped toward them. "Don't touch her!" he ordered.

I blocked his path, smelling the beer and hatred on his breath. "Don't tell them anything else," he said over my head. Inches from his face, I stared hard, thinking he made me sick.

"Out of my way," he said, eyes flicking like rats in a cage.

Monica stood. "Mr. Blanchard," she said.

His eyes left mine for a moment to look at her. I saw dirt in his skin, beard stubble; a y-shaped scar above one eye. Blurred at the corner of my vision was the tattoo of an eagle on his upper arm. We were bare inches apart. I wanted to drive my fists into the soft upper swell of his belly.

He inched toward me. I didn't move. He glared. I glared back. He backed down. Looked away. Sniffed.

"Tend to your wife," Monica said to him.

Carla Blanchard blubbered, her large body shaking. The dog hovered protectively, sympathetically at her side.

"I'll get to that," he said, showing yellow teeth that should have been in the dog's mouth. "You two get out."

26

As I pumped gas, I watched Monica pace the edge of a field separating the service area from the expressway. Hands clasped behind her, neck bent, she seemed lost in sullen thought. When the tank was filled, the skin of dust cleaned off the windows, and I'd paid, I walked over to her.

"Can you imagine living in a place like that?" she asked.

"Bad enough just visiting."

Monica kept staring at the field, then said, "Lord, that woman wanted to talk."

Occasional cars passed on U.S. 31. On the other side of the freeway a huge billboard faced us. Pictured was a slope-headed alien-looking child, his eyes like saucers, neck a string of flesh. Above him was written on the board: "Open Your Mind." To what, I wondered.

"What was she saying?" I asked.

Monica sniffed, shook back her hair. "Something about Kenny being gone to tell somebody something."

"Tell who what?"

She looked up at me with displeasure. "We didn't get that far."

I turned away, noticing wads of fast-food wrappers stuck in weeds. Even though the sky had started to darken, heat still swam around us. It pinched my face, slithered along my back. I had no patience for a domestic dispute. "Maybe I'm crass," I said. "But those two seemed to have a lot to hide."

"I don't doubt that."

Her demeanor was deeply troubled. The threat of violence, that moment I faced off with Webster, had disturbed me, too. "What is wrong with that woman, anyway?" asked Monica. I said I didn't know, although I was thinking again about the Drano. Monica stood staring directly at me. "You know, she looked familiar to me."

"From where?"

"I don't know."

We lapsed into silence. The heat beat on me in waves. Monica fanned a hand over her face. We started back to the car, parked under the overhang of the station. I turned on the air conditioning as we drove. We drove in silence for a time. It was almost 4. The sky was a drab, dreary blue.

"Which softball league are you in?" I asked after awhile. She'd mentioned earlier that she had a game that night.

Monica took in a breath, let it out. It struck me that she had been in prayer and that I had interrupted. She unfolded the hands that had been clasped in her lap. I suspected she'd taken her feelings about Carla Blanchard and her heathen husband to the Lord.

"Didn't mean to butt in," I wanted to say. But I asked, "Are you playing softball in the church league?"

"Co-ed recreational. We play Third Christian Reformed tonight," she responded.

"They let you guys play in the Reformed league?"

"We believe in the same God."

I smiled, driving toward the dusty orange sun. The landscape looked bleaker, less inviting than it had on the way down. "What position do you play?"

"Shortstop."

"Todd on the team?"

"He pitches."

I glued my sandpapery eyes to the road. I wondered what Carla would have told us if we had caught her at home alone. I wondered if we should go back when Webster was on the road. Then I wondered where was I getting off thinking we?

It was odd but pleasing, how well we had worked together this afternoon, a team. Like in the past. Except we often saw things at different ends of the spectrum. Her blacks were my whites. A truck roared by her window. Another followed, then one more. I slowed and cut into the right lane. Open your mind, I thought to myself again. Open it to what?

"Monica," I said, "what if this kid Kenny is wherever Sid Hammersma happens to be?"

"Which is?"

Certainly not Las Vegas, I thought. "Dead." Again we lapsed into silence.

I wondered about the tie between Hammersma and Fortunato. Had Kenny come by the marina to warn Sid of something? Had he come to kill him? Did they run off?

"Monica," I said. She had been gazing out the window, hands in her lap. "I have to make a call."

"Who do you have to call?"

"Marlan."

"Who?"

"Oosterbaan, the chief in Holland."

The phone booth at the next exit was no longer a booth. It had been battered and beaten by the weather and passersby. No matter. It worked. I punched the buttons and waited. In the car, Monica was thinking again, two fingers to her chin, as if trying to decide something. The phone booth stood near an abandoned gas station at the Ganges exit. Five miles down 122nd Avenue to my right was a Hindu monastery. I'd been there twice, watching the shaven monks as they prayed through wafts of incense to their various gods. A many-armed Krishna was my favorite. I knew my ministerial brethren would not think highly of that. But I enjoyed some of what the Hindus had to say about God, even if I knew it was way off track.

"Holland Police Department," I heard. I asked for Marlan. "I'm sorry. He's not available right now?"

Bed springs, bags of garbage, billowed from the dumpster

by the side of the closed service station. I brushed sweat from my brow. "I need to talk to him. This is urgent."

"Are you in trouble, sir?"

I wasn't sure why I said that it was urgent. I'm not sure it was. "I just need to talk to him," I amended.

"Then it can wait?"

With the temperature holding a steady pace just below the boiling point, I felt tense, a little out of control. "I'd just as soon not," I told the dispatcher.

"Who am I speaking to, please?" I told her. "I'll see if I can raise him."

Monica stepped out of the car. I wondered if she was serious about returning to school to become a psychologist. She would be a good one. I thought of her playing with the boys in the storefront church. She sat on the hood, arms folded, gazing across the field. Her strength and loveliness struck me, and I felt again the ache of her loss.

"I'll patch you through," the dispatcher said suddenly.

"Thanks."

What reason would Fortunato have to kill Hammersma? Or he Kenny? It was troubling to think about the church historian in this way. What secrets could Carla Blanchard's hands tell us if they were freed from her husband's grip?

"Marlan?" The connection snapped with static.

"What's up?"

"Sorry to bother you."

"No bother. We've got a coked-up kid holed up in a house is all, threatening to kill himself and his girlfriend."

"Look, Marlan, I've got to talk to you."

"Can't now."

"How about later?"

"Don't know how long this will take. How much later?"

"Nine?"

"If it's about the Hammersma deal, call Slade."

"Got to talk to you first."

"Why?"

"I trust you more."

"You come up with something?"

"I think so."

"What?"

I didn't want to tell him over the phone. "That's why I want to meet. It's important."

There was a long pause; then he said, "Show up at the office at 9:30. Can you do that?"

"That late?"

"Turkstra, it's the best I can do."

"I'll be there," I said, noticing Monica looking at me.

"Wait, one thing I forgot," he said. "I told Slade all you told me. One thing he was wondering. I was, too. What kind of car was that kid driving the day at the marina. The kid you say was talking to the professor."

"I thought I mentioned it to you."

"Maybe, but I forget." I told him. There was a pause; then he said, "Good. I'll see you later."

"Wait." I said. "Why do you want to know the make?"

He didn't answer. The line crackled. "One of our guys got called out to a gravel pit. Looks like this Horizon might've got dumped there."

"What gravel pit?"

"I'll talk to you later."

I stood there a moment, phone in hand. I looked up to see Monica appear on my left. She looked worried, or in some pain. "Our church owns an old Bible camp near here. Could we stop there? I need to talk."

27

I took the two-track past the lodge, through a stand of trees.
Monica pointed to a sandy parking place next to a path
leading through the woods to the lake. Even as we neared the
place, outside the small village of Glenn, I recalled the camp.
I'd attended summer sessions there as a boy. The Christian
Reformed Church, through some missionary organization,
had owned the place. Years back, it had been sold to a Baptist
group. Then, three years before, Rhodes' church purchased it
as a spot at which to hold seminars, meetings and retreats.
Called The Vineyard, it was not busy this day. We saw no one
else as we rode the three-quarters of a mile in, off the road,
drove by the lodge, and parked.

I climbed out first, stretching my legs and back, feeling a
slightly cooler breeze from the lake sift through the lazy-mov-
ing tree branches. I'd already begun to calculate whom I
needed to speak to next. Most important, I knew I had to
somehow learn who had been named as beneficiary on the
insurance policy. I knew for sure now that Sid's wife didn't
know the whole story or wasn't telling me.

Monica's door opened and she slowly got to her feet. Her
eyes shifted over the roof of the car at me. Half-guilty eyes,
vulnerable eyes. I wondered what she needed to talk about.
Without speaking, we stepped around to the front of the car,
where we stood silently, both staring at the sun-shaft-illumi-
nated path that led toward the vast lake, toward the cooler

breeze, toward the deep water. Birds jabbered, soft, cottony balls of pollen danced in the air, and a faint smell of pine pitch filled my nose as we walked.

"Peaceful," I remarked when we reached an opening.

"It is."

Feet dug into the sand, I craned my head and glimpsed a slice of slightly bruised-looking sky through the overhanging web of branches. Again, the hint of rain.

"You say you know this place?" Monica asked.

I turned, looked at the rambling, wood-frame lodge. "I was here, I think, three summers — back in grade school."

Monica had grown up about 200 miles to the northeast in Alpena. The daughter of farmers, she had a mentally retarded brother named Bobby, who lived in a group home in the Grand Rapids area. She had originally moved to this area to live with an aunt and uncle and their daughter Kate, and to attend Redeemer. From there, she'd attended the University of Chicago, where we met. Although we'd gone to the same college, our stay overlapped only one year, and we hadn't known one another. She was eight years younger.

"Was it like this then?" she asked.

"Pretty much." I looked at my feet, still engulfed in the sandy ground. I suddenly recalled the incident in the pond, the night Oosterbaan and Slade and a few others played a cruel joke on me. "They still have that outdoor chapel area with the cross?" I asked.

Monica turned and pointed to her right. A smell of her sweetish sweat mingled with the pine in my nose. "Through there, a little way," she said. Her face swiveled back to me — full cheeks, clear eyes, familiar mouth.

"So," I said.

"You know," she finally said, "Like I said, that woman looked really familiar."

"You've seen her before?"

She nodded to the lake, a massive blue cloth fluttering to the horizon. Fifty miles or so to the left, out there alone, The

Wittenberg Door had nearly crashed into a freighter.

"Where?" I prodded Monica.

A few boats, mostly specks rocking on the blue surface of the lake, floated out there. About 200 feet below, the bright strip of beach led to the right, where I spotted a dock built out into the water. White waves curled almost restfully onto the shore below.

She glanced at me, lips a thin line of either distaste or concentration. "I'm not sure."

We fell into another silence. Monica sat, back to a tree, chin placed on upturned knees. I remained standing, enjoying the soft wind ruffling across the lake. I watched a bank of clouds march overhead. From that spot I couldn't see other cottages, homes, or buildings. We could have been resting on the fringe of the wilderness, except for the few bobbing boats. At the edge of my mind remained memories of this same Bible camp and questions both about the Hammersma case and Monica. I sensed disquiet in her. I worked at calming my thoughts, pretending to be one of those Hindu monks back in Ganges who filled their days with recurrent prayer used to connect them to God. To Krishna. Using incense and pictures, pots of flowers, and carefully stationed statuary around an altar, they worked hard at establishing and maintaining a link with their maker. Too often we Reformed relied unthinkingly on our relationship with God. Through Christ, the Lord made flesh, we had a solid fixture around and through whom we could worship. Still, too often we allowed only our words, our arguments, our theology to serve as our entry into the divine realm. Not that the Hindus, with their belief in bugs being men, had it figured either. Staring out at the welcoming water, I sensed God lived in movement, in wind, in sights and smells, in touch and taste — as much, or even more, than in words. He lived in his son, Christ. But that was a different story. I closed my eyes, letting the rustle of leaves and wash of water move through me.

"Asleep?"

Still awake, but just barely, I'd slouched against the tree next to Monica. My eyes yawned open. The sunlight flashing on the water below stung my pupils. "Drifting off," I replied.

Monica stood facing the lake, shoulders hunched resolutely. "I guess I wanted you to know," she said to the lake, "if I go back to school in Chicago, I plan to go alone." Turning back, she checked my reaction.

"Todd?" I asked.

"A friend." Her gaze remained steady.

"Like me?" I wondered.

Her eyes flickered. She turned back to the lake. I stepped to her side. "Turkstra," she replied, "with you I don't know."

"If I'm even a friend?"

She scowled. "Why couldn't you just let me make a mistake, if that's what I was making?"

"Working for Rhodes?"

She did not answer, remained immobile, sadly staring at the far sky.

"You're starting to see that's what it is?" I pressed.

She examined my face, as if wondering if she should tell me a secret or a riddle. She apparently decided to do neither. "You know," she said simply, "I'm not going to beg."

Although I had an idea what she meant, I felt scared. I knew her strength was a shield. Still, I found it comforting.

She rubbed the side of her face. "Maybe we should just go."

"Beg me?"

"What do you think?"

"Beg me for what?"

"If you have to ask, then you're more brain-dead than I thought."

Rebuked, I nonetheless wanted to touch her, hold her to me. I wondered exactly what made her believe the job at Golgotha Undenominational was a mistake. The name alone, was enough to drive a sane person nutty. Naming a church after a skull seemed in terribly bad taste, almost taunting the worshippers with its reference to their own frailty.

"I guess I'm confused," I said. "Are you saying you'd like to try again? With us?"

She looked up at me with a hint of helplessness in her expression. Then it was quickly replaced with anger. "Forget it, Truman." With that, she turned and stomped off down the path that had brought us to this spot.

I remained behind a few moments. She'd made an unexpected offer. I wasn't exactly sure how to respond. I knew I had no desire to return to the circular relationship we'd had. Close but not too close. Two people locked in a painful dance of indecision. I stuffed my hands in my pockets, thought of the cross not too far away in the wooded chapel, and the pond, the scene of a practical joke that continued to haunt me, a scene brought on by my pretending to be Catholic. A joke ironically played by two men with whom I'd become engaged in the search for what happened to Sid Hammersma. Thinking of Slade and Oosterbaan, I wondered for the first time if they were somehow more involved in the history professor's disappearance than either had said. It was almost 5. I started back down the path.

When I returned to the car, I was surprised to find Monica missing. I glanced around. Shortly, I heard a sound in the trees to the left, back toward the lodge. I stepped over and looked in to see Monica facing a thick tree trunk. Her back shook, face buried in her arms, sobbing. I experienced relief at the same time I felt shame. My stumbling response had led to this. I took a few steps forward, stopped. Hesitantly, I reached out and touched her shoulder. She froze.

"Let me be, Truman," she said. "I'll be back at the car in a few minutes."

28

On the way back, eyes now dry, Monica seemed calmer. She asked that we drive to her church. She then spoke about things she'd heard about Rhodes. Rumors she had dismissed — until today. The trip to Benton Harbor, especially the visit with Carla Blanchard, had brought back what a couple people had said. Misgivings aside, she wondered if a few things fit. I finally asked: "What things?" Monica, animated by her finally spoken suspicions, only said we'd see once we got to the church.

Once there, we slipped in through a back door. It was going on 7 o'clock; no one was around. Monica, without speaking, led me down the steps to the basement, along a couple of corridors and, into the archives.

"Exactly what is it you're looking for?" I asked, stifling a cough.

Wiping hair out of her face with a hand, Monica sighed. A sheen of sweat covered her forehead. "This." She reached up and dragged a box, with some help from me, from the shelf. She wiped dust from the top. I heard movement above, scraping of feet on the floor. The sounds, after a moment, diminished. I turned, heart bumping, well aware that my being here with Monica would cause concern, probably more for her than for me.

She pulled a booklet from the box.

I put a finger to my lips. Her brow rose questioningly. "Upstairs," I said. "I heard someone."

Her eyes rolled to the ceiling. She wiped a forearm over

her forehead. In the other hand she held a booklet. "Probably gathering for softball," she said.

She had told me on the way over that several team members, herself included, normally met at the church and rode to the game in the church van. But she hadn't thought anyone would arrive until 8.

I stepped close. "What is it?" I asked.

Monica was far from pleased by her discovery. I looked at the booklet, held close to her chest. Footsteps creaked over the floor above again. I held out my hand. Monica's large green eyes searched mine. She let me take the book.

"Page 36," she said.

I turned my attention to the cover: "Golgotha Undenominational Church: Its 10th Anniversary — 1965 to 1975." I opened it to the page she'd mentioned, let the light from the archives fall on the open pages. I saw rows of pictures. One of a younger but still handsomely patriarchal Rhodes. I glanced hurriedly at the others. Unable to figure what was here, I looked to Monica for help. Standing next to me, she pointed to a photo of a woman with a strikingly familiar face, an oval face — young, with luminous eyes and sensual mouth, brownish hair piled on her head, a delicately curved throat. Under it, the caption read: "Mrs. Carla Blanchard, Secretary to Pastor Richard Rhodes — 1969 to 1972."

Neither of us had a chance to say a word before we heard someone come down the steps. Monica took the book, stuck it under her arm. Her eyes grew wide as she gazed past me. I took a deep breath and turned. Outlined at the end of the hall was the church's senior pastor. He settled his hands on either side of the doorway. "Reverend Smit?"

I stood in front of her, trying to block his view. He started our way. Monica ducked into the archives. Rhodes continued our way. He wore a suit, the coat open, shoes tapping the tile as he approached. "Turkstra, too," he observed.

"Looks to me, Richard, like we're acquainted with the same people," I responded.

He paused, a look of consternation on his face. Monica reappeared at my side. "Pastor," she said in greeting.

"Pardon?" he wondered of me. I felt Monica tug my wrist, as if to urge me not to confront him.

I plunged on anyway. "Carla Blanchard."

Stopping in front of us, he blinked. "Excuse me?"

Monica pressed harder on my wrist. "A woman who once worked for you."

Rhodes pinched his chin. "Fill me in," he said.

As I did, Monica eased against the wall, gazing at her sandaled feet. When I had finished, Rhodes glanced into the archives. "I remember her well. A fairly high-strung woman."

He was smooth and hard to ruffle. Not only that, I suspected I had made a blunder. I should have heeded Monica's tugs, if for no other reason than he now knew what we'd learned. I realized, too late, he simply had to pedal around this information. "How in the world could she be tied in with what happened to Sid?" he asked.

"That's what I was hoping you might know," I retorted.

He turned down the sides of his mouth in a gesture of innocent curiosity. "No idea, Turkstra. But this certainly sounds like a matter to be taken to the police."

Rhodes remained blithely in front of us, his face an open mask of sincerity. I knew it would be useless to press him further. "I do trust, however," he said, "that your investigation will not require any more unwarranted sneaking around like this." His eyes moved to Monica when he spoke.

"It was my idea to search the archives," I offered.

He smiled, not concerned. "Did Mrs. Blanchard tell you she worked here?"

"She did," I lied.

"And you came down to confirm it?" he asked.

"Correct."

The smile broadened. He picked a shirt cuff out of the arm of his suit coat, examined it. "At any rate, you'll take this to the proper authorities?" I nodded, feeling like a schoolboy caught soaping windows.

Rhodes smoothed the sides of his suit coat with his hand, adjusted his neck. If he was in any way uncomfortable, he didn't show it. He was the model of perfect self-control. "Sorry to barge in on your little scavenger hunt," he said sarcastically.

Monica had begun to look at him again. I couldn't read her expression. Monica seemed cowed, unable to respond. Rhodes' whole bearing spoke of authority, rigidly warm power with a pleasant face on it. "I'm on my way to Chicago on business," he said. "I was wondering if you could help plan the Sunday service."

Monica moved away from the wall. "Of course."

He stared at her, then at me, flicked the cuff again. "Then good."

"You'll be back from Chicago yet this week?" I wondered.

He frowned. "Might I ask why?"

"If the police want to talk to you."

His face clouded only for a second. "If not, my secretary certainly knows where to reach me."

⌢ ⌣

Monica wore a baggy T-shirt with the outline of her church on it. Red shorts stretched over her upper legs; pink socks pulled to her knees; spikes on her feet. She'd changed into the uniform after our visit with Rhodes. I'd suggested she forget playing for the night, but she refused. While a group left from the lot at her church, we climbed into her car and I drove to the park. Neither of us spoke on the 10-minute drive to the brightly lit diamond.

Thunder grumbled again. "You might get rained out," I said, as we stood outside the fence leading to the diamond.

She checked the sky, shielding her eyes against the lights with an open hand. "Probably will hold off."

The pop of a ball smacking an aluminum bat reverberated from the batting cage. I noticed the umpire calling in the coaches for the pre-game run-through of the rules.

When Monica looked back, she asked, "Truman, what did

you think of Pastor Rhodes' reaction?"

We stood to the side of a set of bleachers, 20 feet or so from the dugout in which members of her team milled.

"Took it all in stride." Monica made a you-can-say-that-again face.

"You think so, too?" I queried.

She nodded, scuffed the dirt with a spiked foot. "Still, I could tell he was upset."

"How?"

"That deal he did with his cuffs. He picks at his clothes like that when he's bothered."

I noticed the umpire and coaches break apart at home plate. Game time. "Where's he going in Chicago?" I asked.

"Who knows?"

"Any way to check?"

She winced. I'd already put her in a bad position, even though she'd apparently decided to quit, for exactly what reasons I couldn't say. "I can ask around on the bench."

I nodded, trying to convey by my expression how much I appreciated her help. It struck me as well that she'd put herself in danger. "You sure you don't want me to stay?" I asked, noticing Monica's eyes register the presence of a person behind me whose appearance caused her to bite her lip nervously. I touched her wrist above the baseball glove, below the skin encircled with a white sweat band. Her glance flicked behind me again and back. "I'll be fine."

Then I turned and confronted Todd Engstrom, standing an indiscreet five or six feet away — clad in the church uniform, flipping a softball in his hand. He smiled nervously. He'd greased his hair back, Mafia-style. He nodded an acknowledgment to Monica and said to me, "Turkstra."

"Game's starting!" I heard behind me. Engstrom stopped flipping the ball.

"Todd," someone called. "You're on the mound. Monica, you're at third tonight."

Giving us both a nervous, questioning glance, Monica

started off. Engstrom didn't move "I need to talk," he said.

"About what?" I wondered.

"More or less about why you were at church yesterday."

"You have more to say?"

"I think so."

"Todd!" He waved toward the field.

"When?" I asked.

"After the game?"

"I'm coming back for Monica. You want to do it then?"

He flicked the ball in his hand without letting it go. I sensed he didn't appreciate my butting in with Monica. Even so, he said, "Fine," and jogged off, his long legs loping, to take his place on the mound.

❧ ❧

The woman at the front desk was friendly enough. She apologized twice. But Chief Oosterbaan was not in. He had called minutes before to ask her to inform me, if I stopped by, that he was tied up. Could I call him later, at home, about 11? I told the woman at the desk that I would try. If I didn't, I asked her to have him call and leave a message as to when I could reach him.

Minutes later, I found myself having struck out twice. I hoped Monica was doing better. I stopped by the college and seminary library, hoping to find Al Rozek deep in pursuit of whether Sid Hammersma had written The Outreach article on suicide. Somehow that didn't seem so important now — still, it would be good to know. But Rozek wasn't in. The back door, which he said would be open, was locked.

I stopped on the sidewalk outside the library, looking around, feeling in my pocket. I still had the key to Hammersma's office. Why not go up there and call Slade? I had to tell him what I'd learned, I'd decided.

In the silence of the office, I held my own little seance, asking the spirits of the place to give me direction. I folded my hands by the phone and tried to determine the dimensions of this mystery. God was beyond everything, supremely aloof

199

and yet suffusing it all. In this case, men had created a mess. When it all came to the surface, reputations would be destroyed. Others would be hurt. I let my palms move slowly across the top of the desk, listening intently, hoping the answers would come through my senses. I closed my eyes, smelled the faint mustiness of the room, heard the ticking and hum of far-off machines, felt the desk's slightly cool surface under my hands. I could sense myself reaching out in the dark, trying to discern some cold shape. Some reason for Hammersma's murder — for surely that had to be what it was.

My eyes popped open at some sound. I looked to my right. A blank computer screen stared back at me. Beyond that was a window. I saw movement. Branches scraping glass. I smiled. I was spooking myself. I reached over and thumbed on the desk lamp, which threw down a circle of light that barely extended beyond the top of the desk. To the right of the phone were scraps of paper I'd looked through before. I sifted through them, stopped at one. I read it again. It was a Bible verse, Matthew 18:15: "If your brother sins against you, go and show him his fault, just between the two of you. If he listens to you, you have won your brother over."

Was this important? Last time I didn't think it was. This time I wasn't sure. The verse spoke to the biblical way in which Christians were to handle the sins and wrongdoings of our brethren. We were always to go to them first, if we discovered something in their actions or behavior we believed fell short of God's commands. In Christian love, confrontation was what it was all about. Is that what Sid Hammersma had done? If so, what had he known? To whom had he taken his concerns? Or was this a useless scrap of paper? It seemed the professor kept these slips here as reminders. I closed my eyes again, tried to conjure the image of Hammersma. What formed was a duplicate of the photograph on the other side of the phone, the picture of the professor standing before the mountains, his wife by him in the wheelchair, her hand reaching up and clutching his. In my mind, Hammersma winked, as if I'd caught him in a joke. My eyes opened and fell on the photograph. No winking there.

Knowing it was too much for me, I picked up the receiver and dialed the number for the Ottawa County Sheriff's Department. Slade wasn't there, but the dispatcher said he would relay a message asking him to call me at home.

I set the phone back, kept my hand cupped over it, ruminating. I wondered if anyone had called me at home. On the recorder at the parsonage were several unimportant messages. Only two caught my interest, one from Bradley DeHorn, asking me how I was progressing. The other from Jerry VanderMolen, the reporter from The Press. On the machine, he said, "Turkstra, got some things. The Holiday Inn Plaza in Lansing." He gave me the number.

After figuring how to call long distance from the seminary phone, I punched the buttons, heard the connection link and then the other phone ring. Four times. I was about to give up when VanderMolen answered, breathless, "Hello."

"Jerry, hi."

"Turkstra. I was in the shower, about to go out. Glad you caught me."

To maintain my contemplative mood, I switched off the light and leaned back in the chair. Beyond the window, a square of pale light, branches drooped and waved like arms.

"What've you got?" I asked.

"I'm not sure. You have a few minutes?"

I figured Monica's game was about half over. "A few."

The reason VanderMolen was in Lansing, he told me, was for a meeting of the annual Reformed-Episcopalian Dialogue. "Once a year these guys get together and are supposed to hash over differences," VanderMolen said. "In reality a bunch of church muckedy-mucks meet, babble how one of these days they'll have to work harder to make the two denominations one, study a few Bible verses, then go home after having pledged to do this again next year in some other large city that has nice hotels."

"I'm aware of the dialogue," I told him, feeling the dark

office around me as a kind of comfort. With the lights off, Hammersma's ruddy face didn't peer out at me from a backdrop of mountains.

"Anyhow, I had a couple of very interesting discussions today with several people," the reporter said.

I hoped he wasn't going to draw this out, pile melodrama and sensationalism, rife with his ego, on top of the facts. I rubbed my face with one hand. "I do have to pick someone up from a softball game in about 15 minutes." I wanted to get back to the ball diamond. What had Engstrom wanted? flipping the ball in his hand, he'd been too coy.

"I'll make it fast."

"Why don't you give me the skeleton, then we can talk more about it tomorrow."

I heard a laugh on the other end. "Funny choice of words, Turkstra, given what I'm learning."

I wasn't trying to be funny. The comfort I'd felt a few moments before began to seep away. "Just sketch it for me, please."

"Anyway, you were right. Sid Hammersma was leading quite the double life." He paused, as if waiting for my confirmation; then he went on. "Seems his wife filed for divorce more than once."

"Oh?"

"That's right. But she kept changing her mind, or he kept changing it for her. To save face or something."

"Who told you all this?"

He chuckled. "C'mon, Turkstra. Fair is fair."

"Go on."

"OK," he said. "Seems like the last time she filed, she was pretty darned serious. Fact is, those papers are still in the hopper. Or were. Within the last couple weeks she quietly withdrew them again."

I thought of Virginia Hammersma huddled in her wheelchair on her back deck. Obviously the pain I saw was not all the result of her muscle disease. There was an even worse illness at work in her life. Was it jealousy?

"From what I'm learning, I can't blame her."

"You've heard this, too?"

"Some of it," I admitted.

My watch said it was 9:45. "I do have to get running," I said.

"Maybe you know the rest?" I said nothing. "About his predilections?"

"Homosexuality, you mean?"

"Right."

"I know about it now."

There was a pause, the ocean sound of waves coming in over the static that divided us. "This little story is actually kind of pathetic," he said.

The people weren't, but the way they acted was. "Tell me the story as you know it," I said.

"What's to tell? Sid Hammersma liked to spend weekends, especially in the summer, on the lake, in his boat, in the company of men and boys."

I had suspected as much. "Did your source speculate on what happened to the professor?"

"That he wasn't so free with."

"He make a guess?"

"Only that."

"And it was?"

"That one of Sid Hammersma's friends is involved."

I watched the branches move slowly at the window, an audience that couldn't clap.

"Is that what you think, Turkstra?"

"That one of his lovers killed him?"

"Yes."

"It has crossed my mind." A silence. "That's all?" I asked.

"Pretty much."

It wasn't new, but it fit. Suddenly I had another thought. "Jerry, something else. Does anything come to your mind tying Sid Hammerma to Richard Rhodes?"

"The TV guy?" I grunted assent. "Not really. Why?"

"Just wondering."

"Is flimflam Rhodes in on this?"

"Could be."

"How?"

"I'm not sure." The branch scraped the window outside. I thought of another call I should make.

"You know Rhodes very well?" I asked.

"Not well, but some."

"What do you think of him?"

I heard a mild chuckle. VanderMolen cleared his throat. "About two years ago, I did a story on him and his church. The piece was fluff, said he had few flaws. But the weirdest thing happened."

I recalled photos of Rhodes in church, on the golf course, on his boat, counseling people, in a TV show.

"What's that?"

"After I wrote it, I got a letter from this woman who claimed Rhodes had raped her when she was a secretary at his church. She may have been a crank, but I doubted it. Something about it rang true," he said.

Carla, I thought.

"She wrote she stopped speaking or something like that. Like a caged bird, she stopped singing, I think she wrote."

I wanted to climb through the phone. "What else?"

"That's all."

It made sense. Carla Blanchard. Half-sister of Kenny, lover of Sid Hammersma — possible assault victim, and beneficiary. Or killer? "Anything else?" I asked.

"I've given you the big picture."

The Bible verse glared up at me. Did Sid Hammersma want to bring it to Rhodes? Sections were missing, but the landscape was taking shape. "Anything else you remember from the letter?"

"Something about a child who died or was going to die. That wasn't clear."

"This woman — where was she from?"

"No return address. Wasn't signed. Postmark was Grand Rapids."

"You say you got this letter two years ago?"

"Something like that."

Her daughter would've been in the process of dying, in need of a new heart that never came. A lack of giving that led to the mother's need to reveal herself, if only anonymously, to someone. I could imagine her reaction to a story such as the one VanderMolen crafted out of flossy lies and homey half-truths.

"This important, Turkstra?" I didn't reply. "You've come across her?"

My watch registered 9:52. "I think so."

"She told you all of it?"

"As you say, she can't talk."

On the way back across campus, I learned more. Hustling toward me out of the shadows by the library came Albert Rozek. He was excited. When I told him I was in a hurry, he quickly informed me that he was fairly certain parts of the Hammersma column were a forgery.

"Any idea by who?" I asked.

"Not sure, pastor. But it had to be someone familiar with the church. Someone who knew the words, the ecclesiastical way to argue."

I wanted to know more. I told him I'd call the next day, and jogged off. He stood behind me, the manuscript clutched to his chest — a little crestfallen, I suspected, that I had seemed to dismiss him. But I had to. I knew now more than ever that Rhodes, and probably Engstrom, were not innocent.

29

The lights were on but the field was empty when I arrived just before 10:30. Large drops of rain, the size of quarters, splattered the infield dirt. I left Monica's car running and searched the empty stands, the area behind the backstop where a few people milled, and the park area on the other side of the field. As the fat drops fell faster, people who had been talking in a group broke away beyond home plate and the backstop, trotting for their cars. I put my hands on my hips, struck by worry.

Behind me, I heard, "Pastor Turkstra?" I spun. A wispy woman in a baseball uniform bearing the Golgotha Undenominational Church logo stepped back from me. She put a hand to her throat, startled.

"I'm sorry," I said, feeling cold water trickle down my neck. "I thought you heard me walking up."

"I'm sorry, no." Where was Engstrom? I thought.

Two men hovered a few feet behind her. One carried the bat bag. They watched me carefully. They could apparently tell I was agitated.

"Anyway," she said, "you're him?"

"I am."

"Reverend Smit — well, actually Reverend Engstrom — asked me to give you this message. He said he was driving Monica over to South Shore Marina."

The two men came a little closer, perhaps drawn by my

obvious anxiety. The church van waited behind them.

"What?" I asked. She said it again. "Why?"

"I don't know. Reverend Smit wasn't feeling well, he said, but didn't want to go home. He said something about her wanting to rest on his boat. Being by the water would help." She squinted through raindrops, as if hoping all she said would make perfect sense to me because it probably didn't for her. And she wanted to go.

"Did Monica get sick during the game?" The woman turned to the men, who were of no help. They shrugged. "When did they leave?" I asked.

"Fifteen minutes or so ago."

···

I raced down the street, headlights cutting through rain now falling in silvery sheets. Then I eased up on the pedal, needing to collect my thoughts, realizing again I could use help. I mouthed a prayer, but quickly realized the help I needed was more immediate. I was closer to the marina than the police station, where I could summon Marlan Oosterbaan. I could call Benny. But why not go to the marina first? I wasn't sure that Rhodes was to blame for this, but all fingers were pointing in that direction. Why, I also wondered, had Engstrom left? Maybe he thought the marina would be a safer place to talk. Yet, why didn't he wait? And why did Monica go with him?

The baseball game had been at Prospect Park, a field surrounded by a moderately prosperous residential area. I took 22nd Avenue straight across to Cleveland, up to Crescent and over to South Shore Drive. Winking in the black water out there, as I approached the edge of Lake Macatawa, were lights from boats. My anxiety mounting, I turned into the marina lot and headed through the gate out onto the slippery wood deck that led to the slips and the boats. I looked to the left and right, rain pelting steadily, my shirt stuck to my back. I started toward the office, over which glowed a yellow light encased in wire mesh. Before I knocked on the door, I heard behind me, "Preach!"

I turned and saw Jack, the maintenance guy, walking my way, a flashlight in one hand. He trained the beam on me a moment, as if adding to his greeting or simply making sure it was me. I glanced away from the light, noticed thousands of dancing dots on the water.

"Got a message for you," he said before I could tell him what I needed.

"Message?"

"From — what's his name? — Tom Engstrom?"

"Todd?"

"Guess that's his name." Jack's face was slick with rain, his hair matted to his skull.

"What did he say?" I asked, looking around, assuming Jack was to tell me where the boat was moored.

"That he was leaving."

"What?"

"What he said!"

"But," I said, "I was supposed to meet him — them — here."

"He got me over by the gas tanks. Said you might be coming by, but that he was heading out."

"To where?"

"Some Bible camp near Glenn."

The rain drummed down like nails. My mouth filled with a taste of hot metal. "Was anyone with him?" I asked anxiously.

"A woman. He said you would know who."

"Did you see her?" I wondered.

He wiped rain out of his eyes. The cone of light from his flashlight pointed up and separated us. "She was in the boat, I guess. Something wrong?"

I stood there, my clothes drenched, eyes sweeping the water. Several boats were out there, most heading in. The sky presented a black mask, hiding stars. Lightning flickered in the distance to the north. "Damn!"

"What is it?" Jack looked concerned. Stepped closer, wiped rain from his face.

I shook my head. "Did he say anything else?" Jack shrugged.

"Can I use your phone?" I asked.

Jack had given me a gray sweatshirt to wear. I'd peeled off my T-shirt and was grateful now for the scratchy warmth it provided. I was in Monica's car, parked in the lot to a chiropractor's office, halfway between the marina and the police department. When I called, the dispatcher told me Oosterbaan was expecting me. When I asked where he was, she said she'd check. Moments later, Oosterbaan was on the line. I quickly tried to explain what was occurring. After hearing where I was, he suggested meeting halfway, at the place where I now sat, watching rain wiggle down the windshield in zigzag lines. Even though it was still warm out, I blew on my hands, stomped my soaked shoes on the floor by the accelerator and clutch pedals. I wondered who else to call. I had suggested Slade to Oosterbaan, and he said he would take care of that on his radio on the way to meet me. I smacked the steering wheel with my hand, realizing I'd made a mistake leaving Monica alone.

Moments later, the Holland police cruiser slid next to me, wipers slapping water from the front window. Oosterbaan got out, bent his head and came around to the passenger's side. He wore a dark business suit — the same as this morning. It looked painted on by the rain. He smeared water from his cheeks, then wiped his hand under his arm as he got in. His square face turned to me, chin jutting out above the collar of his white shirt.

I told him about Rhodes, about Carla, about Engstrom taking off. I couldn't keep the fear out of my voice.

"Hold up a second," he said as I chattered on. "You went to the softball field, Miss Smit wasn't there, and another woman told you Engstrom took her to the marina?"

"Right."

"When you got to South Shore, they'd already left. For where?"

"Glenn. Where Rhodes' church has a retreat."

"The old church camp," Oosterbaan said. I nodded.

We were the only ones in the lot of the chiropractor's office. The street on our left was empty of traffic. Calm down, I told myself.

"You say Engstrom wanted to talk?"

"Yeah, but he didn't say he'd take off with Monica."

Oosterbaan shifted around so that he directly faced me. As his suit coat flopped open, I saw the gun on his belt. Somehow being with him, seeing that, made me feel better. I could hand this over.

"Tell me again what you've learned about Rhodes." I went through it, even mentioned the Bible verse by the phone and how it now seemed to it tie in. Oosterbaan listened intently. Rain made dropping pebble sounds on the roof. An occasional car passed, sloshing water on the road, whooshing along to some safe haven. When I was done, Oosterbaan sat back.

He gazed at me as if he thought I was crazy. "This theory has holes all over the place."

"How so?"

"How does AIDS fit in?"

I told him that, too. Sid Hammersma was at the end; he had nothing to lose.

He shook his head sadly. "You're saying that Sid Hammersma had a death wish at the same time he wanted to shake down Rhodes for screw-ups in the past."

Now I turned to him. "You tell me what happened then."

He glowered and narrowed his eyes until they were slits. He stared at me for several moments. Looked away, as if troubled by something. "I don't know," he said softly.

I looked away, too, in the darkness, at the floor. "What about Monica?" I asked. "She's on his boat alone with an ex-con who's got to be a prime suspect."

The eyebrows rose. I detected movement in his face that broke through the professional cynicism and seemed to reflect growing interest.

"Can't we call the Coast Guard and have them intercepted?"

"We could," he said doubtfully.

"But …?"

"But for what reason?"

"Kidnapping?"

Oosterbaan smelled like damp ashes and pungent, acrid sweat. Water shone in the crevices of his face. "How do you know she didn't want to go?"

Jealousy suddenly stung me. I pushed it away. "If she did, it doesn't make sense."

"You're sure of that, Calvin?" His eyes flicked over my face with a kind of practiced calculation. A cop probing the dark side. A side that was always there.

"I am," I replied with as much confidence as I could muster.

Oosterbaan settled back in his seat and gazed out the windshield. Hands in his lap.

"Did you call Slade?" I asked.

Oosterbaan sighed, tugged on his nose. "I just did. No response."

"He's not in?"

"Looks like."

"Can't you get a message to him?"

"They're trying."

I looked away. The rain already was easing. Strands of fog, the heat burning off, curled from the pavement. Leaves on the trees surrounding us in the lot glistened.

"Tell you what, Turkstra," Oosterbaan said. "It's been one heck of a day already. Got a goddamn kid who blew his brains out in his girlfriend's bathroom. I wanted to get home, but you're in luck."

I turned back.

"I'm off tomorrow," he said. "I can sleep in."

I said nothing, watching his face carefully. He still faced the windshield, a puffy, sorrowful expression pinching his mouth together.

"I'll call Slade again and tell him or the dispatcher what is up. If you want, if it will ease your mind, I'll drive down to

Glenn. It's not far. We'll see what's up."

The relief I experienced was mixed with fear. "What if we're too late?" I said.

Oosterbaan smiled. "Still take them a couple hours to get down there in a boat."

"But what if he does something to her before they get there?" I asked.

Oosterbaan shifted in the seat, leaned his neck back. I sensed something pulling at him. "Look," he said, "I'll try to rouse Slade again."

I waited a few minutes while Ooterbaan spoke on the radio in his car, and then he picked up and talked into his cellular phone. A couple times I noticed him glance at me. I looked away, drumming my fingers on the wheel. When he returned, he said, "Christ, what a night!"

Poking his head through the open passenger door, he explained that a witness to the so-called suicide had just shown up. Apparently, there was some doubt that the victim had actually shot himself. As with Hammersma, I thought. Oosterbaan said he had to interview the witness as soon as possible. All of that meant that he would have to let me head up to the retreat alone. When I protested, he said, "Don't worry. I got hold of Slade. He'll meet you there. He knows where it is. He said he'll have a county car there, too. It'll be fine."

"I hope so."

30

Heading south on U.S. 31, the road ahead showing a sheen of misting rain, I recalled the first time I'd met Monica. The afternoon was drab, gritty snow falling, the heater beating hard in the corner of the worship room when she'd walked in off the street. She'd been wearing a red parka with a fur-lined hood. In her hand was a notebook. She told me she was a student at the University of Chicago Divinity School and hoped to interview some street people. The boss wasn't there that day, so I was the only one who could help. Standing by the table near a handful of the regulars playing rummy, I had remarked that the street outside was full of people like that. Why didn't she search for them out there? I was sick of people waltzing into our storefront, academics especially, and wanting us to dish up a tattered-looking but somewhat articulate street person. It was just at the time when homelessness had caught on as a hot media issue. Newspapers, TV, and students of all types were searching for down-and-outers to feature, focus on or analyze. After hearing my quip, Monica gazed at me seriously, and said, "What's with you?" She then turned and walked out. Two weeks later, she showed up at one of our Sunday worship services. After it she approached me again, and we talked. I apologized for being a grump; she said she was sorry for being presumptuous. What followed, slowly, with fits and starts, was a great deal of joy, friendship, intimacy, a falling away and a coming together that had led us here. To my speeding north at

213

nearly midnight on a Thursday in August — nearly five years after our first meeting — to a church retreat in the woods.

Once I left the expressway, I drove 60 down County Park Road to the intersection of B15, where I turned back south a mile. The roads looked slick and shiny. Trees loomed on each side, branches offering shelter in the night. A few stars had broken through the dark, filmy sky. I kept thinking of riding the same road earlier with Monica. I wondered how willingly she had gone with Engstrom. Then again, I thought maybe Engstrom did want to do his talking here and had to get away in the manner that he had — which might well call into question the need to have the police on hand. But, if so, why didn't he leave a message?

Nearing the camp entrance, I looked through the rain-spattered windshield for a county cruiser. I saw none — only wet pavement and the two-track leading into the woods. I stopped, wipers slapping, and peered up and down the road. Oosterbaan had said nothing about waiting for the officers. I'd assumed they'd meet me at the entrance. Figuring if they had arrived that they'd already driven on, I turned down the dirt road. I jounced along the rutted ground. Water splashed and slurped. I pulled my headlights on high, climbed a rise, tires gripping mud, spinning, grinding. At the top, I noticed a path angling to the left and another that continued straight. Rain rapping on the roof, I tried to recall but couldn't which fork we had taken earlier. I wished Oosterbaan was along. Dark, sludgy, the consistency of muck, the water spread beyond the reach of my headlights.

I took the road straight ahead. Within 100 yards, I got stuck. I shifted the car into reverse; the tires slid in useless circles. I jammed it in drive, punched the accelerator. The car bucked and stalled. I twisted the key; the engine sputtered to life. I rocked the car, feeling as if I'd driven onto ice. The vehicle shimmied, slipped, jerked sideways. Damn! I thought, smacking the wheel with my palm. The woods ahead rose darkly, the water an even darker, serpentine movement. It struck me the rain had stopped. Craning up, I glanced through the windshield and spotted a cluster of stars glinting above the pointed tips of trees. The skies had cleared, leaving behind this impassable mess. I had to get out and walk.

My legs slapped with cold, I waded a few yards ahead of the Toyota. I had no flashlight, no boots, no raincoat. I slogged on a few more feet. The water got deeper, but the ground remained stable underfoot. I tried to see through the dark to the lodge. Around me the branches of the trees stirred with help from a crisp breeze. The overpowering heat had left entirely. I was glad again for the sweatshirt. I took in a few breaths, steadying myself. Move ahead. I dug my hands in my pockets, hunched my shoulders and kept walking.

Gulping for breath, my legs feeling the strain of the steep, muddy climb, I stood a few moments later on the top of the dune and tried to make out shapes through the dim, dripping woods. A path led to my left through a stand of slender birches toward a clearing. To my right was a smaller path that disappeared in a patch of matted, twisted darkness. I took the path to the left, started trotting, a pain pinching my side, my chest expanding with anxiety bubbles. Ahead I saw a pale light falling from the sky. The whiteness touched and out-lined a tall shape. I stopped. Some part of me had known, or suspected, it was up here. The cross. I'd taken the wrong fork in the road. Here I was, at the chapel in the pines at which we gathered for prayer every morning and evening during those weeks of summer church camp.

As the sturdy birches ended and the pines began, my way led down to the scooped-out bowl that had been — still was — the worship area, and I slowed my pace. I peered into the area in and around the oval shape of the outdoor chapel. The cross itself was set in a stone slab that measured 10 feet by 10 feet or so. Benches were arranged in a semi-circle around it. I paused a moment and listened intently. Heard faint rustling to my right. I turned, but saw nothing. Just a tree trunk. My feet felt numb from the water and mud I had walked through and had encased my shoes with ooze. I wondered anxiously if Slade was at the lodge.

I turned and surveyed the benches arranged around me and rising back to the lip of the surrounding pines. It was peaceful in here, the air cool, night quiet, benches free of an audience. Up here I sensed the serenity that had come to me years before in this place carved out of sand. My chest quaked. I took a few steadying gulps of humid air. Then I put my hand on the wooden cross. Wet, slick, slightly spongy, as if eaten away by years or termites. I dug out a chunk with my forefinger, corkscrewed my fingernail further in. Leaning against the trunk of the cross with my chest, I swung around the other side, as if sneaking up on somebody. But nothing was there, only wet sand, a pile of twigs, and — further down — the lake, great, black and shimmering. I hopped off the slab, landing in soggy sand. I tried to divine the presence of anyone other than me by closing my eyes and concentrating. My eyelids shut, I smelled more clearly the rich scent of the air and the turgid moistness of the water-logged vegetation.

As I did, the memory flashed though my mind of another time I'd been out here in the dreary, late-night dark. It had started behind the dining hall after dinner. I had gathered a few friends. They had been curious about my connection to the Catholic Church. Probably wanting to show off, I'd agreed to pretend to distribute Holy Communion to a few of my pals — just as I'd seen the priest do in my mom's church. I'd stolen some dry, brittle bread from the kitchen, crumbled it, and handed it out, mouthing prayers, to the others. I had them kneel and placed a chunk of bread, Christ's body, according to the Catholics, on each protruding tongue. As I remembered it, I was nearing the last kid, envisioning myself a papist priest, when arms gripped me from behind. Hands muffled my mouth, and I was dragged and half-carried by a few of the older boys down a path. Razzing me about my Catholic mumbo-jumbo, they tied me to the cross, wrapped a cloth around my mouth, and left. One of them said, upon leaving, "Try playing priest now, weenie."

"Let's see you get down from your Catholic cross," said yet another. Among them had been Slade and Oosterbaan. Both a year older; both Christian Reformed to the core.

I'd clung there a half hour, afraid, angry, near tears, betrayed. In my youthful imagination, I pretended to be a pre-teen Jesus. Or so I tried to view myself. Crucified to the wood, strapped there, imprisoned by rope for my adherence to a godly path. In those days I'd paraded my differences — mainly my Catholic connection — with pride. I let on that I was smarter than the others. That my father's church was mun-dane, far too boring. As a result, I probably did piss a few peo-ple off. Even if that was so, I had been stricken with shame over how I'd been treated. It didn't take long, as I hung there, for the arrogance to drain away. I had felt abandoned and demeaned.

But that night, someone finally emerged from the pines and started down toward me. My high-minded sense of Christ-like persecution had entirely disappeared. Still trapped by the ties and the cloth, I had felt a fierce sense of separate-ness. In a way that I couldn't shake for years, I felt guilty, as if I had justly deserved this roping to the cross by the older boys. After all, we were CRC, not Catholic. Where did I get off with the communion? The person that night years back had stepped up carefully, untied me and told me to go back to camp. He told me not to tell — if I did, I'd be in worse trouble than before. Then he ran off. It had been Marlan.

Standing there now, I swiveled my eyes through the woods. Shook the memory away. Somehow it had been a scourge I'd carried with me for years. I never really forgave any of them, Marlan included. But now, I had no time to be caught in the past. I wondered when the other police would arrive — or if they were already there.

I continued to the south, toward the lodge. Not far along, taking a path overlooking the lake, I saw, motoring toward shore, a boat. Two red lights at the front of the boat made blinking, wavering lines on the water. They were only 100 or so feet from a dock that extended out from the shore and what looked to be a walkway that led up the bluff to where the lodge stood. I remained on the bluff a few moments more, calculating. It had to be Monica and Engstrom. Then I swung around, made one more survey of the amphitheater and woods beyond, as if hoping I'd pick up what I hadn't yet been able to detect, and then I began running along the edge of the dune toward the area where the two of them would soon emerge.

Resting on my knees in wet sand and peering through stalks of thick dune grass, I listened. Tried to make out human voices amid the gurgling wash of waves. Try as I might, I couldn't hear any. Forcing myself to control my breath, I rose and gazed down. I saw the dip and sway of their boat, tied to the dock. I concentrated and finally heard steps. Around a bend in the walkway, I spotted a deeper darkness; then a shadow flickered and rose. I knew it was Monica. Behind her, looming up, came Engstrom. Watching, it suddenly struck me what Rozek had said. Someone had tampered with Sid Hammersma's column. Someone with a theological touch. Someone who knew the lingo. Rhodes! It had to be. I figured I'd better find something to protect myself if needed. I turned, stepped several feet to my left, bent, reached around and found a pile of stones. My hand ran over them quickly, feeling in the dark for one that might be of some use. As I did, I thought of Clarence Venema touching peaches. My hand found a rock — more than fist-sized — and I carried it back to the edge of the steps. I crouched again, training my ears to pick up sounds. Where was Slade?

I heard scraping, a squeak of feet on wood. Not long after, the muffled murmur of voices, one lighter, more musical, but subdued — Monica's. The other even quieter, more gruff and demanding — Engstrom. The first sentence I heard clearly was Monica's. "What time did you say he'd be here?"

"He's probably waiting," Engstrom assured her. Feet scuffed more loudly on the creaking steps.

"Why didn't we see lights on in the lodge then, from out

on the lake?" she asked. It didn't seem she was under any duress, which was good. Still, she sounded worried.

"Place isn't open." Engstrom sounded out of breath.

Monica appeared, slightly bent over from the effort of the climb. She paused, looked around. Hidden in the grass, I waited. Engstrom arrived next, chest heaving. He ran a hand through his hair. Monica turned back to him. "There's no one up here." I detected the apprehension in her voice.

I waited for them to pass, within five feet of where I crouched, just off the path. They crunched on, toward the cabin 100 feet or so in the woods.

"I don't understand," I heard Monica say.

I stood, stepped onto the path, making no attempt to disguise my presence.

"Hello," I said. Hefted the rock. Gripped it tight. A hard skull.

I emerged into the front yard of the lodge. "Turkstra?" asked Engstrom, turning.

"None other."

"Truman," Monica said, stepping from behind him. They had reached the back deck of the cabin. A faint yellow floodlight shone down from above a back door, just under the overhanging, cedar-shingled roof.

Engstrom's face, in shadow, looked worried. "You came alone?" he asked.

"Why?"

"Just wondering."

"Were you expecting me?" I asked.

He said nothing for a moment, seeming to steel himself. "I figured you'd make it."

Engstrom was halfway up the stairs to the back deck. Monica had stepped down to meet me. Her hands slipped under her arms. Her hair looked limp.

"Why'd you want to meet here?" she asked me.

I shot Engstrom a glance. He looked away. He wore a dark windbreaker, and both he and Monica still had on their softball uniforms.

"It wasn't my idea," I said, staring hard at him, flexing my hand on the rock.

"What?"

I replied, "Your friend cooked this up himself."

Engstrom shifted from foot to foot, rubbed a finger under his nose. A couple oily coils of hair looped onto his forehead.

"Todd?" she asked.

He gazed past me, into the dark. "Let's go in; it's chilly out here," he said.

"We can talk out here," I said, shivering in the damp air.

Engstrom's hands were buried in the side pockets of his parka. He looked trapped. His eyes ran beyond me to the darkness again. He bit his lips.

"About what?"

"Why you lied to Monica, to start."

Engstrom looked to his left, to the right, and back at me. Monica had eased to my side. I could feel her warmth.

"Todd," she said, "what's this about?"

He turned. "I'm going in."

"Engstrom!" I called.

He paused, turned languidly back, fighting valiantly to maintain control. A breeze ran through the branches of trees, the sound mixing with the breaking of the waves below.

"Engstrom, what in the hell is going on?"

"Turkstra," he replied, "this wasn't my idea."

"Then whose?"

I felt hard steel poke my back. My head twisted around. "Drop the rock, my friend." I tried to face him. "Drop it!" The stone clunked to my feet. It was Slade.

31

Slade ushered us inside. For a moment we stood in the dark. As I turned, metal jammed under my left shoulder. "No heroics," Slade encouraged. I kept turning, swinging toward him. He jerked hard and the gun barrel pinched flesh against bone. "I mean it," he growled. In the dimness, I saw the animal slant of his eyes, a molten rage on his face. Lights filled the room. At the same time, Slade shoved me in. I stumbled, nearly tripping over an ottoman next to an armchair. I quickly found my balance and faced him.

Monica stood on my left, face drained, hair weak strands of spaghetti, mouth partly open. Engstrom hovered behind her, partly in shadow, nervous but otherwise intact. I didn't remember this pine-paneled room in any way. The furnishings were tasteful, expensive. Prints hung on the walls, an Oriental rug lay underfoot. This was a large living or meeting area. A roll-top desk was shoved into the corner.

"Stand next to him, young lady," Slade said. He had a gun in each hand — a two-fisted gun fighter. One looked like a 35mm revolver — small, chrome-plated. The other was longer, darker blue. My eyes stuck to the service revolver, the shape of the steel, the pearl handle.

"Recognize it?" Slade asked.

"It's mine!" I replied with horror. "Where'd you …?"

"Found it in your closet."

"You broke into my home?"

He nodded. "You told me you had it when we met at Meijer's."

My legs lost strength. My stomach turned. He was going to make it look like I had killed Engstrom and Monica, then turned my own weapon on myself. I reached out to Monica, tried to loop an arm around her shoulder. "Step back," Slade ordered.

He wore a black leather jacket, shaped like a suit coat and slightly beaded with water. Under that was a dark T-shirt. His square face was flushed, his eyes hooded, lethal-looking.

"Mr. Engstrom," Slade said, "step over there, too."

Engstrom's eyebrows rose a half inch. "Me?"

"You too."

The arms that had been crossed over his chest fell. "Why?"

Monica shivered. I settled an arm around her nevertheless. Slade shot me a glance, and turned back to Engstrom. With the barrel of the longer gun, he motioned angrily. "Move."

Engstrom's eyes dropped warily to the weapon. He said, "What is this?" Slade stepped back and glanced from Engstrom to me and back. On his hands were latex surgeon's gloves. No fingerprints. "No more questions," he said.

Slade stepped into the middle of the room. His boots were wet and muddy, staining the rug. He'd have to clean that later, I thought.

"Todd," said Monica in a faltering, painful voice, "what is going on?"

With Slade between us, I could see only Engstrom's upper body. The good looks had fallen into a bag of wrinkles with grimy patches of gray. The ride up here in the boat and now the confrontation with Slade had cracked his boastful veneer of goodwill.

"Monica," he said, eyes flicking over Slade's shoulder in our direction, "I don't know."

"Apologies won't change what your friend is planning to do," I said.

"He's not my friend. Richard said …"

"Shut up!" barked Slade.

I noticed the revolver I'd purchased in the Navy waving in my direction.

"You set us up, Todd," I told him.

He looked frantic with fear. "But, I thought …"

"That you'd cover up a couple of murders for your boss?"

Engstrom's mouth dropped; his eyes expanded into anxious circles. "Murder? I thought …"

"That's the problem, Todd, you're doing too much thinking," I said.

A smile on Slade's face broadened. An evil calm came over him; his hands flexed on the gun aimed our way. My gun.

"Turkstra," he said, "you've always been a little too big for your britches."

"Even when I was a kid, you were a jerk," I said. His eyes grew wide. I wasn't sure why I was provoking him. "I mean, do you really expect to get away with this — with killing us?"

Monica whimpered. "Jesus," she moaned.

Slade's expression grew serious. "Miss Smit, step away from him. Sit on that chair."

She remained where she was. The gun wobbled; the eyes slit; the neck bulged with a corrugated vein. "Tell her, Turkstra. I'm not screwing around."

I gently moved, trying to ease her toward a straight-back chair against a wall by a lace-curtained window.

"Do as he says," I told her. Her eyes bit into mine; she pulled away, slung back her head, stepped over and sat in the chair. She turned her face, chin up, toward Slade.

"That's better," he said.

He was arranging us in the room. The fear that had been in my throat now fell and spread like fire in my belly. My underarms felt clammy. Slade took in a breath. I was not familiar with killers. But I figured few were as calculating as some of us might believe. Slade was on the edge of something; I knew he was capable of the violence he threatened. I was hoping he wouldn't carry it through, or would mess it up in some way. I said a quick prayer.

"How do you expect to get away with it, Slade?" I asked. "We're not the only ones who know we're here."

"Zip it," Slade said to me.

"How are you involved in this?" I asked. "Why are you protecting Rhodes?"

Slade said nothing.

"Is he paying you? And in return, he backs your little run for office?"

As I spoke, Engstrom took another tentative step, raised a hand. "I'm leaving. Whatever you do, I want no part of it."

I saw Monica pierce him with a glance, as if trying to see if he truly was about to go. I suspected he was.

"Really," said Engstrom in a weak voice, hands extended, as if in surrender. "I got them here. I don't want to know anything else. I shouldn't have even done that."

I saw hatred and sorrow and shock on Monica's face. I suspected she also knew Rhodes was behind this. He'd put it all in motion, then slithered off to Chicago.

"Look, Slade," said Engstrom, approaching, forcing a smile onto his square-jawed face. "I'm on your side."

"Punk!" Slade growled.

Then I heard a loud crack. As Engstrom's head swung back gushing blood and Slade moved to us, I leapt forward, right shoulder down, driving across the carpet, expecting a bullet to slam into my skull. I heard an explosion above me; the noise jammed down my ears. But I didn't stop. I gathered Slade's torso in my arms. Trying to swing him around, I spun on my legs, got them twisted and fell over. Slade tumbled on top of me. As we fell, there was more sound — a huge hand clapping. Following the painful explosion I smelled the odor of acrid powdery fire and felt searing in my arm. Slade pummeled me, flopping, trying to pull away. I had his jacket in my hand, yanking him toward me, bucking up with my belly, smashing him on the side with my head, clamping for flesh, a softness inside his shirt, with my teeth.

Wildness filled me. On top of me Slade continued to flop.

He was surprisingly limp for a man his size. I heard gurgling and felt liquid wash my face. My eyes closed, I continued to struggle, ramming into hardness — possibly his forehead — with mine, clutching the leather of the coat and trying to tear it away as if it were skin. In a rage, fueled by fear, I wanted to kill him. Tear open his ribs, rip out the flesh inside. I had begun to shift him off when more noise. a reverberating ring, roared through my ears. Pressing hard against the drums, threatening to pop the tender flesh inside, the noise formed into words. "Truman!" is what I heard.

I had turned Slade over, reached down for the neck. A preacher in a slaughterhouse, doing God's dirty work. But the face under me, the nose flattened and spattering blood, the mouth twisted in a slack grimace of pain, that face was no longer Slade's. I punched him, cupping gristly blood. I punched again, wondering how this had happened.

"Truman! Stop!" I felt tugging from behind. I pulled away, turning slightly to the side.

"Truman!" Monica's face, colored with speckles of blood, was inches from mine. "Stop," she said. "Stop," she said again, collapsing onto her knees on the floor, the soaked carpet, next to me.

"Stop," she said, placing hands over her face and beginning to sob. "Please, stop."

My arms hung limp. Slade, under me, had turned into bones and flesh, a stream of blood winding its gluey way out of the hole that had been his nose. I raised my left hand to my right shoulder, felt matted wetness coming from a dull but widening ache. As I did, my eyes moved up beyond Monica at the man standing behind her, rifle at his side. His sweatshirt with the bold letters Holland P.D. stuck wetly to his chest. His bristly red hair stood straight up like wire that carried electric current. His freckles looked like dabs of mud. A drop of water, possibly sweat, hung precariously from the ridge of his chin. Marlan — come to help.

Monica collapsed into my arms. I clutched her to my

chest; I felt her sob. I rolled off Slade, still holding her, closing my eyes, feeling powerful relief and love wash through me. After awhile, I didn't know how long, I looked up at Oosterbaan. He had stepped over and gazed down at Slade.

"Why?" I asked. "Why'd you come?"

Nudging the barrel of the rifle against Slade's leg, the Holland police officer shrugged. "Finally made sense."

Slade's face looked like half-cooked meat loaf. Not far away sprawled Engstrom. Legs twisted, arms outstretched, mouth open, eyes half shut, face turned our way, a half-dollar-size hole, hardly bleeding, in the middle of his forehead. He looked strangely calm. Why? Why had Slade done it? And what about Rhodes?

I felt Monica pull from me. A mat of red covered her cheek and clumped in her hair. I wanted to respond, find out if she was hurt, too. I wanted to talk to Oosterbaan. But a searing pain in my shoulder and back made words impossible. As I twisted around, trying to stand, something happened. A moan rose in my throat. I passed out.

32

Entering my hospital room in a wheelchair, I saw the broad back, thick neck, curly red hair, wide bottom of Marlan Oosterbaan facing my way. The rest of him was turned to the window. I'd checked the view earlier. It wasn't much. Only showed the south side of Holland.

"I can get it from here," I told the aide. Set my feet on the floor and rocked out of the chair. Took a seat on the side of my bed. Oosterbaan turned, hands in the pockets of his baggy beige pants. Beard bristled on his cheeks; his eyes were redder than his hair. "Calvin."

I greeted him. Winced. The pain a taut hot wire snapping in my upper chest.

"Hurt?"

"Not as bad as it could be."

So far I'd been lucky. The bullet from my own gun had sliced through my body. Doctors in the emergency room at Holland Community Hospital had only to clean, stitch and dress the wound above my breast and the one, slightly larger, in my back. A rib had been nicked, but not shattered, the lung missed entirely. But I couldn't lift my right arm; the doctor thought he might eventually have to operate to re-attach some tendons.

I was grateful to be alive. It was Saturday, two days after the shooting, and chances were good I'd be discharged by noon. The last 36 hours had been hell. Whisked to the ER by

227 DEADLY WATERS

ambulance, I'd undergone a couple hours of intense treatment as state police hovered outside the hospital room. They wanted a statement. Monica had been there as well, hanging on the edges of my sight. The drugs they'd given me for pain had made me groggy and irritable. I'd come to briefly in the ambulance. Monica had been there, seated on a bench, holding my hand.

Now, Oosterbaan sat on the window ledge, legs apart, hands folded over his crotch.

"I need to thank you," I said.

"No need."

"You saved our lives."

"Wish I could've gotten there 10 seconds sooner." Shame moved through me. But it was true — Engstrom's death had not affected me. Much.

"They springing you soon?" Oosterbaan asked.

"In an hour, I hope." He nodded. Mud speckled his loafers. His knit shirt looked stained; faint salt circles showed under his arms. "You've been working?" I asked.

"Haven't slept since the other night."

"That's a long time."

"Tell me about it."

I scooted up in bed. Lay against the raised top of the mattress. Let the pain settle into a knot above my heart. I sensed Marlan had come here with a serious purpose. He yawned and rubbed his face with both hands.

"I heard something about the cemetery?" I said.

Faint sun shone beyond him out the window. Done rubbing his face, he used both hands to mat the sides of his unruly hair. "It'll all be on the news later," he said. I waited.

He twisted a knuckle in the corner of one eye and then in the other. "Talked to old man Venema myself yesterday morning. Then took a walk down there. Found a pile of dirt. Looked new. Our boys dug around. Not too deep, we found the professor and the kid."

"Kenny?" He nodded sadly. "Slade did it?" I asked.

"Looks like, possibly with help from Rhodes."

"Any word on him?"

"None."

Oosterbaan set his palms on his knees. Examined the polished floor. I inched up higher in bed, felt the fire spark in my shoulder. Like a snake bite, a trembling of poison.

I tried to imagine the bodies in the shallow grave. Dumped together. "Were they shot?"

"Both in the head."

"What I can't figure is why?" he said.

I tried my scenario. Kenny, Hammersma's lover, was half-brother to Carla Blanchard. Somehow he knew of what Rhodes had done to her. He told Sid. Maybe there was more that Hammersma learned about Rhodes. Perhaps because he knew he was dying of AIDS anyway, or just out of Christian conscience, or both, the professor took the advice in Matthew. He confronted his brother in Christ with his sin. He told Rhodes he would have to go public with what he knew. Which brought Slade into the picture. What Marlan had just told me about Slade backed me up on this. And Slade, the would-be sheriff, wanted no publicity on either his or Rhodes' past. The confrontation, I told Marlan, led to the graveyard.

Marlan listened to me wearily. Nodded. "Sounds crazy."

"But it makes sense," I countered.

"Maybe."

Marlan stared at the floor. "Another thing we found. Looks like the professor left the marina, docked his boat at an empty beach near the channel to the lake. Guy, probably Kenny, met him. Then they drove to the graveyard. Seems Rhodes and Slade came back later and dumped the boat."

We lapsed into silence. I felt the blood rush through my shoulder.

"Look, Calvin," he finally said, "I want to talk."

With my face, I tried to give him the go-ahead to talk. He turned back to the window. Slouched against the wall.

Scratched behind one ear. A nurse poked her head in the door. Told me the doctor would be in soon. I smiled at her and told her fine.

"You see," Oosterbaan said, "I was wondering if you've talked to the State Police yet."

"Just barely. Why?"

He glanced over his shoulder, eyes narrowed. Pinched his chin with two fingers. "I was just wondering."

Now he had me full of questions. I detected a shade of guilt on his face, a trembling in the eyes. "Is there something I know that telling them would be a problem?"

Marlan sat again on the ledge. He looked pained, his expression troubled, mouth tight. "Might."

"How?" I'd been pondering this part. "It has to do with you and Slade?" I asked.

The eyes widened a fraction, a finger slid parallel to his nostrils. I recalled his face, so much pudgier and worn now, as it had been in our youth. It had always been square, full of bluntness and curiosity. I'd been drawn by its strength. I'd also been repelled by its strength, its hint of violence.

"I suppose," he finally said. Then waited, as if feeling me out.

I had awakened shortly before dawn with a thought, a connection. "You both started on the Holland department about the same time, didn't you?" Slade had later transferred to the sheriff's department.

"Same month, in fact."

"So you knew him professionally, pretty well?"

I glanced down at some notes I had jotted and which I hoped to weave into a sermon for tomorrow. Woven in there were my reflections on this case. "And you knew him when he got off track?" Here I was starting to reach a little.

Oosterbaan's mouth pinched closed. The hands rubbed the knees. "I didn't come here to go to confession, Calvin, or whatever they call it."

"Then what?" Again, he stood. Faced the room. Hand cupping his neck. "I figure you've got something to say," I said.

He sat in the high-back chair at the foot of the bed. Checked the empty doorway, as if searching for my doctor. "Maybe just this. Bruce Slade was involved in so much crap that no one is really ever going to know about."

"Because he's dead?"

"Because he's dead."

Carefully, I twisted around, dangled my legs over the side of the bed. Faced the pale green wall.

"I don't care so much about Slade. How much involves you?" I turned to him.

After a little more verbal fencing, Oosterbaan explained. Almost 20 years ago, he and Slade had been called to the scene of a domestic dispute. Arriving in separate cars, they found a woman who had been beaten by her husband. The man, in a rage, told the cops she'd deserved what she got. That she'd been messing around with the boss, a preacher nonetheless, and she was pregnant. As Oosterbaan started to assist the woman off the floor of their bedroom, Slade took the man, by the name of Webster, outside. Eventually, the woman — her name was Carla — had to be treated at the hospital, this same hospital, for a broken jaw and shattered ribs. Webster had been trying to beat her into an abortion. Oosterbaan went with her to the hospital. Slade arrested Webster. One thing led to another. In the end, Webster was let off. The preacher, who was the father, was never named. But both Oosterbaan and Slade knew it was Richard Rhodes. The woman recovered from her injuries and soon she and her husband left town. Although Oosterbaan wasn't sure, he strongly suspected the incident was the occasion for the start of a relationship between Slade and Rhodes. Oosterbaan figured the preacher used Slade as an intermediary to pay off Webster and his wife. The money was to keep them quiet. How much it was Oosterbaan didn't know. The thing is, Oosterbaan told me, he knew something was up and never called Slade on it. Other situations, some involving Rhodes, and various forms of extortion, also occurred. And Oosterbaan more or less ignored them, too. "You see," said Oosterbaan, "Slade also was a damned good cop. Better than most. He did the job, worked long hours, and put away more than his share of criminals." It's just that Slade used his position to build himself a hefty bank account, said Oosterbaan. At any rate, a run-in that the two of them had over a drug case led to Slade's resignation and move over to the sheriff's department. That was almost a decade ago. Since, Oosterbaan and Slade had maintained a wary relationship. As Slade climbed the ranks and then as he ran for sheriff, it had seemed to Oosterbaan that maybe he was mending his ways. And maybe he was. But then Hammersma turned up missing. Somehow Oosterbaan had not felt right about it, especially when Slade started putting pressure on to clear the case, body or not. Then when I came up with what I had, particularly about the Blanchards in Kibbie, it became clear to Oosterbaan what Slade was up to. The exact tie-in to Hammersma had been foggy, but Marlan strongly assumed that whatever had happened to the professor had occurred with help from Slade.

Still on the edge of the bed, I stared across at Marlan. "How's this tie in with the State Police?"

Oosterbaan slouched in the seat, hands folded over his belly. "They're going to wonder if I was hooked in with Bruce."

"Were you?"

He didn't answer for a moment. "Bruce, when all is said and done, was my friend years back. He was the best man at my wedding, for cripes sakes." Oosterbaan slid down further in the chair, shoulders hunched. "And now I'm the one who killed him." I sensed guilt and sadness, but nothing over-whelming, in the admission.

"I'm not sure what other option you had," I said.

Oosterbaan gazed at the hands on his belly. "I could've jumped in earlier."

"If you'd have known."

The eyes rolled up and engaged mine. I suspected he did know, or have some idea, earlier. Right after, or during, our meeting in the chiropractor's parking lot, for instance. It struck me: Why did he let me go on alone? Why had he called Slade, which as much as sent him after me. The gratitude I felt for Marlan's rescue dimmed. Questions crowded in. I didn't get to ask them.

Oosterbaan stood. "Look, Calvin, tell the state whatever it is they want to know."

"Even if it puts you in a bad light?"

He sighed. "If they try to tie me in knots, I'll call my lawyer." He smiled. I returned the smile. "If they really get in my business, I've got the putt-putt to fall back on."

"What could they hit you with? So you knew Bruce was involved in some things. Will they climb all over you for that?" He shrugged. Yawned. Rubbed his face again.

"Christ Calvin," he said. "I don't know."

I shifted to the edge of the bed as the doctor appeared. "Marlan," I said. He gave me a quizzical look. "Does it strike you that all of this may be part of God's will?"

He set his hands on his hips. Shook his head. "No, Calvin, it doesn't. Not one bit. If God's will is AIDS and adultery and me having to kill the guy who was once my good friend, then I'd have to be looking for another God."

36

My eyes swept the silent, sun-splashed church in Overisel. The Sunday morning light poured with creamy richness through the stained glass windows that faced east. The sun had crested the hill outside. Like a flowing piece of linen, mixed with bands of blue and gold and rose, the light touched the faces turned attentively in my direction.

"Friends," I began, wincing at the pain in my shoulder. A bandage still covered the wound. "Friends," I said again, noticing Benny Plasterman in the back row with his wife and sons.

"The Lord works in wondrous ways," I started, letting it sink in. "But in His creation, His majesty, there is often ambiguity and pain. Not in His word. Not in His orders. Not in His caring or watching over us. That is straight and strong and full and right. Forever. But there is ambiguity and pain, uncertainty in what we, His creation, have made in our responses to Him."

I let my words hang, flitter above their heads, searching for a place to alight. The eyes were fixed on me with avid interest. They wanted to know. I hoped to tell them. The church this morning was packed, almost as full as Easter.

"But in all the fury of forging for us a human nature, our Lord also gave us a mind, a will, an ability to question, demand, debate and complain. And among those great complainers, among those who were willing to face God and stare him straight in the eyes was Job, the man of whom we read today."

Then I paused for a few moments in my preaching. As I did, a door opened in the back. A man shuffled in, followed by a woman whose arms touched his shoulders and guided him into a seat along the far left aisle. Clarence Venema and his wife. This was not their regular church, but I knew why they had come.

As Clarence and his wife settled in the pew, I felt Clarence's stern face, although without sight, train itself on me, as if daring me to go on, to tell a deeper truth.

"What I know," I said, clearing my throat of an itch, "is that why we do what we do, and why God does what He does, is incomprehensible. The motivations of the world are as deep, and sometimes deadly, as any well, pond or lake water."

White walls rose on either side of our old church, climbing to a peaked roof bisected with shiny oak cross-beams. Three fans, large blades twirling, hung from the main beam that ran the length of the sanctuary. I wondered if my words were floating up and being diced into gibberish by those blades. I was afraid I wasn't saying what I wanted. But I pressed on.

"Among us," I continued, "are saints and prophets and wise men full of rage and passion, whose relationship with God is beyond reproach. These are the ones we cannot judge — even if they trouble us by their actions. These are the ones who have built their own bridges into heaven. Shaking their fists, they speak to God for us all." I let that settle, then added, "And yet their bridges are weak and rotten, unless shored up by God's grace."

I saw a few nods, a stifled yawn, a half smile. Clarence Venema's blank, undecipherable eyes bored into me.

"We can blame these men for their sins," I said, "but what do we know?" I paused, looked at my hands on the lectern. Felt a twinge of pain, a shock of electricity, in my arm. "In recent days, in our denomination, we have learned that one of our best has fallen. And fallen in more ways than we can imagine."

Finally, I was talking about the person who was on everybody's mind. "In this man, this leader who showed the fragility of his own being and the obsessiveness of his own wants, we see a finger pointing us toward a place of truth. Truth about ourselves, our fallen nature, our brokenness, our own need for new life and direction." I wondered, was I sentimentalizing his obsession? I hoped not.

"Most of all, in recent days," I went on, "we've encountered, once again, the terrible uncertainty of God's purpose, of a will that we'll never fully understand. The vision we must take from this terrible event is one of common belief and commitment to our own salvation. Because we are seeing — not in the newspapers, not on TV, not in our gossipy conversations — we are seeing how one of our own, however much he failed and fell short, brings us closer to God. To the truth embodied in Christ, in the redemption that came at the cost of blood. We are seeing — we saw — a man who stepped into the fire and in his case lost his life, but will, I predict, come out whole. He took off the veil, both from himself and from a part of the wormy world he wanted us all to see. He was an ordinary man through whom God did an extraordinary thing."

A few in my flock shifted nervously in their seats. Farmers with heavy shoulders and battered hands. Women who defined their days by the work they did for their men. Venema nodded, almost happy. I wondered if he thought I was trying to sound like one of his TV preachers on tape. Next to him, his wife gazed sourly into her lap.

Looking out, I saw many blank faces stare back at me. I felt tired, drained. My shoulder burned. My throat was dry. I thought of the TV images of police officers digging up the graves. I wondered again if Marlan had known more about Slade than he had admitted. As for the State Police, I hadn't told them much. "You all know I'm talking about Sidney Hammersma." My meaning was now plain. "If you take anything away from here this morning, take this: Do not judge him too deeply or harshly."

Venema was shaking his head, smiling. "He was a sinner. But in the end he was not a slave to that sin. If anything, I hope you find it in your hearts to do what Job himself has asked. Let no one condemn him for his sins or punish him for his crimes. Let flowers bloom on that man's grave.

"I believe Sid Hammersma was, in many ways, a modern-day Job. Certainly a plague had befallen him; chances are he brought it on himself, and yet he was the victim of a disease whose ongoing ravages are just beginning to be felt in our denomination and the world at large. Certainly he could have kept it quiet, and in a way he did. But his act of confrontation, his facing down two men with his knowledge of how they had twisted the Christian faith sealed his fate as surely as any lethal injection."

I waited. They were all watching me now.

"In what he did, Sid Hammersma was making a statement, his final statement, about a plague that was rife in organized religion — a plague perhaps more insidious, probably more eternally lethal, than any immune-system-destroying illness could fashion," I preached. "Sid Hammersma, by the way he died, buried in a grave with his brother in sin, left behind a mystery full of sorrow and solace for the rest of us to plunge. He was, no doubt, searching for redemption."

My hands on either side of the pulpit, my eyes searching out the faces in front of me, I found myself empty.

I gazed out over them, feeling deep sadness swallow me. Sunlight still swam and shone through the stained glass windows. I felt my heart pump steadily; my palms hot. I thought of the cross in the woods, of the bees buzzing over the mound of dirt, of Engstrom's head snapping back at the force of the bullet, of the hole in Slade's face. I thought of myself, out of control, scooping blood. The stain of what had happened spread wide. I felt it all rise in me like a fever. I thought of myself in Sid Hammersma's office, making more final calls, closing in on the truth. It struck me that I had been used as a kind of agent. I had been the second act of Hammersma's stab in the dark for a piece of the truth. He had made his statement in the roadside park. It was then up to others to bring his bloody end, and the reason for it, into the light.

I blinked, my face flushed, at the light all around us in the church. I tried to smile, but choked. I had intended to talk about God's will. But instead had made excuses, probably explanations, for Hammersma's behavior. I bowed my head, squeezed my eyes shut, and clasped the edges of the pulpit for support. I saw that lone boat bobbing on the lake, wolf eyes peering, and the smile of a man standing in front of massive mountains, a picture of a young man with a rope coiled over his shoulder. I thought of Monica on her knees, weeping. I thought of Carla Blanchard's hands, trying to express the horror of what had happened.

Gazing out, I felt their attention riveted on me. I seemed to have reached them for a few seconds. I thought then again of Monica, who today was at the other church with her children. We'd been brought back together. Even so, our approaches to theology continued to separate us, especially in the role of women in the church. But that would be another story.

For then, I did what I knew I always had to do. I bowed my head and prayed. And as I did, I thought of the cross in the dark woods. Spongy as it was, it still stood.